Blind response made her murmur his name

Max drew her close and settled her head on his shoulder, his hand against her hair. And in that silence the drumming of her heart was echoed by a stronger rhythm.

"Gail—" Max moved uneasily "—I think you should…."

She looked up and felt his face against her brow. Then somehow her mouth was moving across his cheek and his across hers until their lips touched. They hesitated, and then clung with a fierceness almost painful.

He whispered, "Gail, I don't want you to regret anything…."

She sighed and imprisoned his hand against her breast. He groaned softly. "I'm as human as the next man, you know. If you…."

His words died as he lowered his mouth onto hers.

MARGERY HILTON
is also the author of these

Harlequin Presents

52—A MAN WITHOUT MERCY
163—GIRL CRUSOE
297—THE VELVET TOUCH
357—SNOW BRIDE

and these

Harlequin Romances

1022—YOUNG ELLIS
1068—THE DUTCH UNCLE
1125—DARLING RHADAMANTHUS
1188—THE GROTTO OF JADE
1367—INTERLUDE IN ARCADY
1438—BITTER MASQUERADE
1501—THE WHISPERING GROVE
1536—TRUST IN TOMORROW
1581—THE HOUSE OF THE AMULET
1610—DEAR CONQUISTADOR
1634—THE SPELL OF THE ENCHANTER
1670—FRAIL SANCTUARY
1710—THE INSHINE GIRL
1752—MIRANDA'S MARRIAGE
1950—THE BEACH OF SWEET RETURNS
2135—THE HOUSE OF STRANGE MUSIC
2213—THE DARK SIDE OF MARRIAGE

MARGERY HILTON

the flower of eternity

Harlequin Books

TORONTO • LONDON • LOS ANGELES • AMSTERDAM
SYDNEY • HAMBURG • PARIS • STOCKHOLM • ATHENS • TOKYO

Harlequin Presents edition published August 1975
ISBN 0-373-10103-1

Second printing October 1977
Third printing June 1978
Fourth printing March 1979
Fifth printing March 1980
Sixth printing January 1981

Original hardcover edition published in 1970
by Mills & Boon Limited

Printed in U.S.A.

CHAPTER I

'... and Lima is wonderful! There was an awful moment just as we arrived when I was afraid it wasn't going to be. We were all waiting for that riot of gorgeous tropical colour the airline brochures show you, and the Pacific, of course, and when we got off the plane there was this hot dusty flatness and a fine cloudy mist hanging over everything (apparently it's caused by something called the Humboldt Current—I gather it never actually *rains* in Lima—which is something!), and to cap it all this most unromantic smell of fish! But this, Don Felipe tells us, is from a fertilizer plant nearby. Honestly, I felt awful when he noticed me sniffing, but there was a twinkle in his eye and he is every bit as charming as you said—they're all such happy, friendly people here—and he says I have to send you his felicitations. He is obviously genuinely distressed because you couldn't be with us. His villa is a dream—Clive says we'll have to make the most of this luxury because it'll be our last taste of comfort for a long time. As if I cared about comfort with the expedition of a lifetime to look forward to. We seem to have been planning and dreaming and talking about it for so long I can hardly believe that it's all really beginning at last...'

Gail Denning paused and took a long drink of the delicious iced lime shake on the glass table by her side. The biggest butterfly she had ever seen fluttered rainbow gauze wings over the clusters of shell-pink jasmine along the low wall of the patio, and a little way away from where she was sitting a fountain played its cool, enigmatic music, evoking a languorous dreamlike state which was anything but conducive to concentration.

She bent her head over the half-finished letter and sighed ruefully. She had been in Lima less than a day and a half and already there was so much she wanted to tell her beloved father it would take several letters to cover all the excitement and discovery she wanted to convey. The shadow of sadness returned to her blue eyes. If only he had been well enough to complete the venture he had spent so many months planning for and organizing! It was tragic that he, of all of them, should still be at home in the quiet little Suffolk village which at this moment seemed as remote as the moon.

She smiled to herself; her father would not be waiting anxiously to read her outpourings about the sights she was seeing in the fascinating land of Peru. She must not forget ... Her pen poised for a moment, then descended quickly.

'... there is to be a conference as soon as the great Max Christiern arrives. (I almost feel I should write his name in capitals!) Honestly, Daddy, I don't know why everyone defers at the mere mention of his name. I'm sure he isn't half as brilliant as you. After all, you did the hardest part of the job digging out all the information, but apparently we all have to hang around here waiting for him and his word to get up and go. However, as he seems to be the kingpin this side of the pond and the only one who knows his way round the Andes and all the rest of it to get to our Secret Valley I suppose we must all be suitably meek and obeisant—can you see Clive touching the forelock? I can't—but maybe Max Christiern will be okay once we start to rub along with him. It'll be fun meeting one of those strong, silent explorer types, and after all, nothing matters except finding the Valley and this fabled flower ...'

'So this is where you are!'

A shadow fell across her and she looked up into friendly crinkling brown eyes and the lopsided grin that matched the good-natured personality of one of Gail's favourite persons.

She smiled. 'Hello, Clive. How's tricks?'

'Tricky as ever.' He dropped into the cane lounger beside hers and helped himself to a swig of her lime shake. 'You were looking awfully fierce, girl. Not having words with poor old Roger again?'

'No, not exactly——' She hesitated, her expression troubled. That wasn't strictly true; she had been having words with Roger, and the memory of the incident early that morning brought a sense of guilt that was disturbing. She tucked the half-written letter into her writing-case and looked at up Clive.

'I don't know what to do,' she said slowly. 'I didn't mean to hurt his feelings this morning, but I just felt I couldn't let him buy me that silver ring. It was expensive, for one thing, and for another ... if it had been anything else but a ring ...'

'You know he's in love with you, don't you?' Clive said quietly.

Gail sighed, suddenly aware of relief that Clive had brought the subject into the open and she could confide with trust in the older man. 'That's just the trouble, I didn't. Oh, you know how it is. Roger and I have been practically brought up together, with Uncle Phil adopting him and our two families being so close together. Roger's always been more like a brother to me, until just recently. I just can't think of him in that way, much as I like him. But I don't want to hurt him.'

'It's quite a problem,' Clive said sympathetically. 'Of course I saw this coming a while back, and I knew for certain three weeks ago.'

'You did?'

Clive smiled. 'You didn't see Roger's face when he heard you were coming along with us all on the expedition. You were so cock-a-hoop with joy and your own self-importance because your father finally agreed to let you come and act as his deputy you couldn't see anything or anyone. But Roger looked as though he'd found Klondyke or something.'

'Good heavens!' Gail was genuinely surprised. 'I thought Roger wasn't keen on my coming. He thought it might be dangerous for me, and immediately started being all protective and assuring my father that he would look after me. Good heavens,' she said again, 'I just laughed at him. What on earth *could* happen to me? I've got four of you to look after me—Uncle Phil, and Roger, and Jonathan, and you. And then there'll be the Great Max and the other bod who's coming that we don't know. Quite apart from the fact that I'm perfectly capable of looking after myself, thank you.'

Clive did not respond. He leaned back and regarded her with indulgent eyes, a trace of a smile hovering round his mouth as he took in the short, carelessly cut dark hair, the blue eyes that were clear and honest and expressive of courage, the mouth that was a little wide for classical beauty but smiled without guile, a chin that held determination and a slender form that was almost boyish in the scanty swimwear partly revealed under a white linen play-jacket. At last he said lightly: 'I shouldn't worry too much about Roger. You're both still just a couple of infants. Enjoy yourselves while you're young. Youth doesn't last long, my love.'

'Oh yes! Methuselah! Let me tell you I'm nineteen. I've got the vote. I've been vaccinated against about five hundred hideous diseases. I can solve the big crossword in the *Telegraph*. I can beat you at tennis——'

'That doesn't take any skill!'

'—and Daddy entrusted *me* to look after the diaries and the old maps for the expedition!'

'Bighead!' Clive laughed, and stood up. 'For that I'll throw you in the pool.'

'Oh yes, let's cool off.' She sprang to her feet and held out her hand. 'Come on.'

'Spare me.' Clive pretended to groan. 'You forget, girl, it's all very well for vital young things like you and Jonathan, but I have to remember my advancing years. Just you wait until the venerable forties catch up with you!'

While she giggled he held out his hands and let the spray from the fountain play over them. 'This will suffice for my aquatic capers for today. Unless you couldn't exist if I didn't come and play life-saving with you.'

'Darling Clive, you know I couldn't.' Chuckling, she scooped water into her cupped palms and made a threatening gesture towards him. 'Come on, lazy, and get into training for our big trek.'

'Oh sure.' Clive made an agile grab which had nothing elderly about it and swung her up into his arms. 'You asked for it—oh dear!' After a few steps towards the big swimming pool he pretended to stagger and gasp for breath as he set her down.

From the pool Jonathan watched the horseplay and called an invitation. A few minutes later she was floating lazily in the water while Clive lounged on the terrace alongside and gave the occasional teasing comment on Jonathan's laborious breast-stroke down the length of the blue-tiled pool.

'Your guitar playing is better than that, and that's saying something.'

Jonathan continued to concentrate on his stroke, and Gail began to match him, unfairly changing to a crawl that sent her shooting ahead. She touched the bar and turned to issue a challenge to Clive to come and join the race, then bobbed in the water as she saw he had turned away to greet their host, Don Felipe, and another man. Suddenly she forgot about horseplay and sobered as she looked at the other man. He was dressed informally in pale fawn slacks and a white shirt open at the throat. He was taller than their host and Clive, and his physique under the shirt was broad and powerful, betrayed in the lithe easy control of his movements as he strolled along the terrace.

Near the entrance to the villa he paused, as did his two companions, when Gail's uncle and Roger came out of doors. Don Felipe moved, gestured, obviously making introductions, but Gail did not consciously note the reactions of the other members of the little group which had formed. There was something about the tall central figure that commanded her attention, and she narrowed her eyes against the strong light, trying to see his face more clearly. At the moment his profile was presented to the angle from which she watched, and she studied its strong, intent lines rather wonderingly. The brow was high, the nose straight and the jawline clearly defined to the point of severity. The tilt of the head was authoritative and the bronzed skin helped to add up a total that conveyed power, assurance and someone who would stand no nonsense.

Gail blinked and snapped out of her staring trance. This must be Max Christiern. And Max Christiern meant it was time she got out of this pool. Playtime was over!

At that moment Clive turned and beckoned towards her, and the sun glinted on the chestnut tones in Max Christiern's dark hair as he turned at Clive's movement. Gail lifted her arm to wave and opened her mouth to shout that she was coming, but before a sound could emerge her legs were grabbed and she had a blurred glimpse of Jonathan's grinning face as she was ducked violently.

Spluttering wildly, she struggled back to the surface, forgetting the man on the terrace in an immediate urge to wreak vengeance on her attacker. With an agile twist she turned in pursuit and overtook Jonathan easily, sending showers of spray over his head and shaking her fist. He yelled, accepted the challenge and prepared to do battle, then went down spluttering as Gail grabbed his hair and exacted her revenge. He came up gasping and made a lunge at her, and from the terrace Clive shouted:

'Want any help, old man?'

'Mayday! Mayday!' Jonathan gurgled. 'I'm being drowned by the last of the Amazons!'

'Serve you right for starting it!' Gail aimed another cascade at him, and then bobbed back, honour satisfied, as she joined in his breathless laughter, In leisurely fashion they swam to the edge of the pool and climbed out. By the time they had collected their bits and pieces and wandered into the villa to shower and change the rest of the party were nowhere to be seen.

Jonathan paused as he and Gail crossed the rose and ivory checkerboard tiles of the wide salon. He tilted his head in a listening attitude towards the heavy double doors which led into the main *sala*. Muted sounds of male voices came from behind the gilded panels, and Jonathan said, 'Sounds as though they're in conclave already. Shall we take a dekko?'

'You can if you like,' she cast a pointed glance at her own attire, 'but I'm going to shower and change first.'

'Yes, I suppose you're right,' Jonathan looked back at the door and then fell into step at Gail's side as she began to ascend the lovely curving stairway that swept up in a complete half-circle to the gallery of the first floor. 'I wish the Christiern man had been held up a few more hours. If the conference goes on all night I won't be able to keep my date,' he grumbled.

'What date, for goodness' sake?' she asked. 'You haven't been here long enough to ... oh really, Jonathan!' She began to laugh at the bashful blush in his youthful cheeks.

'It's that girl on the plane. Remember? Her father's in the Corps Diplomatique and they were coming back from leave. She said I could ring her,' Jonathan went on enthusiastically, 'so I did, last night, but she was resting, so I tried again this morning and she said she could see me tonight. Oh hell, blast and damnation! I simply can't be late,' he groaned.

'And you simply can't cut the conference,' Gail grinned.

'No, but I'll be able to slip away,' he decided with a return of his usual optimism. 'After all, it's not as though I have to make the vital decisions on this trip, so I don't suppose I'll be missed.'

Gail had her doubts about this, but she merely smiled as she left him at the door of his room and went on along the gallery to her own. If Jonathan imagined he could evade the gimlet eye of her uncle he was due for disillusion; after all, they were here on a mission, not to enjoy themselves.

The shades had been drawn across the windows of her room to keep it cool and dim. She opened them and stepped out on to the balcony, looking out over the massed blooms of every conceivable tint of rose, from the palest shell pink of the jasmine to the rich flaunting cyclamen winding over the fat curvy urns immediately below. Big velvety bees heavy with nectar drowsed among the blossoms and the soft drone of their flight hung on the hot still air.

Gail sighed, resting her arms on the warm metal rail, letting the languorous sense of sunlit peace enfold her. Already she was falling under the spell of South American magic—and victim to its sensuous malady ... 'Ah, *manaña* ...' she sighed ruefully, turning away reluctantly and making for the shower. Despite young Jonathan's optimistic hopes of romance, it was just as well Max Christiern had arrived to set things moving before they all succumbed to the insidious effects of sub-tropical luxury living and their host's superb hospitality.

Still, as Clive had remarked, they might as well make the most of it ... She showered and tingled under an ice-cold spray in the blue-tiled bathroom adjoining her bedroom and completed her toilet, her musing thoughts running ahead to the journey that awaited them. When she had slipped into a cool lime-green dress she went to her case, the one containing her expedition kit, and took from it the folder which held the precious diary and her father's notes, all of which had been entrusted into her keeping, and again the shadow of regret clouded her eyes. For a moment she was back in time and six thousand miles away, seeing her father's face as he put the folder into her hands. He had not said, 'Take care of them, Gail,' he had said, '*I know* you'll take care of them,' and her heart ached because of the blow ill-health had struck at him. How was he feeling now? So far away and thinking of them, wondering if at last his dream was to come to reality. A dream of finding the key to curing the dread enigma of cancer.

Her father was chief of the botanical research department of the Lealholme–Crosse Foundation, where a ceaseless search for new curative developments in plant pharmacology went on untiringly. Recent research into the properties of a kind of buttercup found in India which secreted a substance with an inhibitory effect on bacteria, and the cyto-toxic 'periwinkle juice' which could kill rapidly developing cells, had caused him to further extend his research along this particular line.

It was a chance remark from a colleague during a conference on steroid chemistry that had started him on a trail begun almost a century previously, a trail that was to lead him all over Europe, seeking old records, many of which had been destroyed during the two dreadful holocausts that had ravaged Europe during the first half of the twentieth century. Then at last, when he was almost convinced that the proof he sought no longer existed, he had found the diary of the young French doctor, Gervaise St Lubin, in a cellar under the archives of the Faugille Institute, and with it the maps and reports made by the German scientist, Von Schaumel, who accompanied Gervaise St Lubin on two expeditions to Brazil and Peru during the latter decade of the last century.

Gail opened the mildewed and crumbling leather covers of the diary and scanned the faded brown writing which would never fail to fascinate her. Was she, nearly a century since this ink dried, to tread the path Gervaise St Lubin had trod? Rediscover this strange hidden valley no one but her father really believed existed, and meet the dwellers therein, whom St Lubin referred to as the Secret People, and find the Flower which grew nowhere else in the world except this forgotten valley?

Gail sighed. Had these two men long dead really believed that a small, insignificant blossom could hold the secret man had dreamed of discovering since the dawn of time? The elixir of eternal life? Did the Secret People really enjoy unbelievable longevity and freedom from the maladies that plague mankind? The search for these answers had cost St Lubin and Von Schaumel their lives. The young Frenchman had contracted an incurable tropical disease during his sojourn in South America. It had killed him a few months after his return to Europe. Von Schaumel had not been deterred. After frantic efforts to raise funds to finance a further expedition, he had set sail the following year for the New World and never returned. Not a trace of him had ever been found.

Gail closed the diary and stared into space. No, the Flower of Eternity would not confer the gift of everlasting life, but there was the chance it might aid the fight against disease, and soon, perhaps in a few weeks, they would be one step nearer——

'Miss Denning!'

The call and the tap on her door brought her back to the present with a guilty start. The young *sirvienta* looked at her gravely and told her that her presence was requested in the *sala.* She was also requested to bring the *documentos—pronto!*

That sounded like Clive! At least she hoped so. Gail thanked the girl and hastily gathered up the papers and put them back in the folder, glancing at her watch as she did so. Surely she hadn't taken all this time! But the deepening violet shadows across the garden told that indeed the afternoon had waned, she rebuked herself.

She hurried along the gallery, pausing once to glance over the ornate balustrade and experience appreciation of the superb sweep down to the great gilded and frescoed hall below. It was quite deserted and she hurried down lightly, to stop before the entrance to the *sala.* Suddenly she did not relish making a solo entrance in front of the gang, especially after having had to be summoned, and particularly with the memory of Max Christiern's forceful expression suddenly coming to life in a mental picture flash. There was no sign of Jonathan to take a share of the disapproval she was certain would be waiting within and for a moment she wished she'd checked to see if he was still in his room before she came downstairs. Oh well ... she smiled ruefully at the door and heard firm steps ringing across the marble checkerboard.

The deep smooth voice of Don Felipe said, '*Buenas tardes, señorita.* So they found you. Yes, this is where you will find them. Allow me ...' He reached past her to open the door for her, and she flashed him a smile.

'I know—thank you, *señor,*' then lowered her voice to a conspiratorial whisper, 'I suspect I've blotted my copy by being late, so I was just bracing myself in readiness.'

Her host pretended to frown at her demure expression as he pushed open the door, and, aware that Don Felipe was reputed to be something of a charmer for the fair sex, Gail had no hesitation in joining the harmless eye-play. 'You've just arrived in time to provide a little moral support.'

'Moral support?' A slight gleam entered Don Felipe's dark eyes. 'Oh come, Señorita Denning, surely we are not so formidable a gathering as all that. Or do they bully you as badly as that?' He touched her arm. 'Take no notice of them. Come, let me introduce you to Señor Christiern, who is to lead you on your journey. I trust you will not find him *too* formidable.'

On the one wall of the *sala* unbroken by entrance or windows hung an enormous tapestry. Below it, on a carved pedestal, stood a magnificently sculptured eagle set in a plaque of glimmering *huamango*. The man who was studying its intricate workmanship did not raise his head until Don Felipe had led Gail almost to his side. Only then did he look up and survey her, the merest of smiles flickering over his mouth as he acknowledged Don Felipe's introduction. He took the hand she had automatically extended and inclined his head.

He said, 'If I am the most formidable hazard you are to encounter you need have no fear of the journey ahead of us, Miss Denning.'

Something in the cool, clear grey eyes holding her gaze with such penetrating steadiness wiped away all the lighthearted banter with which she had entered the *sala*. She withdrew her hand rather quickly and said, 'But I'm not afraid of the journey ahead, Mr. Christiern. On the contrary, I'm looking forward to it more than anything else in my life.'

'I'm glad to hear it,' he said coolly. 'I hope you won't be disappointed.'

'I don't think so.' She decided to ignore the mocking inflection she thought she had detected in his tone and deliberately held his glance, determined not to lose in the clash of wills she instinctively sensed would come with this man who was bound so closely with the immediate future. She held out the folder. 'The papers, Mr. Christiern, with the diary and my father's notes. He entrusted them to me with the instruction to give them to you.'

His lean mouth curved slightly as he took the folder and looked down at it without showing any undue emotion. 'You make it sound as though you were conferring top-secret documents on me.'

'They are valuable, in the sense that they are irreplaceable and are on loan from the Faugille Institute,' she said coldly.

He inclined his head. 'Of course. My sense of humour must have got out of true during the last hour while I waited for these. However, I will take the greatest care of them until I've compared them with my copies, and then I will return them to you. Now,' he appeared not to notice the indrawn breath of affront she gave at the icy snub and turned towards the other, 'perhaps we can get down to work.'

There was a general movement towards the long, carved oak table and a shuffling of chairs into places as seven people took their places round it.

'Are you still in need of that moral support?' Don Felipe was holding the back of a chair and gesturing with his free hand.

'Sadly so,' she responded in a small, rueful voice, relinquishing her hold on the chair she had been about to draw to the table for herself. Then she saw Roger had hurried to perform the same courtesy for her, and she flashed him a propitiatory smile, the quarrel of the morning temporarily forgotten. But inwardly she was seething.

Somehow in the space of a few minutes and few words, Max Christiern had succeeded in making her feel like a banal schoolgirl with an over-developed sense of the dramatic. Making fun of her because of the way she had given him the papers. They *were* precious. It would be a tragedy if they were lost. And he seemed to think it was amusing. To say nothing of that snide little snub about an hour to lose his sense of humour.

She glanced at him where he had taken his place between her uncle and Clive, and her mouth tightened. Perhaps she *had* allowed her sense of importance to get out of proportion. But she *had* felt proud at being allowed to act as her father's emissary when illness had prevented him accompanying his brother, her Uncle Phil, and the rest of the team. Maybe it was childish, but did Max Christiern have to destroy that small measure of pride and make fun of it? Oh hell, I'm being petty, she thought, what does it matter? Nevertheless, she could not help wishing that her father had been present. He had a way with him that seemed to preclude all pettinesses in the people with whom he worked. Whatever happened she must not get off on the wrong foot with the man who was in authority now. And there was one certain thing she must not forget... There had been a great deal of doubt and discouragement to overcome before Gail's father had won the support which made possible this expedition. His colleagues at the Foundation were sharply divided in opinion as to the worth of the project and for a while it had looked as though the whole thing might be vetoed. Then an unexpected ally had arisen in the U.S. parent side of Lealholme-Crosse, in the person of the man who was having so profound an effect on Gail at this very moment. It had been Max Christiern's influence which had tipped the balance...

He had laid down his pen, and his gaze was resting somewhat disconcertingly on her, as though to ascertain whether she was still with them in spiritual as well as physical presence.

Guiltily she realized she hadn't heard a word of what had been said and firmly applied a mental discipline to her erring thoughts. She said, 'I'm sorry. Did you ask me something?'

His mouth compressed slightly. 'I did not—obviously it is just as well I didn't.'

She bit her lip, conscious of a certain interested regard from the others, and said quietly: 'I'm sorry, I was thinking about my father. Please go on, Mr Christiern.'

'I think we'd better forgo the formalities straight away. A few weeks of the primitive living ahead of us will soon rub the shine off our manners.' His glance left her and roved round the circle of faces. 'I think that about ties up the practical side of the business. Our plane leaves at nine-thirty hours tomorrow morning, arrives Sanquitos at noon approximately, where we pick up the rest of our supplies and transfer to the trucks. We have lunch with Señor Perez, then depart for Huamano. From there we go on by mule and if all goes according to plan we should reach Vaquaya three days later. After that, we're on our own.'

He paused, then added dryly, 'It will not be a comfortable journey, I feel bound to warn you. So if you've any doubts...' His glance had come full circle to probe her face.

'I haven't.' Her own gaze did not waver.

He leaned back, and, when no one seemed inclined to comment, went on quietly, 'At the risk of sounding pessimistic and harping on facts which will be well known to you all already, I must stress, particularly to the younger members, the dangers of underestimating the challenge of the rain forest. The buddy system will stand once we leave Huamano. There must be no wandering off on private explorations, anywhere, at any time. You'll have been briefed, I presume, about medical precautions, especially anti-malarial and water discipline. We are carrying a comprehensive medical kit, so there should be no serious setbacks provided that everyone takes reasonable care. Don't neglect the slightest sign of discomfort or infection because it won't stay slight for very long, I can assure you.'

During this harangue his attention had rarely left Gail, and now her sense of humour returned to struggle with pique. She saw the suppressed grins on the faces of her uncle and Clive, and knew that they knew to whom that lecture had been mainly addressed. She assumed a prim expression.

'The secondary infection of prickly heat erupts rather disgustingly, doesn't it?' she observed in sepulchral tones. 'And after the desquamate stage is passed normal perspiration may not be established for several weeks.'

Max Christiern shot her a sharp look and said coldly, 'You've been doing a little homework in the medical library. I'd advise you to forget it, Miss Denning, in favour of day-to-day common sense.'

'A little knowledge . . .' jeered Clive.

She ignored him. 'I thought we'd decided not to wait for the shine to go off our manners, Max. By the way, who's going to be my buddy? Anybody but Clive, please. He snores when he's asleep, and he's nearly always asleep.'

'Exhaustion,' grinned Clive. 'I'm getting too old for the job of keeping you out of mischief.'

'I doubt if Miss Denning will be short of volunteers,' Don Felipe observed, rising to touch a bell by the great stone fireplace. 'I think it is time we relaxed with wine, and then it will be time to dine.'

They had all begun to talk at once as the little meeting broke up from its formal grouping round the table. Under cover of the chatter and lighting of cheroots proffered by their host, Gail made for Clive. In a low voice she said, 'What do you think of him?'

'Who?' Clive pretended blankness.

'Oh—Don Felipe!' she whispered sarcastically. 'Be *serious*, Clive!'

'I'm trying, girl. I was just thinking it's a good job we're leaving tomorrow and you've got us all to protect you. I think Don Felipe has his eye on you. Gr-r-r!'

'*Clive!* I'm not talking about Don Felipe's roving eye,' she hissed. 'I asked you what you thought of *him*.'

'And I'm telling you,' said Clive blandly with an innocent smile. 'He's a widow, you know, and they say Latins make most masterful husbands.'

Gail sent a despairing glance heavenwards and decided to give up. Then Clive said softly, 'The trouble with you, my love, is that you're spoilt. You've had too many of us falling victim to your charm. It's almost undermined the Foundation. But I have a suspicion you've met your match tonight. Fluttering eyelashes and winning ways won't work on this one.'

'I don't,' she denied, 'flutter my eyelashes.'

'A metaphoric example,' he said, grinning. 'You know what I mean.'

'Yes,' she sighed, 'but I wish you'd tell me what you think of him.'

'Has it got you so bad you can't voice his name?' Clive shook his head, then abruptly dropped his teasing manner. 'I'll tell you. I should say he's a man I'd like to have by my side in a crisis. But as to the feminine point of view ... Honey, how do you expect *me* to know?'

'You're so good at judging character.'

'Yes, but not another bloke's sex appeal!'

Gail clenched her hands and glared, but before she could frame a suitably withering retort Roger loomed up and said suspiciously, 'What's all this about sex appeal?'

'You're too young, laddie.' Grinning, Clive moved away leaving her with the one person she didn't want to be alone with at that moment. With a sigh she met Roger's reproachful blue gaze and thought with dismay: Roger's going to go all intense again.

He took her hand and drew her to the side of the great carved eagle, well away from the others, and said, 'Thank goodness I've got you for a moment. Listen, Gail, you're still not mad about this morning? I didn't think until later—I shouldn't have started that ring business while Clive and Jon were around. But when you admired it and——'

'Please, Roger,' she put her hand on his arm, 'forget it. I did feel a bit awkward with the others there, and——'

'I know.' He didn't wait for her to finish. 'I should have waited until we were alone, only it seemed the perfect opportunity to——'

'We're going in to dinner now, children,' said Clive from behind. 'Sorry to break it up and all that.'

He stayed there a moment, waiting, and Roger's thin face tensed with impatience. 'Okay, we're coming. I want to talk to Gail.'

'I think we'd better go through. Can't it wait, Roger?'

'Yes, but——' He ran his hand through his thick fair hair. 'Listen, I've got to talk to you, Gail, before we leave tomorrow, as there won't be much chance once we get away.' He gave a frustrated exclamation as Don Felipe looked back into the otherwise empty room and signalled polite invitation to the dining-room. 'Slip away after the meal. I'll wait for you in my room.'

With a sigh she acquiesced. There was nothing else she could do. It was gradually being borne on her that her relationship with Roger had undergone a change during the past few weeks and she wasn't sure how she was going to cope with this new aspect of it. She went into the candle-lit dining-room and sighed for the easy, uncomplicated friendship she had always known, for the undemanding camaraderie she had shared with Clive and Jonathan and Roger and Tony—who'd had to be left behind—for so long. They were not only the closest and most loyal members of her father's team, they had become part of her daily life, and she wanted it to go on in exactly the same way ...

She had been placed next to her host during the meal, and he was at his most attentive, anticipating her every need almost before she was aware of it herself and ensuring that every part of what was little short of a banquet was served as she desired.

At any other time she might have enjoyed basking in what she fully recognized as simply a charming if ever so slightly wolfish interest in a young and unattached feminine guest. Don Felipe was quite a charmer, and even if he was a bit of a Don Juan and didn't mean a word of it he was more fun than one of the eggheads with their noses in the clouds—like her Uncle Phil.

But now she was conscious of encountering Roger's blue gaze every time she looked across the table. He was sitting next to Max Christiern, and when she evaded one pair of eyes filled with feverish intent she seemed to encounter another pair so coolly and totally different but no less disconcerting. And there was Don Felipe on her right, dark and smiling and shadowy, his eyes seeming to say, 'How sad that all these other people are here,' as he refilled her crystal wine glass, and Clive smirking at the other end of the table as though he fully perceived the trend of her thoughts and thought them highly amusing ... Gail decided to look at her plate and try to sort out logically why she should suddenly feel defensive and touchy and uncertain and all tangled up, and finally decided that it must be the change of air ...

Fortunately the post-prandial discussion turned back to the expedition and might have extended into the small hours of the morning had not Gail's uncle, with a somewhat surprising practicality, announced that they should really turn in at a respectable hour in view of the early start the following morning. There were murmurs of general agreement and the group broke up. Gail was aware of unwonted sleepiness as she murmured a goodnight intended to encompass them all and then bestowed a more individual smile of leavetaking on Don Felipe. But once in her room the sleepiness fled and she thought unwillingly of the assignation with Roger.

For a moment she was tempted to forget it. She could talk to him tomorrow on the plane. Then she decided she might as well get it over with; he would only land along here if she didn't. From childhood they had always barged in and out of each other's rooms when on holiday together with the two families or when visiting each other's homes, but now she was conscious of a reluctance to be alone with Roger, one she had never experienced before. If it wasn't that she had to admit she owed him an apology for being shrewish with him this morning...

Roger's room was on the other side of the gallery, facing the part of the garden where the pool was situated. She left her own room and walked along the deserted gallery. The door of her uncle's room stood ajar and within it sounded the voices of her uncle and Clive. The scent of cigar smoke drifted out and she repressed a smile as she went past the door; so much for her uncle and his 'early' night! She tapped lightly on Roger's door and opened it a fraction as she called the automatic, 'Are you decent? It's me.'

There was no immediate response, and for a moment she thought the room was empty. Then Roger said, 'I'm here,' and she saw the outline of him against the night where he was leaning over the balcony rail.

Slowly she went to join him, and he said, not looking at her, 'Isn't it a perfect night? If only we had nights like this at home, instead of a climate that usually consists of long cold winters and short cold summers.'

She nodded, relaxing slightly as she gazed out into the scented purple darkness. There was no breeze and the heavy breathless warmth was a palpable caress against her bare arms.

Roger gave a soft exclamation. 'Somebody's having a midnight swim. Can you see? Is it old Jon down there?'

Though her eyes were becoming accustomed to the darkness she could not identify the swimmer from this distance.

'He's too smooth for Jonathan,' she said idly, 'and Clive and Uncle Phil are yarning and kippering the air with those lethal-smelling cigars they seem to go in for over here—I heard them in Uncle's room as I came along.'

'It must be Christiern down there,' said Roger, hunching his arms under him as he leaned on the rail. 'I wonder how he's going to fit in,' he went on musingly. 'Somehow he's not a bit as I pictured him. I had the impression that he'd be older, more of a contemporary of Uncle Phil and your father, instead of somewhere in the mid-thirties. What did you think of him, Gail? He looks as though he'd be a bumptious blighter if anyone contradicted him.'

'Could be.' She frowned, not wanting to discuss Max Christiern at that moment, then she said impulsively, 'Roger, I'm sorry I was churlish over that ring business this morning. It was my own fault for admiring it and—— I mean I never thought you'd——' She stopped again in mid-sentence as he turned to face her. 'Only you know what a tease Clive is, and—and it was much more expensive than I dreamed. I couldn't let you buy me such an expensive present . . . I'm sorry if I . . .'

'It wasn't intended to be a present, or a tourist's memento.' Roger hesitated, then said quietly, 'I wanted it to be more than that. I wanted it to be—— Oh, Gail, I know I can't ask you to marry me just yet—it'll be at least another year before I'm sound enough financially to offer you reasonable security—but I want us to have sone definite understanding. Now. That's why I'—he was pulling a small package from the breast pocket of his shirt—'I went back this afternoon and got it. I want you to wear it until we have a proper engagement.'

He was opening the little box and taking her hand, trying to thrust the hard silver circlet on to her finger, and at the cold metallic contact she came out of her frozen astonishment.

'No—— Roger, just a minute.' She backed a pace. 'I—I don't know what to say, but I—I can't take this, not this way. You're going too fast for me. I——'

The ring fell to the balcony floor with a soft tinkle, and automatically she stooped to grope for it. Roger bent at the same time and there was a slight confusion as they peered in the subdued light spilling out from the room behind. Then she spotted it and grabbed it, standing up and making to brush her hair back from her flushed face, and Roger caught her in his arms, in a surprisingly strong embrace. He sought clumsily for her mouth and blotted out her gasp.

For a moment the interlocked figures swayed, then Gail twisted her head and put her hands against his chest. 'No, Roger,' she took a deep breath, 'we've got to get something straight first. Let's go inside and calm down, for heaven's sake.'

Before he could speak she walked into the room and put the silver ring down on the dressing-chest, then sat down on a dressing-chair and thrust out a warding-off hand. 'Sit down, Roger, and listen before you . . .' A little breathless still, she said quickly, 'Isn't it the usual thing to *ask* the girl first? Instead of just taking it for granted that she understands, and is willing, and loves you?'

'But you know I'm in love with you!' he exclaimed. 'I thought it was understood. That it was only a matter of time before . . .'

'But that's just it,' she cried. 'Nothing has been understood, at least as far as I'm concerned. Oh, for goodness' sake, be honest, Roger. There's never been anything but affection, family affection, between us, and you've never given any indication of being crazy with love for me—until now.'

'I couldn't, not until I'd finished with college, and while you were still a kid, and until——'

'Thanks!' she interrupted. 'You're only two years older than me—and about ten years younger in maturity, I'm beginning to think. Oh, Roger,' her face softened. 'I'm not trying to hurt you, it's just that—that I've never thought of you in that way. I do love you, but not ... Roger, are you serious about this?' she asked in a troubled voice.

'I'm serious enough, but it seems you aren't,' he said moodily. He thrust his hands into his pockets and paced across the room, to come to a halt beside her. 'I wanted to talk to you before we left home, but there was such an upheaval of comings and goings, and with your father being ill and everything I thought it best to wait. But this morning, when you picked out that Peruvian silver ring and admired it, I felt sure that it was a sign that you—that you——' He broke off, his mouth tightening, and picked up the ring, weighing it in his hand. Suddenly he swung round.

'Will you wear it, Gail?'

She bit her lip and looked helplessly at him. 'How can I? It wouldn't be fair to you. Because I can't give the answer you want from me. Try to understand, especially at a time like this, I'm not ready for an entanglement, and I'm not sure of my own feelings, or anything. It wouldn't be fair to you,' she repeated.

'I'm only asking you to wear it,' he said flatly. 'I'm not asking you to give me your answer straight away.'

She was silent, staring at the delicate silver engraving and the milky blue stones set round the band. He said, 'I bought it for you, and if you don't accept it I'll drop it down the first drain I come to.'

Typical Roger blackmail! He had always been the same, right through childhood. *'If you don't come and watch me playing cricket I'll hide your book.' 'If you don't tell that ghastly Susan girl to keep away I won't lend you my camera.'* And later, in adolescence, *'If you don't promise to come camping this year I won't take you to meet that skin-diving bod you wanted to meet.'* Yes, there'd been many quarrels; her own spirited pride would never let her give in without a good fight, very often she hadn't given in, but somehow the quarrels had never lasted, they'd remained good friends and good companions, until Roger went to college and time and separations had smoothed out a great deal of youthful impetuosity. But as for love ... She looked up and said curiously, 'Something must have brought this to a head. What and when?'

He smiled without humour. 'Remember that little blonde girl, Miranda, whom I brought home once or twice last year? I thought I'd fallen for her, but she was just as empty-headed as most of your teenage cronies were. I used to feel such a relief when I came home for the vacs and we used to slip back into the old routine. You're always so easy to be with, not worrying and nagging all the time about getting out to parties and swigging cocktails, or getting so dressed up a splash of mud was a tragedy.'

'Yes, I know.' She took a deep breath. 'That's just it, Roger. You want a girl to give you the companionship a man would give you, without the snags but with all the advantages of feminine companionship.'

Suddenly she shook her head and stood up decisively. 'It's no use, I can't wear your ring and make a promise I couldn't keep. Please try to understand. I don't want to hurt you, but I'm trying to be honest. I can't, Roger.'

He said stubbornly, 'I want you to have it, even without any promise. But I shall ask you again. Go on, take it, you can wear it on the other hand if you like, as long as you wear it. After all,' he attempted a laugh, 'if I haven't the right to buy you a souvenir of an event like this trip, then who has?'

Still reluctant and anything but happy, she let him press the ring into her palm and close her fingers round it. 'Very well,' she said slowly, 'but you've got to promise me one thing.'

'What?' His mouth curled slightly.

'That you'll let it rest till the expedition's over. I don't want an emotional involvement, because there'll be enough to cope with without that. And I don't want to quarrel with anybody, least of all you,' she said firmly.

'If that's the way you want it. Until we've seen this through.' He moved, and she thought he was going to embrace her again, but he merely put one arm round her shoulders in the careless way he had always done, and walked her to the door. 'But remember, I'll be waiting. I'm not going to let you go.'

He bent towards her, and she turned her head away. 'You promised. Till we've got back. Nothing's changed—yet.'

'You always were a stubborn little cuss.' Suddenly he seemed to revert back to the Roger she had always known, except that a certain determination had hardened his eyes. 'But remember,' he added, 'I'll expect to see rings on your finger, or ...'

'Maybe the bells on my toes—I'll remember.' Before he could think of anything else she managed a lighthearted smile, murmured, 'Bless you—see you tomorrow,' and slipped out of the room.

The click of the door closing triggered off a sigh of relief that was visible in the sag of Gail's shoulders. She opened her hand and looked down vaguely at the ring. Should she have accepted it? Even though she would never forgive herself if she hurt Roger. And yet the thought of marrying him had never entered her head. Why not? Why was she so surprised at his proposal? He was bound to be fond of her, they'd been so close, as close as brother and sister. But that was just it; one didn't marry a——

The thought died as the shadow fell across her and she looked up into the unsmiling face of Max Christiern.

He was wearing a white towelling jacket loosely over dark red swim trunks and his hair still glistened with droplets from his swim. His glance dropped to the ring on her still open hand and then flickered to the door behind her before returning to her face.

Abruptly she closed her fingers over the ring and shouldered past him, almost running round the angle of the gallery to her own room. When she reached it she could not help glancing over her shoulder to where Max Christiern was about to enter the room next to Roger's. A rectangle of light outlined his broad figure before it was blanked out by the closing door, and Gail raised her hand to her face.

To her dismay it was hot and scarlet.

CHAPTER II

GAIL awakened very early the next morning, before the first rose tendrils reached up from the eastern horizon. She lay for a few minutes, while the tension of excitement crept through her; this was the day of the beginning—the real beginning of a journey into the unknown. Then the other underlying matter erupted disturbingly to the fore of her thoughts and she stirred uneasily. What was she going to do about Roger?

She threw the light covering back and sat up to grope for the light switch. It was hopeless to think of trying to go to sleep again, and even if she could it wouldn't be worth it for an hour. Another memory flash returned from the previous night, and she sat for a moment, listening for sounds of stirring in the depths of the house and hearing none, before she scrambled out of bed and collected her swim things. An early morning swim before the place woke up might help to clear her thoughts and bring them into perspective.

Some ten minutes later she was padding downstairs and letting herself out of the little side door nearest to the pool.

The night had cooled the water and left the air moist but delightfully refreshing. She floated lazily and tried to think of marriage with Roger, of whether she could love Roger sufficiently to accept his proposal. It all depended what one expected of Love with the capital L of reverent poetics, she thought wryly. Perhaps she was in love with Roger without knowing it.

Did the grand passion really exist? The kind which consumed poets' souls and brought thrones toppling? Thinking of her placid parents, and the comfortably wrangling couples who made up their circle of friends, she could not spotlight a single relationship which suggested that a throne might ever have been lost for it—or won! The boy and girl interludes which had been her experiences to date, apart from Roger, also seemed to fall short of the fabled heights—the last one had lost out to a new motor-bike and rally weekends, and then Roger had come home. True, her friend Stella had languished for an entire week after a broken *amour*, and had vowed passionately that it was the end, that she was through with men for ever, but just before Gail left home the tear-stains had dried under layers of creamy eye-shadow and the eyes were speculating dreamily on a new male light shining on the horizon.

The heart seemed a more resilient organ than poetic literature credited, Gail decided, returning to the theory that any two people of opposite sex, given reasonable interests in common combined with affection, respect and a certain amount of physical attraction, could forge a happy and enduring relationship. Propinquity, imagination and nature would do the rest. But it seemed a cold and unsatisfying idea, somehow, far short of the passionate all-consuming fervour which swept one into the very realm of ecstasy where union of heart, mind and spirit transcended even the fleshly rapture. But did it exist?

She thought of Roger, and felt nothing. No quickening of the heartbeat, no firing of the senses, no yearning . . . nothing except a sense of worry, regret and a guilty wish that Roger had never awakened to this unexpected change of heart.

Gail sighed and realised that day had come. The sun glowed through a haze of mist and the scents of awakening blossoms were stealing across the garden. She swam slowly one more length of the pool, and Max Christiern came down the steps from the terrace and strolled deliberately to the edge of the pool.

He halted by the handrails and said, 'I've been looking all over for you.'

'Have you?' She seized the rails, groping with her toes for the rungs, and he bent down and grasped her arm as she scrambled out. She dashed the water out of her eyes and reached for her towel, conscious of her streaming body under his cool gaze. Turning away slightly, she slung the towel round her shoulders and said lightly, 'What can I do for you, Mr Christiern?'

'Forget the formalities first.' He fell into step with her and looked straight ahead. 'I wanted to return your folder. Here it is...' he paused briefly to pick up the folder from one of the garden seats, 'but perhaps you'd better dry off first. Then I suggest that you give them into Don Felipe's care until we return. We'll be spending several days in the rain forest and the damp rots everything.'

'Yes, I was going to do that—except for the maps and my father's notes. I want to take those.' She hesitated. 'If we took those out now ... will you give the diary and the other papers to Don Felipe?'

'Certainly.' He halted and laid the folder on the broad stone top of the terrace balustrade. 'But I thought you would prefer to do that yourself—after you'd made sure I'd returned them all in perfect order. After all, they're very precious.'

For a moment Gail was struck into silence while the strong brown hands sorted out the appropriate items, then indignation came uppermost.

'Just a moment. Do you think for a minute that I'd suspect you of *not* returning them in perfect order?' she said in a low, angry voice. 'And do you have to make fun of me because I tried to be conscientious? Because I don't see the joke. And I don't like what I do see,' she finished furiously.

He had watched her, giving no indication of reaction to her sudden attack, except to hold her indignant gaze quite steadily. Then he nodded. 'All right, I get the message. But I thought you could take it, judging by the little I've gathered of the backchat between you and your own crowd. Maybe I'm mistaken. Or on the wrong wavelength. However, my apologies if the wavelength was as offensive as all that,' he ended coldly.

He held out the bundle of papers she wanted and it was obvious the matter was closed, coldly closed.

She looked at them, making no move to take them, while a quite incomprehensible series of reactions rose to mix with indignation. She was not used to the cool hands-down from any man, and on the few isolated occasions she'd experienced it she'd been able to dismiss it with a shrug and forget the offender. But this time she couldn't. And this time she couldn't leave it at that. She took a deep breath, and decided to come into the open.

'Listen,' she said quietly, 'I don't want to quarrel with you, or anybody else, least of all when we've all this ahead of us. I know I forgot about the time last night and kept you waiting. Well, I'm sorry about that—I'd probably have apologized at the time, straight away, if you'd ... but you—— Oh, it doesn't matter.' She felt the embarrassment of colour come into her cheeks, and a renewal of anger that he could just stand there, making no attempt to meet her halfway, while she made an idiot of herself. 'Forget it.' She snatched at the folder and turned away jerkily.

'No.' He retained his grip on the folder and one that had suddenly closed round her arm. 'It's no use taking that attitude.' He took a deep breath and drew her towards the parapet. 'Sit down for a moment and let's get this straight. *I* don't want to quarrel with anybody, least of all yourself, for the same reason you've already pointed out. So I'll start by admitting that you're the last person I expected to see yesterday when I arrived.'

She stared at him. 'Last person! What do you mean?'

'When I heard of your father's illness, about which I'm extremely sorry, incidentally, and that his daughter was joining the expedition I expected someone totally different.' He shrugged. 'Don't ask me why. I assumed that she'd be older, more ... well, not so incredibly young and slight. I——'

'You mean you expected a great weatherbeaten female clumping in, with a voice like sandpaper and—and'—Gail shook her head, torn between pique and mirth at the mental picture her own words had evoked—'and because I wasn't you immediately jumped to the conclusion that I was young and silly and frivolous.' The moment of mirth had been very brief and her eyes sparkled with defiance. 'Well, I'm not, I can assure you, and if I get the chance I'll prove it. You're not the only one,' she said bitterly. 'Nobody back home was very keen on the idea of letting me take part. They put up all sorts of arguments, until my father and Clive came round to my way of thinking and decided that I was right, that I could compile a full record of the whole business as well as or better than any of the others. I know Daddy's language, how much this means to him and how bitter a blow it was when the doctors flatly forbade him to make the trip. So, if he's to be denied the climax of his months of work and hope, he's going to have the next best thing; see it through my eyes the way only I can convey it to him.'

She stopped, breathless with the force of vehemence, and Max Christiern said, 'All right—I can understand all that. But it's simply that I think the same way as they all thought. I think it's going to be too tough a trip for a girl. It's not that we doubt your ability to keep a clear and comprehensive record—frankly, a job a woman often does do very competently; most men dislike writing reports unless they happen to be writers by inclination. And I'm certainly not disputing your sincerity. But I still maintain it's going to be too tough for you.'

His tone had softened somewhat and she was quick to seize the advantage. 'I knew that was at the bottom of it. Well, please don't worry. Ask any of the others—they'll tell you I've a hide like an ox and an appetite like a goat's. And I don't mind discomfort. So'—she gestured—'won't you accept that, and let's get off on the right foot after a sticky start?'

He smiled then for the first time and stood up. 'You don't leave me much choice after that. I don't want to be a boor, but——'

'Then it's pax!' Impulsively she thrust out her hand, and after a slight hesitation he took it in a firm grasp that allayed some of Gail's inward fear. Maybe it was going to be okay after all. He *was* human! She smiled and relinquished his hand, and was about to make some trite remark to break the funny little silence that had come when she heard steps approaching and saw Roger coming purposefully towards her with Don Felipe in the rear. She grabbed the bundle of papers and thrust the other folder at Max.

'Give that to Don Felipe for me—please. I've got to get in to breakfast or I'll not have time for any. Thanks...'

Clutching the bundle and her towel, she hurried past Roger and her host with hasty murmured greetings and went into the villa, to take the stairs two at a time and almost cannon into Clive at the top.

'Top of the morning, early bird?'

'Smashing!'

Going into her room with Clive's facetious comments floating after her, she grinned to herself. It *was* smashing!

The air of excitement was infectious that morning as the party prepared to depart. The personal luggage they would not require was being stored at the villa until their return and the heap of kit that was eventually stacked near the entrance consisted of the sturdy sensible clothing, groundsheets and sleeping bags, and various other items of equipment they would need. Clive dumped his pack on top of the pile and said, 'I think that's about it. But let's have a quick check, everybody.'

At last everything was stacked in the big station wagon. Max and Clive got into it while the others piled into Don Felipe's car for the drive to the airport. Gail settled back and glanced at her watch. It was still not quite nine o'clock, but she felt as though half a day had been crammed into the past three hours.

Beside her, Roger moved and caught her hand. 'Where is it?'

he whispered.

'Packed where it's safe,' she whispered back, withdrawing her hand gently but firmly, then wondered if she'd been too abrupt. She added, 'It's a dress ring, Roger, and pure silver scratches more easily than harder metals. I don't want to spoil it—or lose it.'

'Oh.' He settled back. 'As long as you've got it.'

'Yes, I've got it safe—don't worry.'

He lapsed into silence and she knew it was not the answer he wanted, but she had no intention of going back on her decision of the previous night. Suddenly she wondered if he was going to abide by her refusal to commit herself until the expedition was over and wished she hadn't accepted the ring at all. But what else could she have done?

The arrival at the airport temporarily drove the thought from her mind. There was more upheaval with the luggage, discussions with airport officials, goodbyes to be said to Don Felipe, then more waiting around while Gail wondered if she had forgotten anything vital.

Roger touched her arm. 'I'm sure we could go aboard. I'm sick of hanging around here.'

'They're still waiting for Harmon,' said Clive, putting his bag down and sitting on it. 'The photographer bod who's to join us. Remember?'

'Well, I vote we move,' said Roger.

'Right, children.' Clive stood up again. 'We might as well bag the best seats. I think that's us over there—among the odds and ends in the tuppenny corner.'

On a far runway a Constellation skimmed down, and Clive added, 'No, children, not that one.'

Gail grinned and pointed. 'Try this one for size.'

'Ye gods!' Clive stopped faintly. 'I didn't know the Incas had invented the original aeroplane.' Eyes narrowed against the sun, he surveyed the old Dakota transport aboard which the party's assortment of supplies was being loaded. He turned to Gail. 'Take it from me—you're going to experience some real flying now.'

'Would you be talking about us?'

They swung round at the unfamiliar voice and saw a tall burly man of about forty-five regarding them with mock indignation. 'You and it belong to each other?' asked Clive, poker-faced.

'We do. That's Dora and I'm Bud Nixon. Glad to meet you.' Bud held out his hand, and Clive made informal introductions. The pilot gave Gail a friendly nod. 'You'll be okay with us. The

Dakota's the best bird ever made. They last.' He waved an oily hand at the solid durable lines of the elderly aircraft. 'She was flying when all your fancy jets were a twinkle in a designer's eye.'

'Yes, I can see that.' Clive wrinkled his nose.

'And she's as good as ever she was,' said the cheerful Bud.

'What do you hold her together with?' asked Clive, strolling on. 'String and chewing gum?'

'Say! I thought we were allies.' Bud dug him in the shoulder. 'Are you trying to start an international incident?'

Gail had dissolved into laughter. 'Take no notice,' she gurgled, 'Clive left his gag-writer at home this trip.'

'I knew it!' Bud groaned. 'Why am I always fated to be a captive audience? Well, if your party's ready I guess we'd better get moving.'

'Hey!' Jonathan hurried up. 'Did you see my guitar go aboard?'

'Your guitar?' Clive was instantly serious. 'Yes, sonny, it's safely aboard. I saw it with my own eyes. It's safely on that Boeing that took off for New York ten minutes ago.'

'You didn't!' Jonathan was visibly shaken, then he aimed a dig at his tormentor's ribs. 'Clive, you're a rat!'

But it was a further twenty minutes before the last member of the team arrived, a sallow-faced man of middle height with lank unkempt hair and a mouth set in surly lines—probably due to trying to hurry airport officialdom through his clearance, Gail decided. South Americans seemed to love stamping and they'd certainly had a field day with the English party if her own papers were anything to go by.

George Harmon was stowed aboard, mellowed a little by a soothing draught from a bottle conjured forth by Clive, and at last the venerable transport was trundling wheezily along the runway. Unbelievably they were off!

After the cushioned luxury of the VC 10 on the journey out the Dakota promised a spartan journey, Gail thought, glancing round the bare interior of the long cabin. In common with most transports of its type the Dakota was equipped for speedy transformation to either passenger transportation or freight carrying, and the hard little seats were the type for quick dismantling when not needed. But what did a bit of discomfort matter? She wondered idly about the state of the pressurization and fiddled experimentally with the little tube clipped to the fuselage at her side. She hoped somebody had remembered to check the oxygen cylinders!

'You know how to use that?'

She turned to find Max leaning over the back of her seat. 'Yes, I think so. I don't suppose I'll need it.'

'Better be sure,' he said calmly, 'we'll touch a pretty high altitude later on.' He got up and leaned across her, uncapping the tube and putting it to his lips. 'It's okay, a bit primitive this type, but it works okay.' He replaced the tube and straightened, looking down at her. 'I'll be here behind you, so if you have any trouble just give me a sign.'

'Thank you,' she said, a little awkward suddenly under his gaze and aware of Roger turning round from the seat in front. Probably Max did not intend to make her feel like a greenhorn, but she could not dismiss the suspicion that he would have preferred a team exclusive of feminine personnel. He nodded, and she settled back, taking the magazine Roger had passed back to her.

But it was difficult to concentrate, and a little while later it was impossible to ignore the majestic presence of the Andes. The foothills passed below and the magazine slipped unheeded from Gail's lap. This crossing was utterly remote from the one three days previously when they arrived. Then, it had been before the dawn. High in the stratosphere, soft lights had glowed in the jetliner, the air hostess had glided along the softly carpeted aisle with drinks, and the grandeur of those peaks far below had been a presence only dimly sensed by those more receptive to travellers' atmosphere—and the suave little commentary coming over the muted tannoy. But now...

Fascinated and almost a little afraid, Gail stared down through the small window. It was all true, everything she'd been told. That the Andes exerted an indescribable sense of wonder no other mountains could equal. It was a spell at once disturbing, awe-inspiring and cruel.

Vast, jagged, enwreathed in coiling mist and capped with white crystal, they were like another world. At one point the plane was flying between two of those leaden-hued peaks, and Gail experienced the uncanny sensation of being suspended motionless between two vast cycloramic cinema screens. The soaring heights parted, opening into a great cavern of sky, reeled past in giant focus and blurred as the gaze was drawn inevitably forward again.

Someone touched her shoulder and she started violently.

Roger said, 'Let's go up front for a better view.'

'Can we?'

'Of course.'

From the observation point up in the nose beside the calm and uninterested Bud Nixon the effect was heightened almost unbearably. She hardly heard what Roger was saying over her shoulder as she crouched in the confined space and stared breathlessly at the scene unfolding. The plane felt dwarfed, a fragile mote amid the grandeur, and suddenly a fanciful notion came to her that she rode a humming bird to some mystic castle whose lofty towers shimmered at the summit of a distant peak.

Half afraid, half exultant, she turned to voice the whimsical notion, and in the second it took to register that Roger no longer stood behind her she felt the world fall away beneath her feet.

The plane dropped like a stone, as though seized in the mad grip of a giant hand, and a wild blurring panorama rushed up before her eyes. Sheer stark panic caught her and it seemed hell was let loose all round. She screamed as she pitched forward, and something caught her, bracing her against ... she did not know ... it was crashing ...

Light-years away a voice shouted, 'It's okay ... we're not crashing ... *it's okay*!'

She had her eyes shut and her teeth clenched, waiting for the dreadful moment that would not come. They said that those last moments before eternity were endless hours; those spinning seconds when death beckoned to desolation. Long enough to live again an entire lifetime ...

The disembodied words floated above her, not registering, then they shaped into sounds and there was a heartfelt blasphemy, and someone *laughing*! ...

'Try opening your eyes. Come on!'

A shuddering sigh ran through her from tip to toe and slowly she raised her head, made her lids part.

Max was looking down at her, his mouth curled in a thin, sardonic grin, and he gave a slow, deliberate sidelong glance of indication. His mouth shaped, 'Go on,' so softly she was not conscious of hearing the words. Unbelieving, she turned her head, saw the blue sky hanging motionless, the long white cloud with a tiny smudge under it, the filmy haze of greeny-grey wavering to meet the blue, and, most wonderful of all, the frantic deafening revving of engines was once more a sweet steady music.

'Well, have you decided to go on living?'

'I—I——' She swallowed hard, still uncertain that her heart and all the rest of her had come down from where she had left it.

'We hit an air pocket,' Max said.

She swallowed again, and behind her she heard the pilot quip, 'Did you have to break the news so soon? With a swell armful like that?'

Time, motion and awareness suddenly all clicked together. It was Max's arm that was clamped like a vice round her waist, Max's body the stay against which she was braced, and at some time during the nightmare her own hands had seized him in a vice hold. Slowly she unclenched her grip and saw the star-shaped creases in the white silkiness of his shirt.

The smile still lingered round his mouth. 'Well . . .?'

The pilot said, 'Gee, I wish I could get them worked up like that.'

Abruptly Max's arm dropped away. 'Keep your mind on your driving, Bud. There's an obstruction ahead.' He touched her shoulder. 'All right now?'

She got her voice back. 'I think so. I—— Oh! The others.'

'Yes.' Max ducked out of the cockpit and she followed him rather unsteadily.

The cabin was a shambles, personal luggage strewn all over, and the still-dazed occupants rubbing the various damaged parts of their anatomies.

Gail's first thought was for her uncle. Professor Denning had been thrown sideways and he was picking himself up, looking white and shaken. She ran to him and he gave a sigh of relief when he saw her. He managed a shaky smile and waved away her anxious hands. 'No, I'm all right, my dear, just getting a bit old for shocks like that.'

'Are you sure?'

'Yes—are you? At least I was sitting down when it happened, but you were on the move.' He looked at Max. 'Any damage?'

'I'm going to check—if everyone's all right?' There were various murmurs and mock groans, and he stepped over a bulky haversack and moved down towards the baggage section in the tail.

'Sure you're okay, Gail?' Roger was dusting himself down. There was a big smudge on his brow and more smudges on the knees of his pants. 'I found myself saying my prayers in the gangway—and I was, too,' he said with a shaky grin.

'I've lost my book,' announced Clive. 'I was just reading, all nice and peaceful and not bothering anybody.' He cast a comical glance upwards. 'I wonder if it's come down yet—I'd just got to an exciting bit.'

'It came down all right!' Jonathan had extricated himself from between two seats. He rubbed his head and held up the offending book with a menacing hand. 'Want it back?'

'Whoa! That was an act of God, sonny.' Clive ducked hastily. 'Gee, that was a shaker. I thought my number was up.'

They were getting over shock now and humour was uppermost as it frequently is once danger is safely past. Gail rescued her own things, stowing them back in her place, and saw that Max was restoring to tidiness the stuff which was strewn around the storage compartment. The others were still grouped round her uncle and without speaking she went down into the other compartment and began to stack the smaller pieces into neat piles along the rack.

Some of the heavier stuff had been strapped in place to distribute its weight, but one large package had broken free and overturned. Max had righted it and opened it to check for damage. He closed the lid and said briefly, 'One item broken. Not too bad, considering.' He bent to heave it back into place and automatically she went to help.

He straightened immediately and motioned her away. 'Go and sit down—you still look pale.'

'Do I?—I'm fine.' A perversive whim suddenly made her want to nullify that earlier betrayal of weakness and assert her practical capabilities. She laid hold on the crate and said airily, 'Come on, I've always been strong.'

'Yes, I've already gathered that,' he said dryly. He rubbed his chest rather pointedly and nodded. 'You pack a tough grip.'

She coloured, seeing the faint marks of the creases still in the front of his shirt, and forgot bravado. 'Did I hurt you? I'm sorry, I——'

'All right—I'll survive.' Abruptly his expression changed and he rested his hands on the crate top, leaning forward slightly and giving her a long, direct stare. 'Listen, Gail, there's something we might as well get straight before we go any further. Don't think you have to play it tough this trip, if that's the idea you've got into your head. You're a girl, and I don't expect you to disown your sex—I loathe swaggering young female Amazons. On the other hand, God help you if you act the helpless female, you'll get no sympathy from me. But in this case'—he rapped a knuckle on the top of the crate—'there's a crowd of men around. They're equipped for crate heaving—you are not. Now go back and sit down, and stay there. And think about what I've just said. Right?'

The temptation to smile during this address had been very shortlived; now it had subsided altogether. Gail looked for long moments at the firm decisive face, found that holding the gaze of those penetrating grey eyes was having a disturbing effect she wasn't quite sure she was happy about, and decided that for the present silence was indicated.

Slowly and thoughtfully she turned and went back to her seat in the passenger compartment.

There were no further shocks. The Dakota ploughed placidly on, over snaking coils of rivers, over the lush green jungle canyons that cut like long fingers into the hills, and from the heights above they looked like part of a great rock-strewn landscape over which a dense carpet of lichen had grown.

The touchdown on the tiny airstrip at Sanquitos was smooth enough, and as Gail alighted she felt her sense of excitement quicken again. The thought of the trek by mule along the tortuous jungle trail to Vaquaya did not worry her in the least. For, if the old diary were true, it was there they would find the key to the Secret Valley and the flower it guarded.

Sanquitos was little more than a big *montana* village. It had no hotel, but Don Felipe had arranged for the party to have lunch with Señor Perez, the manager of the coffee plantation which was the main source of Sanquitos's livelihood.

His car and a big station wagon were waiting at the airstrip with the trucks to take the supplies and in a few minutes the party, excepting Max and Roger, who were to supervise the transfer of the supplies off the plane, was driving along the rough dirt road to Señor Perez's villa.

Gail experienced a twinge of disappointment as the picturesque little town was left behind. It was market day and she would have liked to have peeped at the colourful scene, exploring amid the motley of wares and produce, the noise, and the ebb and flow of bartering humanity glimpsed briefly under the humid, sun-glazed heat of midday. This was where the true essence was found of a country rich in contrasts and legends of Inca wonder, a land already weaving its spell around Gail.

But there was no time. With true Peruvian hospitality Señor Perez thought first of his guests' comfort and doubtless under the impression that the English members of the team longed to escape from the breathless, fly-ridden humidity ensconced them in a cool shaded *salita* and offered them the choice of delicious iced drinks or English tea.

At four o'clock they were on their way again, this time in the trucks, bumping and pitching over the three hour long drive to Huamano. Here the pack-mules awaited, and the two Quechuan guides who were to take the party to Vaquayo, and here, a short distance from the huddled huts of the village, the party made their first camp.

Spirits were gay that first night—the novelty hadn't had time to wear off, but it soon would, Clive prophesied ominously—and Gail, who had never had any doubts about on whom the catering chores would fall, cheerfully concocted her first menu for seven hungry diners. However, there was no shortage of volunteers to help—which would also wear off soon, Clive informed her brightly—and afterwards she lounged on her groundsheet, thinking of tomorrow and riding a mule and the little mission where a long-dead French doctor had stayed on his way to the Secret Valley and written the diary Gail had held in her own hands. Soon she would find shelter under the roof of that mission, and there she would write her story, for the person so dear to her who waited to hear it...

She lit a cigarette and stared up at the stars. This was living! This was fun! She was going to enjoy every moment of it...

* * *

The humming birds were the first wonder to capture Gail's attention in the rain forest. Minute feathered miracles of rainbow hues, their flight so swift the eye could register only the glowing flash of crimson or emerald or blues or rose and try hopelessly to define the brilliant little shape on racing wings.

During those first plodding hours on the back of a small, wiry mule she kept her camera slung at the ready in the vain hope of capturing in colour the flight of the humming birds, and was somewhat comforted by the knowledge that Clive, who rode in front, was also essaying a little photography, and from his occasional exclamations of impatience wasn't too sure about his success, either.

'Sticky, isn't it?'

The voice was close and she looked round sharply, to find she was no longer riding in single file. George Harmon had caught up with her and was now riding alongside. He gave her a cocky grin. 'Bet you're beginning to wish you hadn't come.'

'But I'm not.' She did not return the smile and her response was cool.

He let that ride, but his glance slid sideways under the peak of a shabby green baseball-type cap. Presently he said, 'How about wising me up?'

'What about?' She could not instil a great deal of warmth into the reply, nor did she feel inclined to try. The little contact she had had so far with Harmon had not induced any strong desire to further acquaintance with him.

'Aw, now, honey! Don't be like that. I'm the stranger in the camp. I hope you don't reckon on it staying that way.'

'We're all strangers here,' she said.

He jogged on a few yards, then raised his hands with a resigned gesture. 'All right, you win, honey. I never really believed it, but I guess I do now.'

She sighed, and decided she was being ungracious. 'I'm not sure what you believe, Mr Harmon, but if you think anyone's being unfriendly I'm sure it's not true. No one is intentionally unfriendly, I assure you.'

'No, it's just that traditional British reserve. But I guess it'll break before long—there ain't nothing that can't be broken if you set about it the right way.'

She said nothing. If she could be said to be an example of 'British reserve' she intended to stay that way, and Harmon's approach was more likely to have a reinforcing effect on this intent than otherwise.

Apparently not noticing her silence, he went on, 'Now, for instance, you were trying to get a picture of those pretty little birds back there. Right? Now, if you don't mind my telling you, you won't get a good picture the way you were going about it.'

'Yes, you're the expert, aren't you?'

His shrug and coy expression of repudiation were the original perfect example of smug agreement, she thought wearily, wishing he would go and talk to somebody else. But this intention was obviously far from his mind. He said with that brashness she found so irritating, 'As soon as you're ready to do some more shooting just give me the wire—I'll put you right in the top bracket. It just needs a little patience and the know-how.'

He shuffled the cap around on his head, passed his hand over his moist face and turned to grin. 'I must say it's a turn-up for the book to find a girl in the crew. Makes a——'

'I think we're stopping,' she said with barely disguised relief. 'Nosh time.'

'Great. I'll lend a hand.' Nimbly he dismounted and reached to lift her down before she realized his intention. Hating the lingering feeling of his hands round her waist, she moved away quickly and said over her shoulder, 'You can help Jonathan do the water—it has to be filtered, you know.'

'Sure.' His mocking salute and 'You're the boss-cook, ma'am!' were innocuous enough, but there was a peculiar glint in the pale eyes that returned more than once to study Gail with speculation in their depths during the meal which followed.

The trek was resumed, a slow patient plod into the dense steaming forest, and now, luckily for Gail, the afternoon heat began to have its effect on Harmon, and so also, it seemed, did the flies, judging by his antics and muffled curses as he warded off the small unwelcome company. Roger dropped back and Gail, her shirt pulled loose from the waistband of her slacks for maximum penetration of such air as there was, temporarily forgot about the not very endearing Harmon. But Harmon hadn't forgotten about her.

Nobody seemed terribly hungry that evening when they thankfully called a halt and pitched camp. The lotus life of Don Felipe's villa in Miraflores now seemed as remote as England, and it was difficult to credit that less than thirty-six hours had elapsed since they left its cloistered opulence.

As Clive remarked, the novelty was wearing off and none of them would be sorry to be free of the stifling discomforts of the jungle. Doubtless it was fascinating, the blaze of colours amid the green, the ceaseless chatter and movement of exotic birdlife, the strange seductive beauty of wild orchids incredibly profuse as daisies in an English meadow, there for the taking, but ... as Clive said, he'd swap the lot for an ice-cold shower and an equally ice-cold lager, and this more or less expressed the feelings of the rest of the team. Sticky was the word for it, to say nothing of the itch!

Gail settled down as she had done the previous night to write another instalment of the chronicle for her father, and Roger, though he would obviously have preferred her company, went reluctantly at her bidding to make up a four-hand card school with Clive and Jonathan and the professor. Of Max there was no sign. She'd scarcely seen him all the day, except for the briefest of impersonal contact during halts, which was the way she'd rather keep it, she decided, smiling a little; she'd be less likely to get on his nerves that way.

'So this is where you've hidden yourself!'

A large shadow loomed over her and without waiting for an invitation Harmon dropped lazily on to the corner of her groundsheet. She edged away and the torch she had propped on the top of her pack rolled down. His reflexes seemed instant, for he caught it almost before it reached the ground, but he seemed to be making a lot of restoring it so that its light fell on the open writing-case on which his curious attention was fixed.

She closed it, and he smiled easily. 'I thought for a minute you were pondering over that famous old diary.' He relaxed back and got out his cigarettes, saying casually, 'Do you think there's anything in this miracle herb business? Or are we on a wild-goose chase?'

'The Lealholme–Crosse people must think there's something in it,' she said shortly, 'or they wouldn't finance the trip.'

'Yeah, I guess so, but it makes me wonder if it's worth it.' He swiped at a large moth near his face and watched the crippled insect fall as he said disgustedly, 'To think I could have been in a snazzy hotel tonight, all on exes with a dame thrown in, and instead'—he flicked irritably at another winged intruder—'look what I got!'

She stared. 'Where would you have been? I don't understand.'

'Covering an industrial trade fair at Cincinnati.'

'But you're working for Lealholme–Crosse. We all are.'

'I work for nobody but myself,' he stated with a grin that challenged her to make what she liked of *that*.

Puzzled now, she was silent, and apparently satisfied with the effect of his statement he dragged at his cigarette and went on, 'I'm a freelance industrial photographer. My sister's husband is editor of the Lealholme–Crosse mag—you know—most of these big concerns put out their own journals, the technical kind that nobody but the eggheads can understand. Through my brother-in-law I got the assignment to cover the photographic record of this business, and a lousy assignment it is. But I guess it might be worth it.' He scratched round his ribs and flung his cigarette butt into the darkness with a fine disregard for fire hazard. Then he turned to her. 'What would you say if I told you I'd heard of this so-called Flower of Eternity long before your lot ever got wind of it and started this business?'

'You?' He had her attention now. 'Where did you hear about it?'

'Well, I guess it's a long story,' he drawled, 'but somebody got there before you, I can tell you. All of twenty years ago.'

'Then why didn't somebody investigate it? If there was proof?'

'Because the eggheads at Lealholme–Crosse wouldn't take much notice of the crazy talk of a drunken bum picked up on the 'Frisco waterfront.'

A cloud of moths whirred madly in the torch rays and Gail brushed them away absently. What on earth was Harmon talking about? What story had he heard? Her father had made extensive enquiries during his research; both the U.S. parent company and the Peruvian branch of Lealholme–Crosse had admitted a complete absence of pertinent information at their respective ends. Then where had Harmon got his information? Was his source also European? There couldn't be two Flowers of Eternity.

'Of course there mightn't be anything in it,' Harmon said with apparent disinterest, 'but I wondered if there was any tie-up between the two.'

'What does Max say?' she asked.

'Max? You mean Christiern?' He laughed shortly. 'Think

I'm going to stick my neck out? I like to be sure of my facts before I open my mouth.'

'But if you ... we ought to pool every bit of information we can get hold of,' she exclaimed. 'Who was this man on the waterfront? Had he been here? And——'

'Not so fast, sweetheart. As I said, it's just something I heard. Could be a load of crap for all I knew. On the other hand, if there was anything in it, it could mean the——' He checked himself and laughed throatily. 'I guess that would be painting rainbows, just on account of some crazy old screwball spillin' the hokum. All the same, I'd sure like to see those old papers you have, just to see if it all joins up and makes sense. I guess if——'

'Harmon? Oh—you're here.' Max arrived on unexpectedly silent footfalls. 'We're turning in now.' He stood there firmly, obviously with the intention of seeing Harmon shift before he himself moved again. 'Okay, break it up.'

Grumbling, Harmon got to his feet. 'Lights out? Do you reckon we're a bunch of kids off the campus?'

'You can do what you like,' said Max shortly, 'but I want to see the girl settled safely for the night.'

'Sure, sure.' Harmon waved his hand and grinned at Gail. 'See you in the morning, kid, and we'll have another talk about the business.'

He ambled away and when the darkness had enclosed them again Max said to Gail: 'Is he bothering you?'

'N-no. No, of course not.'

'You don't sound sure.'

'Well,' she gestured, 'I can't refuse to be sociable, can I?'

'Maybe not,' there was a rather noticeable pause, 'but I couldn't imagine you being particularly friendly if you didn't feel so inclined. Either to Harmon or anybody else,' he added after another slight pause.

Gail went taut. What point was that little remark making? 'I haven't been unfriendly—to anybody,' she defended sharply.

'That wasn't what I said.'

The others were standing round the campfire Clive had made, enjoying the last leisurely smoke of the day, and at that moment Gail's uncle tapped out his pipe and turned in search of her. He raised his hand. 'All right, Gail?'

'Yes, fine, thanks. And you?'

'Fine. I'm turning in now. Goodnight, lass.'

'Goodnight, Uncle Phil.' The smile faded from her mouth as she looked back to the shadowed outline of Max Christiern. He shrugged and turned away, and an impulse carried her an impetuous step forward. 'Max . . . ?'

'Yes?' He halted immediately.

'There is something . . .' She stopped, already regretting her impulse.

'I thought there was. What's worrying you?'

'It's not exactly worrying, just curious.'

As though he sensed the uncertainty behind her restraint he said in a more encouraging tone, 'You'd better tell me about it. Come on, we'll take a turn along the track.' He saw her involuntary glance at the eerie, impenetrable darkness outside the perimeter of the clearing and touched her shoulder. 'It's all right, I won't let you get lost.'

'Buddies?' She smiled faintly and heard him laugh. He flicked on a large rubber-covered torch and then briefly she recounted the conversation with Harmon. 'I don't know what story he's got hold of, or who this other man is,' she concluded, 'but I think he ought to be made to spill it.'

'Probably he would have done, if I hadn't interrupted.'

'But that's just it.' She turned to look up at the dark profile. 'He had no intention of putting me wise. I could tell. He was stalling to see what he could find out from me.'

'Why should he?' Max asked in equable tones. 'There's no secrecy about the Flower, or mystery that I know of, apart from the sheer inaccessibility of the place where we hope to find it. After all,' he went on in the patient manner of one explaining what should be obvious, 'there's nothing new or unusual about investigating jungle lore in search of old plant potions which might yield unexpected results if applied scientifically. The ancient Egyptians distilled an essence from the poppy to kill pain long before we extracted morphine from the same source. One doctor has made several journeys to visit witch doctors to seek knowledge and sources of their herbal cures.' Max halted and played the torch rays over the tangle of liana above before he turned and looked down at Gail. He gave a slight shake of his head. 'I fail to see what interest the old diary can have for him. I should say it's well out of his line. Unless he read French and German he wouldn't make much out of it, except for photographic purposes.'

'I don't think that's what he had in mind, and after all, he'll see it all for himself very soon—that is, if it exists.' She spotted a massive old tree trunk which had fallen partly across the track and moved towards it with the intention of sitting down. 'But I still feel there's something about him—don't ask me what—that I don't like.'

'There's something about Harmon none of us seems to like

very much, but I still fail to see—— Don't do that!' he said sharply.

'Do what?'

'Sit down. It'll be alive with termites.'

'The whole place is alive with termites, and a few million other varieties.' She stood up and brushed at her clothes. 'But why should he seem so interested? The way he talked about a tie-up between——'

'Let's get back.' Through the dimness a faint smile was discernible on his face. 'I think you've forgotten something.'

'Oh.'

'You're the only girl in the party—it's probably Harmon's idea of a line likely to hook you. By the way,' he interjected abruptly, 'how long have you been going around with your shirt flapping loose?'

'All day—it's cooler. Listen, it wasn't a line—not that sort of a line.'

'No? I'm beginning to wonder if you would recognize any sort of a line, and don't do that again,' he nodded at the offending shirt, 'even if it feels cooler. It's an invitation to be bitten. I thought you knew the rules: pant legs tucked into socks, no sandals, bush hats after dusk—where's yours?—mosquito veils at night. And no loose shirts, either.'

She sighed. He wasn't interested in Harmon, he was only interested in dictatorial enforcement of the rules. She made another effort, restraining irritation. 'Okay, lesson taken as read, I'll conform. Now, do I show Harmon those papers?'

'Why not? You'll find out where his interest really lies. When it does, just holler, we'll all be around to rescue you.'

An exclamation of annoyance escaped her and she said tartly, 'You needn't bother. I won't be hollering, nor will I need any protection, from Harmon or anybody else. But you're wrong, I know it. Just as I know that Harmon's on to something.' They had reached the line of tethered mules and the two curled-up forms of the sleeping guides, and she lowered her voice. 'What's more, I intend to find out.'

He flicked the torchlight at the small tent which was hers and said calmly, 'Yes, you do, and you can keep me posted.'

His light tone infuriated her and she turned sharply. 'Why should I? Go and find out for yourself. But you won't, you're only concerned about keeping the rules and whether I get bitten. Well, I'm more concerned with the main purpose and I'm going to play along with Harmon till I find out what it's all about. Because I don't believe he's only here to take photographs. So go on, laugh! Goodnight!'

'Just a moment.' The hand that closed round her arm was much more forceful than the words as it arrested her ducking movement into the tent. 'Listen, miss, we'd better get a few things straight. I thought at first that basically you were a sensible girl and the high spirits were the effects of the trip. Which is quite understandable. But now I'm not so sure. I think you've got an over-developed sense of drama. Two and two never made five and well you know it. So just forget all this nonsense, and to make sure we continue to have a trouble-free trip I'm going to watch you in future to make sure you obey all those rules which apparently don't interest you. I'm also going to insist that you hand over those papers and any copies you have into my care. If you want to refer to them you'll know where they are.' He paused and his mouth tightened grimly. 'Lastly, keep away from Harmon. I personally will see that he keeps away from you. Is that clear?'

Clear. She stared at him, for the moment too astonished to be angry. Now who was being dramatic? 'And suppose I choose otherwise?' she dared to say at last.

'If you're sensible you won't.'

Was there a subtle undertone of threat? Or was she imagining it? His attitude had changed completely, and the short exchange with him had altered her own, but it had happened too quickly to be pinned down and analysed. What had begun as a fleeting, nebulous curiosity raised by Harmon and turned into a careless impulse to confide in Max seemed to have run unto a headlong collision—with the very object of her confidence. He'd practically scoffed at her speculations about Harmon's disclosures, then he'd gone all grim and officious. Too officious!

'Are you afraid I'll meddle, or refuse to toe the line?' she asked, determined not to bow down.

'Meddling makes trouble, and the other objection is merely childish. I'll take those papers now.'

She opened her mouth to voice defiance, then something emanating from the implacable man planted solidly before her stilled the impulse. She ducked into the tent and unlocked her case. From it she took the oiled silk packet and silently handed it over.

He nodded, murmured a brief goodnight and walked unhurriedly into the darkness.

Slowly and thoughtfully Gail began her preparations for the night. It was not until quite a while later, curled in her sleeping bag, the uncomfortable netting obediently swathed about her head, that it occurred to her to reflect on the astonishing meekness with which she had obeyed Max Christiern.

CHAPTER III

THE first hint of personal disaster manifested itself on the third morning.

Gail wakened with a dull heaviness that wasn't yet a headache but promised to develop into one very soon and an unpleasant listlessness which made her reluctant to mount her mule when the time came to start again. The thought of another day of slow jogging discomfort like that of yesterday filled her with depression before she even started.

Dutifully she managed to take half her salt quota and swallowed a couple of aspirins, thankful that her 'buddy' for the day was Clive. Of all of them Clive was by far the easiest companion, invariably good-humoured, but understanding enough to cease his teasing when her response became half-hearted.

He swatted automatically at the cloud of insects perpetually overhead and said softly: 'Cheer up, love, the end's in sight.'

'Yes, mine,' she said lugubriously.

'Bad as that?' He reached over and patted her hand. 'The heat's got you—it's hellish, I'll admit, but you'll be all right when we get to the mission and have a bath and a proper rest.'

She nodded, too weary to reply or wonder what had happened to the vitality she'd blithely assumed would carry her through anything. Yesterday she'd been tired, but not at the start of the day, and the whole party had showed signs of weariness by night time, except Max. But he was used to the climate, and roughing it only seemed to reveal how hard and tough he was, right through. He'd certainly fulfilled his promise, she thought bitterly. Harmon had been kept well out of her way, but only Harmon. She'd been so hedged in with protective company she had grown first suspicious and then angry, sure that Max was responsible for the watchfulness. She had simmered in silence, restrained only by the innate common sense which told her that protest or argument would merely lead to a flare-up which in the end would hurt her most. Not for worlds would she risk the proving of the obvious doubts Max harboured about her inclusion in the party. But this morning ... she mustn't be ill ... she couldn't be, anyway, because she'd only eaten the same food and drunk the same fluids as the others, and they were all right. Probably because of Max's insistence on obeying the rules. *His* rules! And those insect bites; it was galling to admit that he'd been right. But *they* weren't serious, only uncomfortable, so Clive must be right; it was the heat ...

Roger, who was riding in front with Jonathan, turned at that moment and called to her, and she waved a response, forcing herself to smile.

Clive said, 'Like me to drop back and let him ride beside you?'

'No, thanks,' she said under her breath, so that only Clive could hear.

'What? Not fallen out again? Poor old Roger.'

'He fusses so,' she grumbled. 'I can't stand possessive people. He nearly drove me crackers yesterday, asking me every five minutes if I was all right, if I'd remembered my paludrine, then I feel guilty if I snap at him because I know he's a dear and all that. But he's started going into those moody silences ever since...' She bit her lip. 'He never used to be as bad as this.'

'He's growing up, and so are you,' said Clive calmly. 'He's realizing that the kid he played with isn't a kid any longer. I warned you, honey, that the romantic teething troubles were about to start.'

'They have,' she groaned, 'and I wish they hadn't.'

'Why not?'

'Because ... because I can't feel that way about him. I'm not in love with him. I'm not in love with anybody, and at the moment I don't think I want to be.'

'Hm,' Clive gave his funny, whimsical little smile, 'that sounds as though you were and don't want to admit it.'

'Well, I'm not, except perhaps'—she turned and made a face at him—'you'd better watch out, I might decide I'd like to marry *you* one of these days.'

'Me?' Clive widened his eyes. 'Is this a proposal? Or a warning?'

'That would be telling.' She was silent, for the first time struck by the thought that Clive had never married. Why not? He was still attractive, not nearly so sere as he jokingly pretended, and his most endearing virtue in Gail's eyes was that one could say anything to him without having to pretend. 'Why haven't you married?' she asked.

'Never been asked.'

'Oh, Clive!' She began to laugh, then stopped on a little choked exclamation; it hurt her head to laugh. Aware of his enquiring turn of his head, she said quickly, 'It's time you threw out a few hints. I think you'd make a super husband.'

'Too late,' he said in sepulchral tones. 'I'm too old to be a gigolo and I haven't enough money to be a sugar-daddy, and certainly I've no intention of being a father figure to any mixed-up girl-child, which includes you, young lady,' he ended sternly.

'I'm not mixed up.'

'The entire feminine gender is mixed up, the trouble is it never knows it. Doesn't even know that ladies wait for leap year before they snatch at a defenceless male. The answer's no, by the way,' he added hurriedly, 'just in case the message wasn't clear.'

'I'm heartbroken,' she sighed.

Clive chuckled, and they lapsed into companionable silence as they journeyed stolidly on under the great dense canopy through which the sun's rays percolated only in occasional small glimmers. The forest seemed even denser here, Gail thought, giving no indication that they were nearing its end. Its moist breathless stillness hung heavily in a perpetual green twilight that seemed to sap every vestige of energy from the traveller. Her clothes stuck clammily to her and she was stiff and sore from the long spells of unaccustomed riding. Thank heaven this afternoon would bring the way out of the forest.

They broke trek a little while later in a small clearing near the tributary and began the automatic rigmarole with the water filters. Gail toyed with the unappetizing mixture of corned beef and pulses, willing herself to finish it, although the swallowing of each mouthful entailed a major effort.

She became aware of Max's glance straying to her as he talked to her uncle a short distance away. Almost defiantly she put down her unfinished portion. Why couldn't Max Christiern relax like anybody else? Beside her, Clive had covered his face and was napping, Roger and Jonathan were smoking, and Harmon was dozing, his mouth slightly open and his lank black hair falling in untidy strands over his brow. He looked more repulsive asleep than awake, she thought with a flash of distaste. Max had probably been right; Harmon had been pulling her leg, he would probably have been raucously amused if she'd taken him up seriously over his story of hearing about the Flower.

She finished her coffee and hoped it would revive her sufficiently to collect the utensils and clean them. Every movement a heat-laden effort, she scoured them and repacked them in the food hamper. The others showed no sign of moving and she wandered to the edge of the clearing, picking her way along the side of the sluggish stream in search of a coolness she knew did not exist.

Her headache was getting worse and her entire body felt as though it was throbbing with dull dry heat, even her eyeballs felt scraped dry of their natural moisture. She uncorked her water flask and splashed some on her forehead before she drank a few mouthfuls of the tepid, unpalatable fluid. The chlorate of lime and hypo that had to be added made it too unpleasant for long satisfying draughts.

The replacing of the cap seemed inordinately difficult and was suddenly of immense importance as she fought against the strange disorientation which was swamping balance and senses. She dropped the flask and leaned back against the bole of a tree, trying to summon the effort to make it back to the clearing. She shook her head and took a deep breath, trying to stir leaden limbs to action. How far had she come? Twenty yards? It was so silent. The cries of the birds sounded queer, muffled, as though passing through layers of cotton wool. Twenty yards ... only a few steps ... she must move ... How many twenty yards in the six miles somebody had said they still had to go? Funny, it was all sixes. She closed her eyes. Six miles to go, six men in the team, six days since they started ... she must move ... she'd left Clive ... he might be feeling funny as well ... she'd better see ... he was her buddy ... he liked her ... Max didn't. She was only here on sufferance. She mustn't let him see she was feeling groggy. The first time she proved a hindrance he would send her back. She mustn't give him the excuse. *She must get back* ... but if she moved she would faint ... all the heat in the world was concentrated on her ... it was coming from the tree against her back. If only she could get cool ... they would wait a few minutes ... she would dip her face in the river ... dream of coolness ... snow, drifting in cool flakes ... rush of waters ... ice crackling ... wonderful ice, melting the heat ...

Gail slid deeper into euphoria. Now she was cool, under those needle-sharp stings of an icy shower, cold and dark and cooling. She stirred fitfully, her lips moving faintly, shaping whispers: don't wake me ... not yet ... not for a little while. I'm so tired ... please ...

But her hair had got wet under the shower. No, in the river. She must get back to the others. They'd be worried. She put up her hand—something seemed to be stopping it—to pull the wet strands away from her face and opened her eyes.

It was quite dark and very still and quiet. She blinked, full consciousness returning with a rush, and panic followed. Where was she? Not still asleep under that tree? It was night! Had they all gone on and left her there? But she wasn't under that tree, or——

She struggled wildly to sit up and a hand pressed on her shoulder, thrusting her back.

'Now, no fighting! You'll do.'

A large dark outline swam into focus and the voice clicked into place in her memory and filled in a mental picture of Max Christiern.

'Where...?' Again she tried to sit up and free herself from the thin cloudiness in which she—— It was a sheet! A cold damp sheet! So that was why she was so deliciously cool, her whole being moist and——! Shock coursed through her—entirely unclothed!

'Keep calm.' The voice was unperturbed. 'I'll light the lamp.'

The amber light of the storm lamp glowed to life, illuminating her own small tent, and black leaping shadows grew on the canvas. She saw Max outlined against his own shadow as he adjusted the lantern and hastily she wriggled down under the sheet, painfully aghast at the long shape of herself scarcely concealed under the damp clinging folds.

He came back to her side, shaking down a thermometer, and said, 'Cooler now?'

She nodded, watching the hand and the thermometer with a slightly hypnotized gaze. He reached for the sheet, and she clutched its edge in instinctive protest. He stood still and she relaxed her grip and sighed. His tone and his mien were so detached, so coldly professional that she might have been something on a slab for all the concern he was showing. The thermometer was thrust into her mouth, and a slight frown stayed between his brows while the second-hand of his watch ticked round and his fingers curved lightly on her wrist.

For a few moments he was silent and she felt a stab of fear. Surely she wasn't really ill? And why was it so quiet? Suddenly she sensed the jungle pressing close outside and a strong feeling of isolation. He was turning away, replacing the thermometer in its tube, and she reached out and caught at his arm.

'Max, what happened? Please tell me. I'm—I'm not——?'

He turned back to her, his expression softening a little as he saw her worried face.

'You collapsed with heat exhaustion after lunch.'

'Yes, but...' She could not keep agitation under control. 'I can't remember. What time is it?'

'About eight o'clock.'

'Are we still in camp?'

'*We* are.'

She noticed the stressed pronoun and repeated in a startled voice, 'We? What do you mean? Where are the others?'

'They've pushed on. They were all aching for a decent night's rest and a bath. There was no sense in depriving the rest of the team needlessly.'

'What about us?'

'We'll follow on in the morning, if you're fit enough.'

She stared. 'I'm all right now.'

His smile was tinged with cynicism. 'Not yet—not quite.' Then his expression became grim. 'Don't ever do that again.'

'Do what?' she said. 'I couldn't help it.'

'I don't mean taking ill. I mean wandering away alone. You'd gone quite a distance. It took us nearly an hour to find you. No——' he gestured abruptly as she began to protest, 'I know you don't remember. I don't expect you to, as your temperature was tipping a hundred and three and you were light-headed when we got you round.'

'But I can't remember. What have I been doing since then?'

'Sleeping.'

'I remember going to sleep. I was dreaming of snow and swimming through a deluge of icy water.'

'That would be the treatment I was forced to give you.'

She fingered the damp sheet and looked up doubtfully. 'This?'

He nodded. 'And buckets of water.' He came and squatted on a small folding stool, and the ghost of a quirk at the corners of his mouth disappeared. 'You see, Gail, when a person, particularly someone who is not used to the tropics, succumbs to heat it's vital to bring down the temperature as speedily as possible. What happens is that the body's natural cooling mechanism starts to give up. Heat-stroke follows and it can be fatal. So lacking ice-packs the only remedy was that of stripping you, wrapping you in a sheet and swilling you with water.'

He paused, and the little quirks came back to lighten the seriousness of his expression as he said, 'That you are now perfectly lucid, your temperature practically back to normal, proves the efficacy of a somewhat primitive treatment.'

She frowned, digesting this information, then asked, 'You sound like a doctor?'

He smiled. 'I am a doctor, though I've veered into another line now. I did a three-year residency in a Boston hospital not long after I came out from home.'

'Where's home?'

'Wherever I happen to be.'

She looked down. It didn't seem a very satisfactory answer, but if he didn't want to talk she wouldn't ask.

He stood up and turned away. She watched silently while he filled a cup with water from a Millbanke filter and dropped two tablets into it. He shook the cup, then held it out to her.

'Oh no!' Her mouth twisted into a grimace. 'Not more salt—please!'

'Sodium chloride—ten grains.' He was smiling now, a smile that curved his lean mouth with lazy humour and gave him a wickedly attractive look that Gail had not previously noticed.

She sighed and drank slowly, watching him over the rim of the cup, and wondered why she had never realized how attractive he was—or could be if he so chose, she amended to herself. The dark eyes held her gaze and she felt warmth creep into her cheeks. She became aware that she was holding an empty cup to her lips and put it down hastily, where it promptly overturned.

He caught it as it rolled and when he straightened his face was quite sober again. With unflurried movements he opened one of the waterproofed canvas packs and drew out a bundle. He came back to her side. 'I think we can dispense with any more treatment. You'd better get into your sleeping bag—and don't forget your net.'

He ducked out of the tent and she unrolled the bundle, to find her clothes neatly folded within. Someone—Max?—had made another neat bundle of her toilet case and pyjamas and a clean dry towel which didn't belong to her. Thankfully she threw off the sheet and towelled and talcumed herself, and she was feeling considerably more recovered and refreshed when, hair tidied, face creamed and teeth scrubbed, she had put on the muslin pyjamas and wriggled into her sleeping bag.

Five minutes elapsed and she lay uncertainly, listening. The sounds of movements outside had ceased and she knew an unreasoning disappointment. Where had he gone? Was he just going to leave her alone now until the next morning. She might have a relapse! Also, she was beginning to feel like eating.

'Are you settled in there?'

'Yes.' Her spirits took a surprising upward spiral and she looked expectantly towards the tent flap.

He came in, pinned the flap back while he brought in two metal cooking containers and the billycan. He adjusted the inner net and left the tent flap open to the night, then said briskly, 'I'm afraid it isn't anything very exciting—I could only keep two of the mules back, so we'll have to make do with cereal and concentrates. But I've made some tea.'

'It doesn't matter,' she said happily, accepting the big plain biscuits and the bowl of reconstituted packet soup, 'this is fine.'

After a silence which seemed to be getting a trifle lengthy she remarked, 'We're lucky today compared with old-time travellers. I mean regarding the variety of dried and compressed foods available. So much lighter and less bulky. One doesn't have to carry one's own cow along and milk it for every cup of tea.'

He smiled but made no response, reaching to take the empty bowl and standing up. He poured tea from the can, added a spoonful of dried milk and handed it to her. 'I'll leave you to drink this at your leisure. I'll take the lamp and leave you the torch, but get to sleep as soon as you can.'

She watched him move in the swinging light of the lamp and said hurriedly, 'Thanks, but where are you going? I mean, have the men taken the shelter?'

He turned. 'I won't be far. If you get panicky just yell.'

'I won't get panicky.' She settled back. 'I was just wondering if you—watch out for snakes if you're going to sleep in the open,' she said abruptly.

'I can't very well sleep in here, can I?' His face was expressionless. 'So I haven't much choice.' He watched her look down and added, 'All right. That wasn't very fair, was it? Don't worry, snakes don't usually live up to their fearsome reputation. Keep out of their way and they'll keep out of yours. Goodnight.' He gave her an unexpectedly sweet smile and ducked out into the night.

For a long while she lay wakeful, wondering if he was yet asleep, and, for a whimsical moment, if he were wakeful and his thoughts following the same pattern of her own; of the awe-inspiring nature of their surroundings. Suddenly she had become aware of the smallness of herself and the frailness of the little canvas shelter deep in the heart of the untamed sleepless jungle. All around, pressing close against the canvas, were the mysterious nocturnal whisperings and rustlings, an alien zone of steamy darkness and unknown danger ever present.

Gail switched off the torch and closed her eyes. She felt neither alone nor afraid—only strangely content.

* * *

They reached the mission at Vaquaya late the following afternoon, by which time Gail's brief mood of content had long since vanished.

After her dreamless refreshing sleep Max had coldly and clinically checked her temperature and pulse and pronounced her fit enough to travel. She was not allowed to escape consuming her full quota of the beastly salt and copious draughts of the water Max patiently filtered and treated. Her protest that it was spoiling her breakfast and that too much salt was an emetic met with a brusque:

'Nonsense. You know it's necessary. Don't think about it and you won't be sick.'

'Auto-suggestion?'

He smiled sardonically. 'Where a woman is concerned? Never. Nothing so psychologically simple. I never yet knew a woman who couldn't imagine any given situation into something wholly convincing and suitable to her own way of thinking.'

'We don't!' She stared at him. 'It—it isn't even a logical theory.'

'And when is a woman's imagination ever logical?'

My! He's in a sarky mood this morning, she thought, then flashed, 'Is a man's always logical? It depends on the person's viewpoint. Anyway, why pick on us?' she accused, nettled by the arrogant assumption in his tone. 'Haven't you ever listened to a group of men when they get together in a pub after a fishing trip? The one that got away! And that's only one instance—I could think of a few more as well.'

His teeth glimmered in a smile that irritated Gail intensely. 'No. You're thinking of exaggeration. Something quite different from imagination. Exaggeration elasticizes a fact in existence; imagination creates a fantasy.'

'I don't need the definitions, even the finer shades, thank you,' she said coldly.

His mouth twitched. 'I must grant that the former is somewhat of a male prerogative, where fishing is concerned, but still merely a man's extension of a given situation. So I'm afraid you must admit you missed my meaning altogether.'

'Did I?' She raised her brows. 'I'm afraid my imagination isn't vivid enough to fathom the finer shades of your masculine analysis.'

'Perhaps it's jaded with all that salt,' he said with amusement, and turned away to complete his methodical packing. 'Don't let it worry you,' he added over his shoulder, 'I'm sure the journey will soon restore it.'

She looked at the broad shoulders curved over the pack he was strapping securely and tried to clamp down her annoyance as she attended to her own packing with unnecessary force. It didn't take long, and when she straightened he was watching her, his face betraying impatience.

'Haven't you learned to conserve your energy?'

'Of course.' She eyed him warily.

'Then why tear into it like that?'

'We've lost a lot of time—through me.' She heaved the pack outside the tent and turned back briskly. 'I've no wish to be the cause of losing any more. Shall we get the tent down now?'

'No.'

'No?' She stared her puzzlement.

He added his sleeping bag to the two packs beside the two placid mules and repeated, 'No. On the contrary, we have plenty of time, so you can sit down while I pack the tent.'

'But why not? I'm not tired. I've had a long rest—a very long one,' she said with an exasperated gesture.

'Maybe you have, but this is why.'

To her surprise he came across to her and drew his finger lightly along her brow. He held it before her eyes so that she could see the faint film of moisture on it. 'You'll sit down and cool down,' he told her firmly. 'You're not yet acclimatized, and I don't want another little performance like that of yesterday.'

He looked quite capable of enforcing his order, and unwillingly she sat down on one of the packs, bitterly aware that the few minutes of exertion plus sheer annoyance *had* made her uncomfortably hot and sticky. Moodily she watched him dismantle the little shelter, fold up the canvas and close up the lightweight telescopic alloy frame. Perhaps he was right, even though it was galling to have to admit it; she was not yet proof against the torrid heat of the jungle valley. But acceptance of something beyond the control of willpower was not easy, especially on top of the uncomfortable suspicion that he considered her as a possible impediment, one he would have preferred to be without.

She was silent after that and conversation was limited to essential communication during the resumption of the journey. Now, their destination in sight, she reined to a halt and looked wonderingly at the whitewashed adobe walls of the little mission which was the last milestone of their journey.

It was peaceful and mellow in the rich gold of the waning sun and she gave a small sigh, suddenly aware of the return of lethargy. Stiffly she dismounted and took down her pack while Max unloaded the other animal. He had trekked on foot all day, showing compassion for his loaded mount and refusing Gail's tentative suggestions that he should take her mule for spells. After her third attempt at persuasion his refusal had been brusque, to say the least, and she'd desisted from any further mention of the matter. His stamina was phenomenal, she thought, watching him lead the patient beast to a drinking trough at the side of the mission compound. She had yet to see him betray either fatigue or those bouts of irritability to which the others had all given vent at one time or another during the three days in the rain forest.

Suddenly she was overtaken by a mixture of guilt and shame. Perhaps she was mistaken to allow the antagonism he seemed to evoke so easily in her to override common sense. Even if he did restrain human feelings of annoyance and irritability behind that arrogant irony of his he was putting the expedition first, as she must do. He was doing his job, watching over the welfare of all of them, herself no exception—the reverse, rather! It was too much to expect all that *and* a blissful soul-communion of kindred spirits, she reminded herself with a flash of wry humour. All the same, it would be fun if he would...

She shook her head and gave an encouraging murmur to the placid animal which had carried her safely over the journey. 'I expect you could do with a drink, old chap. Come on.' She led it across to the trough and ventured a smile at Max.

For an instant he looked down at her, his eyes considering, then he nodded in response and took the bridle from her hand, looping it over a post. 'You'll do. I think you've got your bounce back.'

'Bounce?' She pretended to sag at the knees and saw his smile broaden. 'I don't know about bouncing, but I don't think I'll want to sit down again for weeks,' she added feelingly.

'You've an awfully long stand ahead of you, then,' he remarked dryly. 'Are you serious?'

'I certainly am.'

'Really saddle-sore?'

'A bit,' she admitted. 'More stiff than anything else. I've never ridden in my life, but I didn't think that a couple of days just jogging along would have any effects.'

'Oh.' His mouth quivered ominously and remained straight with an effort which was perfectly obvious. 'I wondered why you wanted to be so self-sacrificing and let *me* ride. Never mind, with a bit of luck the mission house will be able to supply hot water and some kind of a tub so that you can soak out the saddle sores.' His gaze shifted past her and he exclaimed, 'Ah, this must be Father Lorenzo—and your welcome home party!'

Instinctively she looked for sarcasm behind this last statement, but there was none in his expression or in the hand he rested just under her shoulder blade to motion her forward. The light touch stayed there, unexpectedly friendly, but there was little time to reflect on this little pleasantry, or the equally unexpected indulgent lift of his brows as he met her glance.

A rotund, elderly priest was hurrying across the compound, his soutane flowing in the light breeze and his face wreathed in welcoming smiles. The others were following him and the next moment Gail was surrounded by affectionate greetings and sympathetic enquiries about her recovery. All except that of her uncle.

'You gave us a fright, young lady,' he said gruffly, after a brief survey of her perfectly healthy-looking young person. 'Whatever possessed you to go wandering off like that? And why didn't you tell me you were feeling dicky?'

'One of those things, Professor.' Max spoke up crisply. 'It could have happened to any of us. And now...' He turned abruptly, and Professor Denning recollected himself and made the introductions.

The invasion of seven guests was quite a strain on the accommodation in the little mission house, but Father Lorenzo's welcome gave no hint of this as he showed Gail to a small, spotlessly clean room, which though spartanly furnished, seemed like heaven after the three nights sleeping rough.

Max and her uncle were sharing the room next to hers and the others were to sleep in the little dispensary at the other side of the compound, much to Clive's amusement. He wanted to know if the nurses were pretty and if they had cool soothing hands for his fevered brow.

Father Lorenzo laughed heartily. 'We have one nurse—an Indian woman who is a tower of strength—but I doubt if she is quite what you have in mind.' He was obviously overjoyed at the advent of the visitors and as the evening wore on and, over a simple but homely meal, he told them something of his work. Gail gained a new insight into the unbounded selflessness of those who gave their life work to the service of humanity.

On the last part of the journey that afternoon, after they had at last emerged thankfully from the rain forest into the dusty heat of the molten yellow sun, they had passed an Indian village and she had seen the rough-thatched adobe huts, the dull-skinned women, the children with sticklike limbs and enormous eyes who pursued a horde of big black mangy dogs, the men lolling in the sun, and she had smelled the sickly sweet smell of drying coca leaves. The slow, listless movements of the men's jaws, the rolling of the ash granule which released the cocaine content of the coca leaf as it was chewed told more than any words of when hunger seeks relief in numbness.

How could one man bring more than hope where such poverty and defeat reigned?

But in two short years Father Lorenzo had done a great deal; the little mission held not the gleam of chalice, nor the richness of vestments. A simple Cross hung on its whitewashed wall, above an altar which was a hand-carved board, but the Hand of God was in the orderly plantations of manioc and banana, the newly tilled strip along the riverside where the tender green shoots rose to the sun ... and in the heart of the man who sighed because he had achieved so little, and not quickly enough.

'But you have heard enough of my parish and the little school which stayed empty of pupils until the day Chief Tapibos decided to indulge his curiosity and see what it was all about.' Father Lorenzo's smile of reminiscence faded and he said, 'How can I help you, my friends?'

They exchanged glances, which somehow ended on Max. Calmly and concisely he recounted the story to date and finally placed the diary and the two maps on the table before the priest. There was a long silence after he had finished speaking, and at last Father Lorenzo looked up and his expression held a trace of sadness.

'Yes, this is the area so marked here. But I'm afraid you have come too late, my friends.' He leaned back and shook his head, his calm gaze scanning the intent faces turned to him. 'The one man I know who might have been able to help you died two years ago. Perhaps you noticed—as you arrived—the ruin of a dwelling on the other side of the river? It was the first mission to be founded here, by a Scottish missionary who came from Manaus, many years ago. I met him twice, once when I was still a young man and at theological college, later—much later—when I was about to come here to take up the work he had begun so long ago and been forced to renounce because of ill-health. He gave me immeasurable help and advice, among other things he had worked on a translation into the Quechuan tongue of the four Gospels, and it was then he told me of the valley on the other side of the hills and the people who dwelled there. There is no doubt that they and the valley are the ones you seek.'

Max said gently, 'Did he speak of the legend?'

Father Lorenzo smiled. 'The elixir of life and this flower? No, my friends, not as you hope. The Secret People are as frail as the rest of the humanity and their numbers decreasing. Dougal—my predecessor—had a theory that they were the last surviving descendants of the pre-Inca era. That because their valley was so ringed by hills to be well-nigh impregnable and set in the heart of a vast, virtually unknown territory, their existence had remained inviolate. Very few white men have come this far, but two did, a long time ago. They were adventurers, gun-runners fugitive from an uprising in Ecuador which they had helped to ferment. They came to the pass through the hills and stumbled into the Secret Valley. One was wounded, the other delirious with fever. The Secret People brought them to the mission, where Dougal tended them as best he could. But the man with the wound haemorrhaged and died that night; the other talked wildly of the valley and the strange things he had seen, of a sun temple and mystical rites, of the elixir he had drunk, and the *Blüte aus Ewigkeit.*'

Clive gave a soft exclamation. 'German! *Blüte aus*—— Blossom! The——'

'Yes. What you have called the Flower of Eternity.' Father Lorenzo sighed. 'Naturally Dougal assumed all this to be the ravings of delirium. But the man passed into a long deep sleep. By the following day his fever had abated. He was weak, but calm and perfectly lucid. However, he repeated none of his strange ramblings; on the contrary, he closed up like a clam on the subject and departed soon afterwards, saying only that he would return and bring others. However, he did not do so and gradually it all passed from Dougal's mind. Until the time we talked of Vaquaya and he remembered.'

'Had he actually been to the valley?' Gail asked.

'On several occasions.' Father Lorenzo read the unspoken question in her eyes and shook his head. 'I asked the same thing. But he had found a green and peaceful valley, and a people quite different from the jungle tribes among whom he worked. A people who lived simply and peaceably, wishing only to be left in their unchanging seclusion. He respected that wish, my child.'

There was a long silence, each one of the group pursuing their own wondering thoughts. Many puzzling links remained to be filled in, but the certainty that they were on the brink of what they sought burned like a slow fuse behind each outwardly calm exterior. Harmon was leaning forward, his eyes alight with an avid, intent gleam, and he seemed about to exclaim sharply when Max said quickly:

'The pass? There *is* a pass?'

Gail's glance shifted, seeing the priest sigh and the compassion in his expression for the hope he was about to dash. He said slowly, 'Not now. A little while after the happening of which I've told you there was a cataclysmic storm. Earth tremors and floods, and a landslide in the hills. It blocked the pass and sealed off the valley—completely.'

CHAPTER IV

MAX was the first to break the spell of despair and disappointment which stunned the entire party. His expression grim, he stood up and moved to the window, to stare bleakly at the long indigo shadows deepening across the copper-hazed compound.

The padre bent over the map, tracing its lines with a stubby, work-roughened forefinger, and Clive lit cigarettes for Jonathan and the moody-visaged Harmon. Roger touched Gail's arm and drew her to one side, away from the others.

He said, 'You know, this just makes me more convinced that we went the wrong way about this route. I've had another look at the map and I'm sure we've come a long way round, doubling back in a big loop.'

'How do you mean?' she asked in a low voice. 'There isn't any other way. We went into all this months ago and finally agreed this was the best direction from which to approach. We couldn't possibly have come up the Amazon and travelled south.'

'I think we could,' he said stubbornly. 'We should have made for Iquitos anyway, whichever way we came and flown from there over the Maranon, or alternatively, taken La Marginal to Tarapato and made our way cross-country from the north-west. I'm sure it would have been better. Then we'd have approached from the other side. There's almost certain to be a way in from there.'

'In theory, yes,' came Max's cool tones from behind, 'but in practice, no. Our nearest focal point north-west is *not* Tarapato. It's Porto Manan, which does not have an airstrip; in fact it doesn't have anything, and the section of highway which will eventually connect it with La Marginal isn't even begun. We would have faced a three-week trek instead of three days, plus the crossing of a gorge two thousand feet deep, and the problems of altitude.'

He turned away and Roger drew a deep breath. 'He's an arrogant cuss,' he muttered, 'he hasn't even considered any alternative routes, if the truth was known. And I think he had a nerve to take over the way he did.'

'Oh, Roger, don't be silly.' Gail kept her voice subdued. 'He didn't take over. He does live here and has contacts who've moved around. We are the strangers. We all knew that we'd be dependent on him before we ever started. I think we were lucky to get him.'

'I don't mean just that angle. I mean the way he sent us all packing yesterday and stayed with you himself.'

'Somebody had to stay with me,' she pointed out wryly. 'It was the only sensible way.'

'Well, I didn't like it, and I said so at the time. *I* should have been the one to stay behind, or Uncle Phil, at least, not him, but Christiern wouldn't hear of it. Didn't seem to think he could trust me either to look after you or get us both safely back here.'

Gail sighed deeply, somewhat dismayed to learn that there had been an argument about which she had known nothing. She said placatingly, 'I'm sure it wasn't like that. He probably did what he thought best for everybody, not just me. And he is a doctor as well.'

'So what?' Roger was not mollified. 'Uncle's a research chemist and I'm his assistant; we're not so damned dense that we couldn't cope with a straightforward case of heat syncope.'

'All right—all right,' she said hastily. 'I know you could. You have a strong feeling of responsibility, but so has Max. Can't you give another man credit for it?' She smiled, wanting to emphasize her point and for the moment completely unconscious of having taking up a defensive stand on behalf of Max Christiern. 'Do stop worrying about it, Roger; we've got far more important things to worry about now.'

'Yes.' His expression altered as the same thought occurred to him as had occurred to Gail; had they come all this way to failure? So near . . .

Suddenly she realized that the medley of voices had ceased, that Clive was saying something about the other way and that Father Lorenzo was speaking. Afraid she was missing something, she broke away from Roger and pressed eagerly back into the circle of lamplight. Her uncle checked her with an impatient lift of his hand as she leaned over the back of his chair, and Father Lorenzo, who had paused to smile at her interruption, returned his grave glance to Max.

'I only know it is reputed to lead into the valley and through it, but having no personal experience I can't tell how navigable it is, or what conditions you would meet. There's always been a great deal of Indian superstition around it—not that I imagine that aspect worrying you—but I——'

Gail's impatience and puzzlement increased until she turned an imploring glance and whisper to Clive, who grinned and mouthed against her ear, '*River—underground. Supposed to be haunted!*'

'The Indians shun it, won't even cross the compound after dark,' Father Lorenzo was continuing. 'Spirit River—you can see it from the northern end of the compound, running into the cavern under the hill.'

Max frowned. 'It's getting too dark now to reconnoitre.' He tugged at his lower lip. 'Could we hire canoes?'

'I think so, but you won't get a guide,' the priest warned. He shook his head. 'Are you sure it's wise to risk it? You don't know where it might lead.'

'We haven't come this far to give up so easily,' Max said, and there was a murmur of agreement. 'Would you mediate on our behalf, Father? I should like to investigate this River of Spirits.'

The idea of a subterranean river, especially one reputed to be haunted, caught the imagination of all of them, and there was a great deal of excited discussion during the leisurely meal that evening and afterwards, until Max, mindful of consideration for their host and the lateness of the hour, broke up the discussion and Clive good-humouredly marshalled his dispensary mates across the compound to their sleeping quarters.

Their voices diminished, and Professor Denning turned to go indoors. Gail stayed where she was, her hands resting lightly on the single bar that railed off the small veranda. Her thoughts were too full of conjecture to allow the relaxing prospect of sleep come immediately. In fact, she felt more wide-awake now than she'd felt all day, even though she knew she should follow Max's advice as the others had done. Max...

'Gail...'

She started and saw the shadowy figure of Roger coming across the compound. He came up the steps and she repressed a sigh. 'I thought you'd turned in,' she said lightly.

'I changed my mind.' He took up a stance beside her, leaning on the rail and putting his arm round her shoulders. 'I thought it was you here, so—— I never seem to get you to myself for more than a couple of minutes these days,' he exclaimed impatiently. 'There's always *somebody* around.'

'Naturally,' she tried to keep her voice casual, 'seeing that that's one of the main rules; no wandering off alone. So I keep the rules, and so should you.'

He was silent for a moment, then he said moodily, 'Are you sure that's all? I get the feeling that you're trying to avoid me these days. You——'

'That's nonsense. Of course I don't,' she retorted. 'All I'm trying to dodge are the midges!'

He did not seem reassured, drawing her to him possessively. 'That business yesterday with you and Christiern made me furious. To start with he pitched us all out of the shelter, except Uncle Phil, and sent us to cart buckets of water for him, then had the nerve to order us all to carry on without you.' Roger drew a deep, angry breath. 'When I think of him stripping you and—and then staying there with you all night, it makes me... it's not decent!'

'Just a minute!' She twisted free and faced him sharply. 'What do you mean by that? If you think—— Somebody had to do it, or I wouldn't be here now. And for what it matters he was about as unfeeling as a—a stone! Anyway, would it have been any more decent if it had been you, or Clive, or Jonathan? And if you think *I* wanted it to happen like it did you must have a pretty warped opinion of me.'

'No! Oh, Gail, I didn't mean it like that,' he exclaimed hotly. 'It was the high-handed way he——'

'I don't want to talk about it,' she said flatly, 'and I don't want to talk about Max Christiern. Now,' she made her tone firm, 'it's time we turned in. Goodnight, Roger.'

'Gail . . . please . . .' He caught her arm and pulled her against him. 'Not like this. I only want to——'

'But I don't. You've forgotten something. You promised, Roger, and I meant what I said. I'm not getting involved, or even thinking about it, before we get home again.' She turned away. 'Now leave me alone, will you?'

For a moment he did respond, then he said sulkily, 'Very well, if that's the way you want it.'

'It is.' Hardening her heart against him, she stood there unmoving until she heard his steps go slowly across the compound and the slight sound of the closing door told her she was alone again.

She took a deep breath and stared into the night, forcing her anger to subside, then abruptly went down the steps and began to walk towards the opposite end of the compound. Why couldn't Roger leave her alone? He had never seemed so ineffectual and immature a youth as he had during these past few days.

Oh, to hell with Roger! They were here on a mission, and that was all that mattered. She lit a cigarette, trying to push the irritating little interlude from her thoughts and recapture her previous mood of well-being.

The moon was out now, bright and almost full, except for one dark blue shadowy bite out of it, and a milky shower of stars rode high across the heavens. The air felt cooler after the oppressive clamminess of the nights in the rain forest, and there was no longer the unnerving sense of being constantly besieged by unseen and often noisy forest life. She looked up at the stars, the same stars that guided those pioneers of olden days, and wondered how those intrepid men felt as they set sail in their frail boats for unknown shores. They had only their courage and resourcefulness, no wonders of twentieth-century technology to help them chart their way and maintain a link with the loved ones left at home. Perhaps they also wrote their journals and recounted the wonders they had found, as she filled page after page for her beloved father all those miles away.

She came to the end of the compound and the rough fence which edged it near the river bank. It was a narrow stream here, some two hundred yards from where it curved and came into confluence with another tributary. Although the moon cast pearly streaks across the ripples it was not bright enough to reveal more than the hazy outlines of the shimballo trees that hung over the bend, their squat and twisted shapes made fantastic by the web of creepers that festooned the branches, and it did not reveal the cavern under the hillside where the river disappeared underground.

She sighed and flung her cigarette into the water, then turned away, reflecting that she had better get back before somebody decided to take a roll-call. It was then she saw the dark figure standing a short distance away, its presence betrayed by the small crimson glow of a cigarette.

Her first thought was that Roger had followed her, and instinctively she backed with the intention of escaping unseen. Then a voice instantly recognizable shouted, 'Stay where you are! There's a mudbank along there.'

She might have known it would be Max. She stayed still and he came to her side with firm unhurried strides, the tiny red glow wavering gently as he moved. He halted, his features dark above the pale luminosity of his shirt, and suddenly she found herself unexpectedly bereft of words as she looked up at him.

'Well, have the spirits cast a spell on your tongue?' he asked lightly.

'No.' The funny little trance snapped and she laughed. 'I was trying to get *en rapport*—to ask them to guide us through their Stygian hideout tomorrow.'

There was no reply, and she said on a quick little breath, 'You *are* going to try to get through? You're not going to turn back?'

'No, I'm not going to turn back.' As she had done a few moments ago he sent his cigarette flying with a shower of sparks into the water.

She watched the tiny blurred movement into the current and said idly, 'I wonder where it'll be an hour from now.'

'Where what will be?' He rested his hands on the fence rail.

She made a small wry face into the darkness. 'That cigarette end. Perhaps in the Secret Valley.'

'Disintegrated, more likely.'

She sighed, determined that his dispassionate attitude should not dispel her mood of romanticism. 'I wonder what it'll be like,' she mused. 'The Cavern of Shades, the Cauldron of Fire, the Burning Waters. You know, Father Lorenzo sounded almost as though he believed in their existence when he was telling us of the Indians' superstitions.'

Max stirred and looked down at the dark waters. 'I don't

think so. He didn't want to encourage us to venture needlessly into danger.'

'But it may not be dangerous. I mean, if the Indians shun it and the Valley how can they know? It's probably founded on some old story that's lost in legend. After all, think of our own superstitions. Like seeing the new moon through glass and walking under ladders. But nobody takes much notice of them these days.'

'I doubt if this instance quite fits into the same category.'

'Maybe not,' she said slowly, 'but there's one thing I'm sure of; that river will lead us into the Valley. I know it.' She raised her arm and glanced at the luminous dial of her wristwatch. 'And this time tomorrow we'll know.'

'You sound convinced,' he said after a perceptible pause.

'I am.'

'A pity. Because I'm afraid it's going to come second-hand to you.'

'Second-hand!' Her head jerked round. 'To me? What do you mean?'

He straightened. 'I'm sorry, Gail—you're going to hate my guts for this—but you'll have to stay behind at the mission during this part of the trip.'

'Stay behind?' she echoed, wondering if she'd heard it properly. 'Me? But why? You can't be serious, Max. Why, I—I——' Her eyes went as blank as her voice and she took a small step back, trying to see him more clearly through the darkness. 'Oh, but you can't! I——'

'But I can.' The slight note of sympathy had gone from his voice. 'If what I suspect proves to be fact it won't be a comfortable ride on that haunted river, certainly not for a girl.'

'Well, if that's all that's worrying you ...' she sighed on a rising note of relief, '*I'm* not worried. Not in the least.'

'Maybe you're not, but I am,' he said flatly. 'In any case, I intend to make the preliminary trip alone. I see no sense in subjecting the whole team to possible danger.'

Gail felt as though she had just awakened from a very bad dream without having reached the moment of awareness that it was only a dream. Surely he didn't mean it! She could understand him wanting to make a preliminary survey before the entire party set sail on these unknown waters, but to bar her altogether ... She wasn't going to submit to this without a fight. About to renew protests, she hesitated. This was suspiciously like sheer male dominance and the fear of femininity proving a weak link in the chain. Her mouth set; there was more than one road to Rome...

'You've forgotten something,' she said softly.

'Oh?' He sounded guarded.

'Yes,' her eyelids dropped to veil the gleam beneath them, people who make rules should obey them themselves and set a good example.'

'Meaning exactly . . . ?'

'The buddy system.' It was an effort to keep triumph out of her tone but she succeeded, then softened her voice. 'You can't go alone, Max.'

'Are you volunteering for the job?'

'Yes, if you need a volunteer.'

There was a silence and she was aware of him turning, the shifting of his hand along the rail. His breath feathered her hair as he said coolly, 'You wouldn't be trying to inveigle me into retracting anything?'

'Of course not,' she said innocently. 'I'm beginning to see your point of view and it's making me feel worried. It's also making me feel guilty.' She sighed. 'I suppose if I were you *I'd* feel hampered by having a girl in the team, wondering if she was going to be a nuisance as soon as the going got difficult. I mean, if I hadn't been here you wouldn't have had a hold-up yesterday, and you'd have bashed on and taken the snags in your stride as you came to them. Isn't that true?'

'To an extent.'

'I thought it was.' She gave a large sigh and looked mournfully at a spot just to the right of his shoulder. 'I blotted my copy-book yesterday as far as you are concerned, and I never even said thank you. Oh, I understand all right. But, Max'—she contrived a sad little catch in her breath—'couldn't you change your mind?'

'No, I could not. So you can forget the arguments—and the feminine wiles as well.'

A soft exclamation escaped her as he turned his head and added in the same coldly dispassionate tones, 'They don't fit in with the tough little hoyden image you've worked so hard to achieve.'

'*Oh!*' Feminine wiles melted rapidly in a flare of hoydenish temperament. 'That's the most unfair accusation I've ever heard. And the most old-fashioned! Or didn't you know that girls today can face as much hardship and discomfort as any man, and without moaning? And they do! But maybe you thought it would have been all right if I'd been one of those hefty globe-trotting females without any feminine wiles, or—or feelings. Well, I'm not, but that doesn't mean I'm going to crack.'

'But you did, yesterday,' he said quietly.

'That could have happened to any of us,' she said stubbornly. 'Heat syncope can attack anybody, regardless of whether they're male or female.'

'But it didn't.'

She bit her lip, silenced by the quiet finality of his voice and lost for fresh means to combat it.

He said, 'Why don't you stop trying so hard, Gail? We don't think any less of you for—for being what you are.'

'For being a girl?' she said bitterly. 'Thanks!'

He sighed. 'It's getting late. Time you went in.' To her surprise he put his arm round her shoulder as he turned her towards the mission. 'Try to be sensible. Stay at the mission where you're safe.'

'And if I don't want to be safe?'

'This time you haven't any choice. Go on, in you go. Goodnight.'

There was a great deal to occupy Gail's thoughts when she settled down amid the now familiar smell of insecticide and the ghostly shrouding of mosquito netting. But one certain scathing observation persisted in her mind with increasing chagrin; so Max considered her a tough little hoyden, did he? So why didn't she live up to it? She'd be a fool if she let it hurt her! Anyway, why should it?

* * *

By breakfast-time next morning the news of the ban had got round the team. Faces expressive of sympathy were turned on Gail and there seemed to be a tacit avoidance of the subject, until Clive, more perceptive than the others, noticed that Gail's grin wasn't quite as forced as might have been expected in the circumstances.

He said curiously, 'Aren't you disappointed, girl? I expected fireworks for breakfast. Or have you turned chicken at last?' he added dryly.

'I have not,' she returned tartly, 'and if you think I'm going to crawl to His Nibs and beg and pray of him to let me come you've got another think coming.' *But I almost did*, she thought bitterly.

'Well, I do think it's a bit grim,' said Jonathan. 'I mean, even if it is a bit rough, surely, among us all, we can look after you all right.'

'Can he stop her?' Clive said. 'It's a free country, isn't it? Or is it?' He assumed an expression of mock sympathy.

Only Roger remained silent, his face still bearing traces of the previous evening's sulkiness, while a mild argument broke out on the sensibility or unfairness of Max Christiern's embargo on Gail. She listened, her thoughts busy as she glanced occasionally at her uncle, who was being tactfully non-committal. She wondered if he had informed the party of the full extent of Max's high-handed intentions and in a suitable lull said sweetly:

'I'm not worried. I'm going to have lots of company—all of you.'

'All of——!' They gaped at her, and she grinned.

'Our leader is going alone!'

'You're kidding!' They turned in concerted movement to Professor Denning, and Gail sat back, making a smug face at her uncle's furious glare. Disgust and rancour began to fly freely in unrestrained male language, and Clive cried, 'What the hell does he think we are? A bunch of wet first-year students, or something?'

Professor Denning waved his hand and tried to start explanations, and a low yet icy voice said in Gail's ear, 'Stirred up a nice little hornet's nest, haven't you? You might have waited till I gave them the true construction. I hope you're satisfied with your revenge.'

She looked up defiantly into Max's angry face and met his furious gaze without wavering. 'Yes,' she said calmly, 'I hope you get well stung.' Without giving him a chance to reply she marched out of the room, already conscious of encroaching guilt at her lapse into the kind of behaviour of which she should be ashamed, even though there had been provocation. Well, he *had* said he was going alone, and the others would never agree to this. As Clive would say: there was safety in numbers where reconnaissance of this kind was concerned. But her uncle liked Max; they would soon reach an amicable plan, and she had an awful suspicion that it would take them all on together—without herself.

Her expression determined, she slipped quietly away from the mission.

An hour later all was peaceful in the mission. Max and the Professor and Roger also departed, following the same route as Gail had discovered by instinct, and a further hour later the party was assembling by the riverside landing stage.

Three canoes bobbed in the shallow inlet at the side of the compound, and a group of Indians clustered around Father Lorenzo, their dark eyes filled with superstitious awe. In broad daylight it was possible to see beyond the confluence, where the swift flowing stream disappeared into a black cavern under the hillside, dark, unwelcoming, and faintly foreboding, even in golden sunlight.

Max glanced at his watch and said briskly, 'Right, let's go.' He looked at Professor Denning. 'Shall we take the first one? Clive and Roger following, and Harmon and Jonathan in the third.'

The Professor nodded absently. He looked round. 'Where's Gail?'

'Staying behind. I thought you knew.' Max gestured towards the cavern. 'I think there's too much risk involved.'

'I quite agree.' A gleam of unwilling admiration showed in Professor Denning's smile. 'I'm glad you finally persuaded her—more than I could do.'

'Or anybody.' Clive and Jonathan suddenly broke into simultaneous roars of laughter. 'All aboard for Spookey River! Ahoy, there!'

Max and the Professor turned sharply, the Professor looking amazed and Max's expression darkening with disbelief and anger.

A canoe was skimming downstream, propelled by an aged Indian of shrivelled visage. In the bow sat Gail, her red neckerchief fluttering in the breeze, her eyes glowing with triumph and defiance. If she had tried she could not have timed her entrance more perfectly for dramatic effect. Her entire demeanour radiating glee and determination, she raised her paddle and tried to twirl it baton-wise, and uttered a singing 'Ahoy!'

Speechless, the men watched the Indian swing the frail craft into the inlet, slip a frayed painter over the post, and then scramble out and hurry across the compound with an agility that belied his venerable appearance.

'Well,' she said, 'I'm ready and not unreasonable. I'll let you all lead the way.'

'Gail!' said her uncle weakly.

'Oh, would you bring my pack, Roger, please?' she cried. 'I'm not getting out.'

Max came to life. 'Oh, but you are!' He advanced grimly towards her. 'Out!'

'No.' She watched him warily, her hand reaching for the painter. *'Oh!'*

He had lunged forward and too late she had tried to slip the painter and tug it from his hand. He gripped the prow of the canoe and slowly, without any apparent effort, began to draw it up on to the bank.

She clung to the sides, scarlet patches of fury glowing in her cheeks, and looked desperately for aid.

Clive laughed again, unmercifully. 'Now I know what all the chortling was about down in the *aldea* this morning. The mad gringo squaw and her canoe. Oh, Gail! Attagirl!'

'You might come and help me instead of grinning like a hyena!' she cried brokenly as the canoe gave a final lurch and came to rest high and dry in the mud with her still sitting in it helplessly. She glared at Max. 'You can't do this to me. This is mine. I bought it.' Her mouth tightened with a fresh spurt of defiance.

'You——!' Max straightened and ran an exasperated glance over the dilapidated little craft. 'You bought *this*?'

'Yes. I happen to be part of this expedition and I don't intend to be dumped here until you choose to say I can move.'

'My God! How far do you think you'll get in that?' He turned away and gestured to Roger, who had gone obediently at Gail's behest and was now emerging from the mission with her pack. Max said resignedly, 'Shove it in there and transfer the medical kit as well. Will you take number two with Clive and Roger?' He glanced at the Professor and awaited the older man's nod of agreement before he swung round to Gail.

The dawn of surprised triumph and delight faded rapidly before the icy glimmers in his eyes. He said curtly, 'Right, you win. We've wasted enough time on this nonsense. On second thoughts you'll prove less of a liability where I can keep my eye on you than left alone here to devise any more infantile defiance.'

The canoe teetered as he let go of it and she climbed out. He caught her arm to save her from stumbling and released his anything but gentle grip the instant she had regained her balance. Aware that Clive and Jonathan had ceased to chuckle, she went to the leading canoe of the string and got into the seat Max indicated. Resentment of him showed in every line of her taut face and stiff little body as she sat there, shoulders ramrod straight and chin thrust out. She had got her own way, but the triumph had been shortlived, for the real victory had been his. In the space of a few short moments and a single brief decisive action he had made her look ridiculous and feel exactly as he had described her in those curt words: infantile and defiant.

He climbed in without a word and cast off. She picked up the paddle, trying to match her rhythm to his, and the canoe moved sluggishly out of the inlet and into the main stream. She felt the tug of the current and over his shoulder Max said, 'Ship that paddle. It's not needed.'

With a bitter glance at the broad muscular back she obeyed,

under no illusions as to the correct interpretation of that clipped order; he didn't even trust her to paddle a canoe without tipping it over.

The river narrowed as it approached the cavern and she eyed it grimly, recalling Max's last-minute instructions. She twisted cautiously and looked over her shoulder. Jonathan and Clive waved gaily, and Clive stopped paddling a moment to give her a thumbs-up gesture of sardonic victory, then patted his head to remind her to duck her head.

Max had fixed the big battery lamps in the prows of the canoes and he leaned forward to switch theirs on and slightly adjust the angle. The entrance was very near, and instinctively Gail hunched her shoulders as the moment came and the canoe swept under the great rocky arch. The sunlight was extinguished like the light of a snuffed-out candle, there was an instant chilling of the atmosphere, and a pervading sense of fatality as blackness descended and only the thin yellow rays probed out into the eerie gloom.

There was no means of knowing how many miles of unknown waters lay ahead, and Gail could not suppress a shiver of apprehension mingled with excitement. Superstitious fears could be scorned and laughed at in the friendly warmth of the lamplit mission, secure in the friendly, indulgent companionship of the men. But now ... Spirit River, shunned by the locals, reputed to be haunted by the legendary victims claimed by the Mountain of Doom. Of course it was all just superstition!

She peered ahead, trying not to look at the gaunt twisting shadows cast among the convolutions in the tunnelled rock, and forcing herself to maintain a practical frame of mind. Imagination and primitive fear could produce the Cavern of Shades from which none returned—supposing they survived the Cauldron of Fire! A fire under a mountain! Gail tried to smile, but somehow couldn't find conviction in telling herself: ridiculous! If it were volcanic, yes. She tried to remember the exact location of volcanic areas in the Andes, and comforted herself with the assurance that there wasn't an active volcano within hundreds of miles of this pimple below the foothills of that vast chain of mountains which stretched down an equally vast continent.

'Head down!'

She started and ducked only just in time. The roof of rock was sagging in low convex loops overhead, dangerously low for the careless voyager. Doubled up, she tried still to peer ahead at the churning waters like a black tongue rooted in an endlessly narrowing throat. The current was increasing in power now and there was little need of paddle power as the three canoes were swept on headlong, deeper and deeper into the unknown.

'All right back there?'

'Yes,' she said in tones as cool and clipped, and lapsed back into silence.

Still there was no sign of the underground stream widening or the chasm enlarging. Once she felt the rock above actually brush her hair, and there was a muffled oath from the canoe at the rear as someone suffered a grazed head. She slithered lower into the canoe, suddenly aware of her nerve cracking and longing to voice the fearful thought; suppose the river didn't end in the Secret Valley? Supposing it just got smaller and smaller until it filled the chasm, until everything was submerged? But pride and determination would never allow her to breathe a word of her fear to the hard unfeeling man crouched intently over the prow.

Suddenly, just as she felt her nerve had reached the limit of endurance, Max gave a warning shout and she tightened her grip on the sides of the canoe. There was a lurch and a grating under the base, then the bottom seemed to fall out of the world, the rock walls spun dizzily, the craft nose-dived and tossed through a thunderous roaring water, and Gail felt herself thrown violently from side to side. She closed her eyes and waited for the end, then suddenly it came in a vast splash that drenched her to the skin, and the canoe, miraculously, was drifting in widening, gradually slowing circles. Tremulously she raised her head to look, and saw that Max was already paddling to the far side of the enormous cavern they had entered.

Even as she realized that he was getting them well clear of the rapids before the following canoe rounded those tortuous zig-zag bends she was aware of disappointment. There was no beauty here, no wonder of crystalline formations caused by calcification through the millennia, no delicate beauty of colour, only a big sluggish circle of inky water and a great gloomy vault that held the chill of the grave.

The lamp splashed oily yellow patches of light on the sullen ripples and silhouetted the dripping paddle as Max shipped it. He said, 'They should be round by now.'

His voice echoed mournfully and Gail felt the cold desolate atmosphere of the soulless place pervade her both mentally and physically. She forgot her resentment of Max, knew only that he was living and human and strong. She said in a small voice, 'This must be the Cavern of Shades.'

He swung round, and she thought he smiled faintly. But the brief flicker of his lips was gone in a second. 'Nothing supernatural about this—provided one lands in it right way up. Here they are!'

The second canoe came over, carrying her uncle and Clive and Roger. For a heart-stopping moment she thought they were going to capsize, then Clive shifted his weight adroitly and chortled, 'How was that for the Big Dipper? Okay, you two?'

With swift easy movements he paddled across till he was alongside Gail and Max. Five pairs of eyes watched anxiously, striving to pierce the inky gloom over the turbulent waters. Then there was a wild icy cry and the third canoe appeared. For a breathless instant it seemed to be suspended in mid-air before it spun wildly and capsized.

The displaced water swamped wildly over it, and Gail gave a cry of horror as she saw that only Harmon remained clinging desperately to the upturned craft.

Her cry of Jonathan's name was jerked from her as Max sent their canoe skimming into the spray. There was a blur of confused movement and then Jonathan's flaxen head bobbed up in the seething foam. He was only a few feet away from the other canoe and he struggled desperately towards it.

'Harmon!' she screamed. 'He's there! Right beside you.' She stood up, leaning forward, trying to get nearer, faster. Couldn't Harmon grab Jonathan? He had the boat to hang on to. She grabbed the paddle and leaned over, reaching, praying, and Max snapped, 'Stay back! Grab Clive's side and hang on.'

Feverishly she obeyed, seeing the pattern of his plan and the third canoe closing in. While she grabbed the side of it, holding the two craft close together, Max leaned out at a perilous angle and snatched at the struggling Jonathan. A moment later Jonathan was hanging on to safety and Max thrust the end of the paddle to Harmon. 'Haul in and drag it with you,' he snapped.

Clive had swung the prow of the other canoe and between them he and Max uprighted the unlucky craft and held it steady until the luckless pair scrambled aboard again.

It had been near tragedy and only Max's quick thinking and Clive's instinctive, faultless co-operation had averted disaster. Gail drew a deep breath and looked anxiously at Jonathan, who despite his white face was forcing a grin as he stopped spluttering and shook the wet hair out of his eyes.

'At least it was a warm dip, but the flavour ... Ugh!' He spat disgustedly and began to strip off his shirt.

'Never mind. Here...' Gail tossed over the towel she had grabbed from her pack. 'Sorry it's not very big.'

'Thanks.' He towelled himself, attempting a shaky laugh, and Clive obliged with his own hastily rummaged-for towel, tossing it to Harmon.

Gail sat back, aware she was trembling a little, then she noticed Max and stared, momentarily forgetting the frightening event. He was plunging one hand into the oily, unpleasant-looking water, and there was an intent frown between his brows. She saw his nostrils dilate and for the first time she noticed a certain dryness in the air, almost an acridity bearing a faint odour which for the moment she couldn't identify.

The others, relaxing now and alternately teasing and commiserating with the victims, apparently had not noticed anything out of the ordinary, and she said in an uneasy undertone, 'Max, what is it?'

'You've noticed something?'

'I'm not sure.' Although the happenings of the frightening journey into darkness had banished all her former acrimony she was still a little wary of him and had no desire to appear any more idiotic in his eyes than she could help. 'It's probably just stale air,' she said uncertainly, 'but it's making my nose tickle.'

'It's sulphur dioxide,' he said grimly. 'The temperature of the water was the first warning. We're running into the thrust fault.'

'Oh.' She looked blankly at him, experiencing a fresh sense of unease. She knew little or nothing of thrust faults, subterranean cracks in the earth's crust, but that Max looked worried was in itself sufficient to cause her a tremor of alarm.

'I half expected this,' he said. 'The natural explanation for the superstition. Put your hand in the water.'

She did so, and gasped at its heat.

'Now this.' He reached up to an overhanging lip of rock.

Slowly her fingertips obeyed, to come away from warmth, and coated with a fine dust.

'Lava ash.' He dusted his hands down his pants. 'This is the centre of the fault, I think. Periodically there'll be an upheaval. The water will boil and spout like a geyser. See the funnels?'

'What do we do?' she whispered.

'Try and ride it. We've no alternative. This is why I wanted you to stay where you were safe.'

'Yes, I see. I'm sorry,' she said in a low voice. 'But I'm here now.'

'Not scared?'

'No.'

She met his gaze levelly, and for the first time saw a softening in his eyes as they studied her rather curiously. 'I believe you mean that.'

An intense pleasure ran through her, even while she realised that her determined negative had been perfectly truthful. She wasn't scared now. She might be later on, but whatever happened she didn't want to be anywhere else at this moment than here in this great cavern, which, if Max had surmised correctly, could become the terrifying Cauldron of Fire.

He said suddenly, 'Do you happen to have any smelling salts in your personal belongings?'

'Yes.' She looked a little puzzled. 'I packed some in case anybody was overcome with heat.'

'You didn't use them on yourself the other day,' he observed dryly. 'Could I have them now, please?'

'Yes, of course.' She found the tin in which she kept her own small first-aid kit and took out the smelling salts.

He weighed the little flask in his hand and said ruefully, 'Not very much, but better than nothing. I'll have to use the lot.'

'The lot?' She stared. 'But it's ammonia. It's frightfully pungent, you only——'

He wasn't listening and her puzzlement increased as he unpacked a drinking cup and put a little fresh water into it. Rather brusquely he bade Clive take a packet of gauze from the medical box and then instructed her to cut it into seven big squares. While she did this he carefully emptied the contents of the bottle of smelling salts into the cup of water.

The others were silent now, and the expressions on the faces of her uncle and Clive told her that Max wasn't indulging in time-wasting experiments. Roger was frowning a little, Jonathan looked puzzled, and Harmon was openly truculent when Max had soaked the squares of gauze in the diluted ammonia solution and handed one to each member of the party.

'Tie them over the nose and mouth to act as a mask,' he said.

Harmon's face darkened and he held the gauze at arm's length. 'What the hell is this for? Are we a bunch of fainting schoolmarms or something?'

'Listen,' said Max patiently, 'there'll be a build-up of sulphur dioxide fumes in there,' he pointed to the opening in the rock where the river continued to flow, 'and the fumes are irritant to throat and lungs. There'll also be lava ash. These masks will help to neutralize the acid in the fumes.'

'How about soaking our shirts?' suggested Jonathan, who seemed to have completely recovered. 'They'd keep us cool.'

'Oh yes,' jeered Clive, 'just because you took a bath.'

Max shook his head. 'There could be other irritant contents in the water.' He turned to Gail and took the wet gauze from her hand. 'This won't be very pleasant,' he said quietly, 'but it's the best protection we have to hand.' He folded it into a triangle and gently placed it over her face, tying it firmly at the back of her head.

Glancing at each other, the men followed Max's example and adjusted their own improvised masks. The completed effect was bizarre and would have been amusing, but for the seriousness of the situation and the unpleasantness that lay ahead.

Gail looked at the white-masked figures sitting in the canoes which bobbed gently under the great arch of rock and found it difficult to believe it was all happening. Then Max picked up the paddle and gave the signal to start. Slowly they moved forward, the great rift in the rock wall enclosed them, and they slid cautiously over the yellow reflections into the blackness ahead.

The light from the following canoe sent Gail's own shadow looming over the broad shoulders of Max and she wondered inconsequently what he was thinking at this moment. Did he feel fear? Was he as taut and apprehensive as she? Apprehensive! She might as well admit it; she couldn't utter a truthful denial at this moment. It was the waiting, the not knowing what to expect. Choking fumes ... suppose there was an eruption of boiling lava before ... would they ever ... ?

'Gail.'

'Yes?' She choked through the clinging wetness over her mouth.

'I want you to lean forward ... wriggle into the bottom of the boat if you can't reach. Grip the back of my belt ... can you reach? Or hang on to me.'

Cautiously she relinquished her hold on the gunwales and slithered down into the space behind the thwart. She reached for the faint burnished sheen of the leather belt round Max's waist and he said, 'Right? Now hook your fingers through it and don't let go.'

'Yes.'

'And close your eyes.'

She obeyed instinctively, thinking that he meant they would smart, then the grey, choking cloud was suddenly all around her, stinging, stifling, and heat was a living curtain against her panting body. She tried to keep upright, but blind instinct sent her head burrowing against the hard muscular back that was safe and unyielding. It was impossible to draw breath through throat and lungs that seemed on fire, impossible to open eyes to release the burning tears that stung like acid against her lids. The hard edges of the belt dug into her fingers, and she released one hand, thrusting it desperately round the hard, muscular waist, before everything dissolved into velvet and went far away, down into deep, deep darkness...

CHAPTER V

THE first thing Gail became conscious of was a hot glare forcing her eyelids apart, then tightly shut in protest, and a vaguely stirring impression that her sins had finally caught up with her during a nightmare excursion through Dante's Inferno. There was a silence, a slight motion that was perplexing and not unpleasant but doubtless merely a devilish lull before unspoken horror yet to come, and then a smothering sensation that fulfilled every delirious foreboding.

She struggled, was aware of a vile taste and limbs that didn't want to respond, and the smothering sensation abruptly ceased.

'Take it easy.'

The voice came from somewhere above her head and sounded disembodied and curiously hollow. A pressure seemed to resist her effort to move, and a sudden wave of nausea more effectively quelled her attempt to move. She subsided, grimacing, willing the unpleasant qualms to pass, then opened sore smarting eyes and blinked with horror at the apparition looking down on her.

'All right—take it easy,' the voice repeated. 'You'll be all right soon.'

Awareness was almost complete and things were swimming into normal focus: a heavenly blue sky, a calm, sun-rippled stretch of water, a vista of peaceful greens touched with silvery fern and patches of rose and white, an outline of hills hazy at the perimeter of her vision, and the extension of her own limp self, legs sprawled along the well of the canoe, Max's knees the pillow on which her head rested, and his blue eyes regarding her with a hint of grim amusement in their depths. But his face!

Her lips parted, stifling an aghast exclamation, and his mouth curved sardonically. 'We're all the same,' he said. 'You haven't escaped, either.'

'B-but you're—you're *yellow*!' she gasped. 'All over! Am I—is *my* face?...' The peculiar caked sensation became apparent as she spoke and she raised her hand to her face, regarding the startling hue of her hand and wondering if her own normally sun-gilded healthy complexion had suffered the alarming transformation that had overtaken Max.

She stared at his clean-cut features, all quite yellow, a particularly obnoxious greyish yellow that dulled his dark hair, coated his brows, even his lashes, and merged into his shirt, the folds of his rolled-up sleeves, his bare arms, the sides of the canoe, her own shirt and pants and feet and arms ... everything! Yellow!

'It'll wash off,' he said calmly. 'How do you feel?'

'Ghastly. Was it the ... ?'

'The thrust fault?' he nodded. 'It's mostly lava ash. You'll feel pretty groggy for a bit, but it'll pass off.'

She moistened her parched lips and shuddered. 'I feel as though I'd been baked in a mudbath.'

'You have been—almost literally. We all have.' He soaked his handkerchief and dabbed at his own face, leaving streaks and smudges, and she realized that the 'pressure' she had experienced as she returned to consciousness had been Max bathing her face. His rescuing administrations seemed to be becoming a habit as far as she was concerned! What next? She wriggled into a sitting position and took the handkerchief from him.

'It's still all over you—let me.' Gently, and avoiding meeting his eyes, she dabbed methodically at the sulphurous grime on his cheeks. 'Didn't you pass out?'

'Not quite. Another moment or so, though, and I would have gone over. It was an unpleasant experience.'

She shivered again, then remembered. 'Oh, the others ... Are they——?'

As he nodded, she glanced round, and he said dryly, 'They're coming round as well, but I should wait until they've regained their sense of humour before you start enquiring after their health.'

She looked across the dazzling stream and saw her uncle sitting up in the big canoe, dabbing at his face with a handkerchief, and beside him Roger was clinging to the gunwale, apparently incapable of anything else, while Clive was leaning over the other side and scooping handfuls of water against his face.

There was no sign of life in the other small canoe. Then a red-and-blue-checked hump resolved into Jonathan's shoulders and he struggled upright, blinking around dazedly before he spotted her and gave a feeble wave. A moment or so later Harmon also sat up, grimaced, and was promptly sick over the side of the canoe.

Gail averted her gaze and Max said wryly, 'If you think you're immune I'd like to shift upstream a bit. There's a shallow stretch of bank up there where we can land.'

'I'm not going to disgrace myself, if that's what you mean,' she said coldly.

'I merely asked. In the circumstances it would hardly be a disgrace,' he said dryly, reaching for the paddle. 'Sit tight.'

A few strong strokes and he had the canoe shooting upstream to the sandy inlet he had spotted. He beached the canoe and put a strong steadying grip on her arms to help her out. She watched him turn to rummage among the gear in the canoe and reflected once more on his indefatigable stamina. Her own legs felt reluctant to support her and every breath or spoken word still rasped painfully against a throat that felt as though it had been scorched with white-hot grit. But Max seemed untouched or unmoved by the recent nightmare experience; he seemed to have shaken it off as a dog would shake off water, yet he held infinite patience for others not so fortunately hardy.

He came with her pack and dropped it beside her. 'I should wash off the filth and change into clean things.'

'Oh yes...' Still unable to shake off the dazed feeling, she looked doubtfully at the clear, placid water, wondering if it could really be that same terrifying torrent that had plunged them underground into fear and the unknown.

He said, 'If you stay under the shadow of this spur you'll have reasonable cover. I'll go back downstream and see to the others—and keep them from barging along until you've dressed.'

'Thanks...' She still hesitated, reminded of the privacy aspect which had not occurred until he spoke. 'Supposing anybody else comes along? Indians, or...'

'You'll have to duck and holler for help, won't you?' he said, not unkindly. 'Don't take all day and don't drink any river water.' With that he loped up over the verdant incline and dropped down out of sight at the other side.

After a cautious glance round the sylvan scene she stripped off her clothes and immersed herself in the shallow waters under the shadow of the spur. The water was beautifully clear and cool, but mindful of Max's edict she resisted the temptation to rinse out her mouth; the acrid, stinging unpleasantness would have to be suffered until they were sure the water was safe to drink.

A little while later, bathed and refreshed and in varying degrees of recovery, the party gathered together and discussed the next move. Clive and Jonathan were in favour of moving on along the valley, but Gail's uncle was still shaken and unwell from the effects of the trip and Max decided that it would be best to make camp for a while until everyone was rested. They made a meal and then Clive, ever practical, rigged a makeshift clothes-line and announced that the launderette was open for business.

Gail watched him pounding away with a small stone, attacking the shirt which he had spread over the grass at the river's edge, and she giggled.

'What are you laughing at?' he demanded, mock-injured. 'This is the proper old-fashioned way. Beats the dirt out.'

'Beats the life out as well. Here, give it to me.'

'Well,' Clive grinned slyly, 'I didn't like to ask, but if you're feeling energetic...'

'I'm not, but you could give Max a hand with the other tent.' She rescued the maltreated shirt and, as Clive saluted solemnly, added in a casual tone, 'You might bring my uncle's things and Max's—I may as well rinse them out as well.'

Clive raised his brows but made no comment, returning with the armful of clothes and then departing to make himself useful elsewhere. Soon the clothes were strung along the line where they would soon dry in the hot sun, and it did not occur to Gail why she should take a more particular loving care over Max's plain, sturdy drill shirt, pulling it into shape and using the only folding hanger she had with her to place it on and merely slinging her own garment carelessly over the line as she did the others. Later, she returned it, neatly folded, and he said, 'You didn't need to bother, you know, but thanks,' and his smile sparked off a warm inward glow that persisted for quite a long time, until the moment that shattered the curious sense of peace which had gradually enfolded the evening.

They were sprawled indolently on their groundsheets, some of them smoking, chatting idly, and Gail was staring up at the deepening blue of the night sky when Roger said suddenly:

'Anybody noticed how different the terrain is in this valley?'

'Yes, it's not so wild, not so—so violent as some of the country we've seen,' Gail hesitated, glancing at the hills hidden behind the veil of night and imagining the mountains rising in wild grandeur beyond, before she went on slowly, 'If you didn't know the Andes were all around you could almost imagine you'd strayed into another country.'

'Maybe we have,' said Jonathan, lying back and putting his hands under his head. 'Anything could happen here.'

There was a silence. Soft, misty curls of smoke rose from Professor Denning's pipe, then Clive said musingly, 'Another thing; have you noticed how silent it is? Deserted silent, I mean.'

'Yes.' Gail stared into the darkness. She was acutely perceptive to the quality Clive had noticed. There was a sensation of being the only living entities on the face of the land. There had been no sign of tracks, of man, mule or anything else, nothing to indicate any living presence in this lovely wild lost valley in which they had awakened from the dark horror beneath the mountain.

And yet ... there was something. Something Gail couldn't begin to analyse; an intangible air of something waiting, of ... She shook her head and stared into the infinity of night. Perhaps the valley *was* haunted. Perhaps it was the Valhalla of the spirits who haunted the river. Perhaps...

Roger landed beside her and looked questioningly into her face. 'What's the matter? You look worried.' He hesitated, then shifted closer, reaching for her hand and entwining his fingers in hers. 'Gail, I'm sorry about the other night. I didn't mean to——' He tugged at her hand. 'Come on, let's go for five minutes' stroll.'

'Ssh!' She turned her head sharply, her suddenly tensed grip thrusting him away.

He stared. 'What's the matter now? Are you——?'

'Didn't you see?' She was sitting bolt upright, staring at a patch of inky shadow behind her tent. 'Over there. It moved.'

'I can't see anything.' Roger frowned. 'It's just the shadows. They play tricks with your eyes, you know. Come on, let's——'

'It's gone now.' She scrambled to her feet. 'But there *was* something there.'

The others were moving now, glancing towards her and then following as she went slowly towards the tent. Their voices stilled, and Clive called, 'What's up?'

'I don't know.' Gail completed her prowl round the tent and stared into the blackness beyond. It held no movement, no sound, except the faint sussuration of the river at the foot of the incline. Roger came to her side and spread puzzled hands. 'I can't see a thing. There's nothing there. You must have imagined it.'

Max looked down at her. 'What did you see, Gail?'

'A child,' she said simply.

There was a moment of silence, then murmurs, a disbelieving snigger from Harmon and grins. 'You're imagining things,' said Roger, putting his arm round her shoulder and making to steer her back into the circle of the camp. 'It's probably a hangover from this afternoon.'

She shrugged and smiled ruefully. 'Maybe it is. I expect——'

'Just a moment.' There was a slight frown between Max's brows. 'Tell me exactly what you saw, or thought you saw.'

'Well, it was just a child,' she said helplessly. 'At least, it was a small figure. It had on something greyish—I couldn't see properly—it was only a glimpse, then it disappeared.'

'Where?'

'Over there.' She pointed. 'He—or she—seemed to be looking at us. Then it simply went.'

'I think you've got a secret hoard of *pisco* that you haven't let on about,' chaffed Clive. 'Come on, we could all do with a snifter and new light in our eyes.'

'But I did see a child,' she protested.

Clive sniffed. 'Well, where is it now?'

'Gone to fetch its mum,' suggested Jonathan.

'And the rest of the family,' said Clive. 'Don't be frightened, girl, we'll guard you with our lives.'

Amid laughter the little group broke up and there was a general movement towards sleeping bags or the shelter of the bivouac. Only Max did not join in the laughter and his goodnight was quiet and non-committal.

Gradually the voices died away and through the pinned back flap of her tent Gail could see the faint outline of the bivouac canopy. A moon was gaining strength, lending a ghostly radiance to the leaves of a lone eucalyptus tree that overhung the clearing. Had she imagined it all? The glimpse had been so brief she was beginning to believe her eyes had played her a trick.

But the child was not a trick of her imagination; nor was the reception committee to which the team awoke at dawn.

* * *

There were at least two dozen of the strangers.

They stood silently in a close-ranked group along the river bank. They wore long robes similar in style to the poncho, but there the resemblance ended. There were no gaudy colours, none of the big colourful hats Gail had seen the Peruvian Indians wearing; the material appeared to be a soft textured homespun of creamy browns and dark red tones, and bore little in the way of decorative trimmings. The newcomers were all male, all adult, except for one child of about eight or nine who wore a brief, skinny tunic-like garment and stood in the centre of the group, close to a tall, elderly man whose gravity and imposing stature set him apart from his companions. Their skins were light, no browner than the team's own sun-bronzed skins, and they did not look like Indians, nor did their features suggest they might be of Latin extraction. Except for the rather high thin cheekbones and prominent brows they might have belonged to any north European land.

'Well, who's going to volunteer as interpreter?' asked Clive. 'Don't all rush at once.'

Max moved forward, and his movement acted as a signal, bringing them out of their state of surprise. They all stepped forward, except Clive, who put an out-thrust arm in front of Gail. 'You stay here, my girl, until we establish friendly relations.'

'And suppose you don't?'

Clive did not reply and she watched the men approach the waiting strangers. When the distance narrowed to a couple of yards Max halted and spoke. The strangers had made no move and their intent expressions did not flicker.

Gail drifted forward until she was within earshot, watching Max hold out his hands and greet them in Quechuan.

For a moment there was no response, then the man who seemed to be the leader of the strangers raised his hands in a gesture clearly expressing non-comprehension. Max tried again, in another dialect, and met the same negative gesture.

'Try Spanish,' said Roger in an aside. Still no response.

Clive took over, a rapid fire of colloquial and pidgin which Gail couldn't follow at all but which she guessed was a relic of his years of army service. Roger tried French, Jonathan a smattering of Italian, and Max a slow, articulated Portuguese.

It seemed like deadlock. The men looked despairing at each other while the child looked at Gail and nudged the leader. He looked down at the child, murmured to him, and then looked back to Max, his lips framing a guttural syllable.

An exclamation broke from the Professor, almost of disbelief, and he cried, '*Einen Augenblich! Verstehen Sie? Ich*——'

The effect was instantaneous. The leader gesticulated, his grave lined features filled with animation, and he began to speak, while the others exclaimed among themselves.

Clive whistled softly. 'It's incredible! They speak or understand German. Here. I——'

'But there are lots of German settlements in different parts of South America,' Gail said.

'Yes, but not here. I wonder...' Roger's frown was puzzled.

Suddenly Clive exclaimed aloud, 'Remember? Back at the mission? When Father Lorenzo was on about it? They called it *Blüte aus Ewigkeit*!'

'Which means—I'm not sure what—but we'll find out soon, with——' Clive stopped as Professor Denning came towards them. Normally unflappable, he now looked like a man in the grip of a great excitement.

'I can't stop and explain everything now,' he said quickly,

There was a moment of silence, an exchange of glances, and then he came to her side without waiting the outcome of the halting question and answer between the elder and Professor Denning.

'Don't worry,' Max said quickly under his breath. 'I should imagine there's a certain amount of segregation and they're probably going to take you to the women's quarters.'

'Yes, but...' She stared uncertainly at him. 'I'm not sure I want to be taken to the women's quarters. I'd prefer to stay with you—and the others,' she added hurriedly.

The two women had fallen back. Their expressions were almost as uneasy as Gail's own, and for a moment Max looked worried. Then Professor Denning hurried across.

'It's all right, my dear,' he said. 'You are to go with them, for refreshment. We are being treated as guests, not prisoners, you know.'

After a doubtful glance at him she looked back to the two women. The younger one did not smile, but she put out her hand almost timidly, her large dark eyes not wavering in their sad regard of the newcomer, and Gail sighed, moving forward unwillingly. She glanced over her shoulder. 'If you see my shirt fluttering from the ramparts you'd better all come quickly,' she muttered darkly, and surrendered herself to the strangers.

She was led through an arched opening into a small antechamber devoid of furnishings and from it into a long low stone-walled passageway. It was instantly cool, cool enough to be shivery, and the effect of the sunlight casting bars through the narrow window openings all the way along created a bizarre light and shade that reminded Gail incongruously of a never-ending pedestrian crossing. Where on earth were they taking her? There were openings on the right, all obscured with hangings that seemed to be made of a coarse flax-like canvas painted in strange designs of vivid blues and reds, which she supposed led to various departments. Departments of what?

All the way, the women spoke not one word, although every few steps they turned to glance at her with undisguised curiosity, a curiosity which seemed to centre round her plain, workmanlike apparel, particularly the now most fashionably shrunk blue levis she was wearing, alas, the traces of the rigours they had survived.

But why did these two women look so sad? She ventured a smile at the girl and saw the dark eyes widen and almost return it, only to look away again. The older woman's expression had the same air of some secret grief, some care that depressed the spirit as well as her thin shoulders. Gail suppressed a sigh and hoped the air of grief wouldn't prove too contagious.

At last the passageway ended and opened into a wide room, also of stone, but rendered less severe and chill by the same type of hangings as she had previously noticed. But this was not the end of the journey. There was another doorway, another passageway, and at last the women halted and indicated a doorway draped with the now familiar curtain. Gail entered, prepared for almost anything, and gave an audible sigh of relief; this was the bathing apartment!

When she became accustomed to the grey-green eeriness—there were no windows except for horizontal slits high in the stone walls—and the constant sound of running water she began to enjoy the novel experience of climbing a little stairway of cool brick steps to climb into a great bath that reminded her more of a brick-built tank than any bath she had ever seen. Water flowed constantly into it from a big cistern high above it and overflowed at one end into the sunken gulley in the floor beneath and drained away through a grille in the wall at one side.

The woman brought a bowl of dark, oily-looking liquid which Gail presumed was soap and then, to Gail's secret amusement, retreated to the other end of the apartment and sat down, obviously to make sure that the rules of cleanliness were obeyed. When Gail had bathed and dried herself on the length of flax-like material supplied the woman came forward carrying a soft cream-coloured bundle and made signs to indicate that Gail was to take it.

Gail stared at the long robe and shook her head, then saw to her dismay that the girl was already dealing with her discarded clothes. They were being soundly drubbed in a trough she had not previously noticed, and as she watched the girl shook them vigorously, placed them in a big bowl and bore it away.

There was nothing else for it but to don the robe, which proved surprisingly soft against her skin, and fasten it about herself as best she could. Then she heard a soft jingle and found the woman standing behind her and holding out a girdle that seemed to be formed of fine gold chain.

Having reached the stage where it seemed easier to go along with fate than try to resist, Gail fastened the chain girdle about her waist—it couldn't possibly be real gold!—and allowed herself to be conducted further into the mystery.

By now she had begun to lose her sense of direction, and when she was taken into the room which apparently was to be her apartment she was glad to sink down on a low divan and look about her new surroundings. Here were the strangely patterned hangings all round the walls, the same narrow windows which were too high to see out from, and the same flooring of terracotta bricks about six inches square, all set beautifully evenly without any visible means of cementing or plastering. The furnishings were simple, low benches and stools of a dull black unfamiliar timber, and vividly dyed materials covering the big square divan on which she was sitting.

She got up, smoothing down the clinging robe, and padded round the room, then picked up one of the disconcertingly heavy stools and placed it under the window. She was standing on it, feeling a soft draught of air playing on her face and looking out on the quadrangle, when the woman entered, followed by two other girls.

They were carrying large platters of a dull, silvery metal which they placed on the long bench table by the divan. Gail stepped down from her perch and surveyed the refreshments which seemed to be for her, as the woman and girls had retreated again, and hoped she wouldn't be breaking some code of hospitality if she didn't consume it all.

There were two jugs, one holding water and the other a creamy liquid that looked like milk, a bowl of fruit, all unknown to Gail except for some tiny bluish-coloured grapes and avocado pears, some cakes that looked like maize, a jar holding honey, and a huge dish holding eggplant, potatoes and salad greens. There was also a kind of condiment set holding dark spices and what looked like red chutney.

Wondering how the men were faring, she began cautiously to sample her lunch...

But when she had finished and the girls had taken away the platters unease claimed Gail again. The silence was beginning to fray her nerves and at last she resolved to take the initiative.

The woman made no attempt to stop her when she walked firmly to the doorway and stepped outside. Trying to ignore the flowing folds of the long robe and forget the silent shadow at her heels, she began to retrace her steps, until she found herself back in the long passageway and almost running in her eagerness to emerge into the open air. She came to the archway, set off across the quadrangle without once glancing back, and neared the part of the building where she was certain the men had been taken. But there was no entrance that she could see, only a wall that continued the enclosing of the quadrangle, and the gateway was barred. Gail thrust at it and then turned to the woman.

The woman gestured, and it was clearly negative. Gail bit her lip, then turned with a hint of desperation towards the way they had first entered.

It still stood open and after a quick glance at the woman Gail stepped outside and looked along the great avenue. Slowly, then with quickening steps, she went on until she was back at the landing place by the river. There were no adults to be seen and the avenue was deserted, but she could hear voices and childish cries near by. A moment or so later she saw the children.

There were about a dozen of them, and they were racing downstream in small coracles which they paddled swiftly and skilfully. If they noticed her they gave no sign, seemingly intent on their race, and when their voices faded the unnerving silence descended once more.

Half prepared for signs of restraint from the woman, Gail began to pace along the riverside, and was surprised to find that the woman made no move to follow her. It seemed she was free enough in that respect.

But what was the use of freedom if it didn't lead anywhere except along the riverside or up that great avenue to the huge gateway which seemed to mark the boundary of the city? She stood for a long time, staring up towards the temple towering above the vast green amphitheatre, and turned at last to go back the way she had come. The whole place seemed deserted. There was only the sad-faced woman patiently awaiting her return, the silent room, and more refreshments she didn't really want. The only thing she *did* want...

Almost ready to believe that the men had vanished off the face of the earth, Gail sank wearily on the divan and fell into an uneasy sleep.

* * *

She awakened abruptly to stifling darkness and a strong sense of tumult about her. She sat up, discovering that the stifling sensation had been caused by a layer of heavy but soft blankets with which she had been covered while she slept, and peered at her watch, to discover also that she had slept for several hours. Then she heard the sounds she thought she had dreamt, and stiffened: she was not alone. Someone was in the darkness, weeping.

'Who's that?'

There was a stifled gasp, the rush of soft footsteps, and then the flicker of light beyond the doorway. The woman came into the room, her form shadowy in the glow of a primitive lamp which she set by the divan. She reached for the blankets, began to fold them, and Gail saw that her features were taut with grief.

Gail forgot that she couldn't make herself understood. Knowing only the impulse of sympathy, she scrambled off the bed and put her hand round the woman's shoulder.

'What's wrong? Why do you cry? Try to tell me, please ...' She attempted to make the woman sit down, patting her shoulder as she realised her helplessness to break the language barrier.

But the woman seeemed to respond, looking searchingly at Gail, and then stood up, taking Gail's hand and indicating that she was to follow.

Her heart beating fast and knowing instinctively that the strange sense of tumult to which she awakened had not been imagined, Gail followed the woman along the passageway. It was illuminated by flaring torches fixed in metallic baskets set high in the walls, and the flickering radiance seemed to heighten the sense of drama that gripped Gail as the woman halted before a shallow flight of steps set in a recess. At the top there was an archway, and grouped beneath it a cluster of silent women.

They looked up as Gail approached, but betrayed no expression beyond a dull, frozen apathy as she was led into the room behind the heavy curtain which the woman drew aside.

Gail halted, almost overcome by the wall of heat behind the hangings, and barely restrained a gasp as she stared at the strange scene. She was looking into an enormous domed room which glimmered like burnished bronze. Walls, ceiling, all were covered with the metallic glow. At least thirty torches flared and flickered all round the chamber, and in niches beneath them strange twisted vessels held burning incense which added its heavy fumes to the already overpowering heat. There were at least a dozen women sitting silently in small groups of twos and threes, but it was the central focal point that brought the gasp to Gail's lips.

On a dais was a high divan which bore a sinister resemblance to a bier in its shape and bizarre ornamentation, and on the divan lay a girl.

She was lying quite still, her eyes closed, her long dark hair tumbled wildly over the rich burnished covering of her pillow, her form as slender as a child's beneath the thin white robe in which she was clad. She was obviously very young, and she was obviously very ill.

At each side of her two women sat. They had bowls on their laps, and as Gail watched they dipped cloth into the bowls and sponged the girl's forehead.

Gail felt a touch on her arm. She looked round and met the intent gaze of her companion. The woman pointed at the sick girl and said, 'Azzuni.'

'Azzuni,' Gail repeated, and the woman nodded.

A sigh whispered through the chamber, and Gail went forward slowly, mounting the three steps to the dais and looking down on the sick girl. She whispered the name again, a strange, musical name, and the girl's eyes opened. But they held no recognition, only the dark, feverish brilliance of pain. Immediately an older woman came forward. She held a beautifully chased drinking cup that seemed to hold a pale, almost colourless fluid, and one of the other attendants raised the girl's head while she held the cup to her lips. But the girl turned her head away and sank back, moaning fretfully.

Suddenly Gail felt a wave of unsteadiness and perspiration beading her face. She fought back the weakness and bent over the girl, wondering if she would be breaking some taboo by touching her. Gently she laid her hand on Azzuni's forehead, feeling a shock at the burning dryness of it. The protest she had half expected did not come. Instead there was a sudden air of intentness, almost expectancy, and she knew instinctively that these people desperately needed help to heal someone who was special in their society.

Wishing she had a thermometer and a great deal more knowledge than she possessed, Gail took the girl's wrist and checked the pulse rate against the second hand of her watch. When the full minute had elapsed she felt unease. The pulse rate indicated that the temperature was probably at least four degrees above normal. She listened to the thin, shallow breathing, noted that there was no rash or outward indication of tropical infection, and shook her head. But unless something was done soon...

Suddenly all her innate practicality came uppermost. How could anyone breathe in this sickly, overpowering atmosphere, laden as it was with the fumes of the incense and the reek of the torches? Abruptly she descended and looked for the hidden windows, seeking to draw aside the hangings and let the sweet clean air into the room. The girl needed breathing space, and all these people shifted out of her sickroom; most of all she needed a doctor.

But here Gail met her first barrier of antagonism. Shocked hands drew her away, replacing the hanging she had drawn aside, expressed horror in a way that was unmistakable, despite the language barrier.

Gail tried to explain, to mime, and gave up helplessly before the lack of incomprehension. It was hopeless. But she had to do something, and soon. If only she could find Max ... but she *had* to find Max...

The babble had subsided; the women had returned to their

vigil, the useless sponging and attempts to make Azzuni drink their brew. Gail turned abruptly and slipped outside. She hurried back to her apartment and seized the lamp, hoping she could carry it without dousing the wick, and set off to locate the men.

As she ran she wondered who and what Azzuni might be. Judging by the ceremony and air of tragic concern surrounding her she was someone of high rank or symbolic importance. What had struck her down? And how long had she lain stricken?

Gail emerged into the open and found the night bathed in the silvery radiance of an almost full moon. Thankfully she set the lamp down in the lee of the entrance and made her way out into the avenue. No use wasting time groping across the maze of terraced gardens with their intersecting walls or hoping the gate across the quadrangle would be open. There had to be another way in.

A white ghostly figure in the long pale robe she had forgotten she was wearing, she followed the high outer wall, trusting her instinct. It seemed to extend for miles, and she had rounded two angles and was almost on the point of turning back in despair when she heard the voices.

She froze, hardly daring to believe her ears, then shouted wildly, 'Uncle Phil! Is that you? Uncle Phil! Max! Where——'

'Gail!' After the cry there was a moment of silence, then hurrying footsteps on the other side of the wall, and Max's voice, 'Stay where you are. We're coming.'

But she was running now, looking at the dark blank solidness, seeking for the gate that didn't seem to exist.

'Gail... stand clear!'

The voice was above her head. She halted and saw a head and shoulders outlined against the sky. Then Max was hanging by his hands for a second before he dropped to the ground and turned towards her, dusting his hands against his thighs.

'Oh, Max... !' She ran forward, reaching out. 'I was beginning to think I'd never——'

'Steady.' He held her by the shoulders and smiled faintly. 'Did you think we'd—— Good heavens!' He noticed the robe and his brows shot up. 'They have transformed you. Have they looked after——?'

'I tried to find you this afternoon,' she interrupted, 'but——'

'Yes, I'm sorry about that, but we got into conclave, and there's a great deal to explain. What with——'

'Yes, I know, but—Max, you've got to come with me, now.

There's a girl back there. She——'

'Shall we take it easy?' he checked her quietly. 'And start at the beginning.' He turned away, raising his voice. 'Hello there. Make your way down to the river and meet us there. Okay?'

'Okay,' came the response from the other side. 'All right, Gail?'

'Yes, but listen,' she drew back, 'we've got to do something right away about this girl. She's terribly sick, and she's lying there in a steam bath of fug and stinking fumes and—her temperature's sky-high, and—— She's called Azzuni, and——'

'Yes, we know about Azzuni,' Max broke in, 'but we can't do anything. We want to, but we can't.'

'But why not?' Gail's eyes dilated as she stared at him. 'You could. You're the only one of us who could. Max, you're not going to stand back and not do anything to help her? I tell you, she's terribly ill.' Gail's voice rose in shocked disbelief. 'You must, Max! If you don't, I think she'll die!'

'Gail, I can't. Do you think I don't want to? Do you think I'd sit back and not raise a finger to help? This is what I'm trying to tell you. Azzuni is the Chosen One. She is the Bride of the Sun. But until the marriage ceremony is over no man may touch her, even look upon her.'

Max took a deep breath and let his hands drop to his sides.

'God knows, I want to save life. But Azzuni's taboo. Taboo to all men. Even to a doctor. That's why I can't help her, Gail.'

CHAPTER VI

It was a strange tale that Max began to unfold as they walked down to the moonlit riverside.

The men's experience had been similar to Gail's own. They had been taken to bathe and refresh themselves, offered clean robes, and shown to spacious apartments where food and drink was brought to them. Afterwards, they had gathered in the meeting hall of the council and begun the long difficult job of breaking down the barrier of communication. The leaders of the Secret People had seemed as anxious as the expedition team to reach understanding, and gradually it emerged that the Secret People possessed three tongues; an everyday language which proved completely incomprehensible to the team, an Indian dialect which bore certain similarities to the Quechuan widely spoken by South American Indians, and their puzzling knowledge of German, which, however, was known only by the elders.

And so it had taken a great deal of time and patience before some of the answers began to come clear, and a mystery that was half a century old was a mystery no more.

'So von Schaumel made his home here, and lived with the Secret People for fifteen years before he died,' Max said wonderingly. 'He learned their tongue, and taught them his own, and added his scientific knowledge to the already considerable ingenuity of these people. They had long shunned the river, believing it to be poisonous, and built a fantastic irrigation system to trap and tap the mountain streams, but von Schaumel discovered the thrust fault and the resultant effect on the water, and devised a series of filters so that the water could be utilised for domestic purposes. He bred from the two mares among the pack animals which had carried his supplies and thus provided a sturdier mode of transport than the llamas on which the Secret People had previously depended. Llamas are not happy in lowlands, and though these people have considerable herds of them grazing up in the hills to provide wool and meat, they lacked the stronger beast of burden.'

'And the Flower? Does it really exist?' Gail asked impatiently.

The Professor and Max looked at one another, then Max shook his head doubtfully. 'It's too soon to tell. There *is* a flower, it's part of their legend, but they believe its magic is fading. For as long as they can remember they've used an extract from this flower for its herbal qualities. The roots are made into a balm or salve for outward application and the petals are used in the manufacture of an elixir which has been their standby remedy for infection and fever since ...' He shrugged. 'They've given us permission to take samples of this flower, apparently it grows like a weed everywhere, but they are deeply worried about its failing properties, believing that for some reason their god is displeased with them, and——'

'Is their god the sun?' Gail interrupted.

'Not exactly,' the Professor put in. 'They believe in a supreme invisible god, and believe that the sun is the outward manifestation of that being, and is thus the focal point of their rites and worship.'

'Then ... are they of Inca origin?'

Professor Denning smiled. 'That we do not know, and I doubt if we ever shall, my dear. For they don't know themselves. Until the coming of von Schaumel they had no written word. Everything was handed down by word of mouth from father to son.'

'Yes, but it sounds as though they could be. After all, a lot of the Indians are descendants of the Incas who survived the Spanish conquest,' Gail persisted, 'and Macchu Picchu wasn't found until 1911, nobody knew it existed and that it was supposed to be the last refuge of the Incas. How can we know for certain that they didn't retreat across the Andes and make a fresh start?'

'Because it's known that they lost heart. Their legend told them that they were to have an allotted number of rulers, after which an invader would arrive from the unknown and rule them. And their prophecy was fulfilled—in the form of Pizarro.'

Gail looked doubtful and Max smiled. 'It's a question that has puzzled a lot of romantic minds beside yours, Gail. And now,' he glanced at his watch and stood up, 'I think it's time we made our way back.'

She did not move, except to look up at him. 'What about Azzuni? Surely somebody can think of some way to help her. I mean, it might be something we could treat. We've a fair supply left in the medical kit. But if she's left the way she is . . .'

'My dear, we realize that,' said Professor Denning, 'but we can't flout the wishes or beliefs of these people. It is their choice, the same as it is ours, whether they accept medical treatment or not.'

'But their own elixir isn't working,' said Clive quietly.

'Nevertheless, we can't force our beliefs on them. Nor do we want to risk antagonizing them at this early stage,' said the Professor.

'Listen, I know all about medical ethics,' argued Gail, 'but there are times when rules are meant to be broken. *I've* seen her; you haven't. And there's one thing I'd like to say,' she looked directly at Max, 'could you, knowing you might have the power to save her, live with yourself afterwards if you stood back and she died?'

There was a small ripple of shock through the others, then Max said quietly, 'But we don't know, Gail, and it isn't as easy as that.'

He touched her shoulder with a gesture that indicated it was time to go and suddenly she felt contrition over her outburst, and that unwittingly she had directed it against him in particular. She stood up and looked away. 'I'm sorry, Max. I—I didn't mean that personally. I——'

'Forget it,' he broke in curtly, 'I know how you feel. Believe me, I've experienced the same situation. It's not a pleasant one.'

There was a silence for a while as they turned to walk back to their quarters. Between Max and Clive, Gail felt her steps lagging, and depression creep back into her. The memory of Azzuni haunted her and heightened the sense of unease which was gradually replacing the first feeling of wonder at the discovery of the valley. She would never admit to fear, but the strangeness did threaten to be overwhelming, especially when she was the one who was forced to face it alone. They were very near the point where she must leave her companions and subconsciously seeking to postpone the moment she said, 'Tell me about this Bride of the Sun business. What exactly does it——' A dreadful thought struck her and she exclaimed sharply, 'They're not going to—to sacrifice her, or——?'

'No!' Max and Clive said simultaneously. 'They're——' Clive's voice checked and Max finished, 'They're not as barbarous as that. As far as we can gather, Azzuni was born at the moment of the sun's greatest supremacy, roughly what we call noon on midsummer's day. From the moment of birth she is prepared for the purpose they believe she is born for: to provide the next Leader. In ten days' time the ceremony is to take place in the Temple. The son of Zarco, the present Leader, becomes the proxy bridegroom, that is for the Sun, and is married to Azzuni. The child of the union will be the next Leader.'

'And'—Gail stared—'if she doesn't have a son? What then?'

'If she disgraces herself by producing a daughter I guess it's too bad for her,' said Clive, making a gesture across his throat.

'It's not funny.' Gail turned away from him. 'So that's why they're in such a state! But she's only a child, if she's more than thirteen or fourteen I'll be very surprised. It seems...' She shook her head and lapsed into silence.

They reached the gate and halted, and she looked round the circle of faces, then at the darkness she must return to alone. She thought of the eerie flickering torchlight, the lonely apartment, the silence, and that weird chamber where the sick Azzuni lay amid the scents of burning incense. She took a step forward.

'I can't. I don't want to go back there. Oh, please, can't you do anything about me? Don't you understand?' she begged. 'I can't communicate. I want to be with you all. Can't we camp out for the night?'

There was a pause, then the Professor cleared his throat. 'Now, Gail,' he began, 'this isn't like you. You know we can't camp out. It would be churlish to refuse these people's hospitality. They——'

'It's all right for you, *you* can talk to them and you're all together. Oh, it doesn't matter!' she turned blindly away, as furious with herself for this unwonted betrayal of weakness as she was with her uncle's lack of understanding.

They began to murmur and Clive and Roger both tried to put their arms round her at the same time, gestures which she shrugged off angrily. 'Don't worry. I'll survive. Goodnight.' She ran through the great arch without a backward glance, vowing bitterly that never again would she let them see she was scared, let them think she couldn't take it, think she was being childish. It *was* childish...

'Gail!' Max caught up with her and yanked her to a standstill. 'Are you really scared? Because there's no need. If I thought there was any——'

'No, I'm not scared. Don't worry, I'll behave myself,' she said coldly. 'I know Uncle Phil's blind and deaf to everything but the cause of history and discovery. Well, I won't——'

'Listen to me,' he interrupted in a low voice, 'don't get the idea that we're deserting you, or that we don't realize it might be a bit unnerving at first, but be honest; has there been a single indication in the way you've been treated to cause you fear?'

He looked down at her set face and his voice softened. 'All right, I know it hasn't worked out very well for you, but remember that these people have offered hospitality according to their custom; that it doesn't concur with our own is to be expected, but I don't suspect for one moment that we have any reason to distrust them. Now try and stick it for one night and tomorrow I'll try to do something about getting you shifted a bit nearer us. Okay?'

'Max, you don't have to baby me,' she sighed. 'But my clothes have vanished and heaven knows where the rest of my gear is. I haven't even got a comb. That's what I'm moaning about as much as anything. If I could make myself understood it wouldn't be so bad,' she added resignedly.

'Well,' his brows went up and he fished a small comb out of his shirt pocket, 'at least I can remedy one lack. Anything else? A hankie?'

'No, but I'll have your torch,' she said in a small voice. 'I can stand anything as long as I have a ray of light when things go bump in the darkness.'

He handed over the torch, flicking the beam briefly into her face before he did so, and said, 'It's a new battery—oh, Gail, you're a funny girl. Now don't worry.' His arm went round her and held her rather clumsily against his side as he spoke, and the movement took her by surprise. She felt the folds of his shirt against her face and the warmth of him during the brief contact suddenly banished all her misgivings.

Then he pushed her away and said, 'Go on—I'm not very

good at babying girls—and don't worry.'

'Yes—no—thanks.' The torch stabbing a wide dancing circle along the path in front of her, she followed the friendly radiance until she reached the entrance. The little lamp was still glowing where she had left it and she picked it up, carrying it in one outstretched hand as she went with slower steps now back to her room.

There was no sign of the woman and utter silence was everywhere. Gail sat down on the divan and after a moment began to comb her hair into some semblance of tidiness. When she had finished she sat still, running one finger down the comb and making soft little trills of sound, and a thought occurred which brought a slight smile to her mouth: they were strange circumstances which could bring her to using another person's hair comb—without the slightest feeling of repugnance!

So Max wasn't very good at babying girls. Now she came to think of it, during the last two days he had begun to betray the same tendency towards her as the rest of the team; a kind of indulgence—protective babying was near enough to an apt definition if she was strictly honest, she decided wryly.

Her head tilting a little to one side, she frowned and considered the thought; somehow, the thought of Max aligning himself with the others in his attitude towards her didn't bring any satisfaction at all. In fact, there was something almost disappointing in it, the more she thought about it. Babying...

* * *

Gail was awakened next morning by a light touch on her shoulder. Sunlight was streaming into the room and the woman was holding a tall, beaker-shaped cup. Instead of a handle there was a ridge round it about an inch below the rim, and when Gail took it she realized it was to serve as an insulating grip instead of a handle. There was a clear, dark liquid steaming in it and a faintly scented herby smell that was pleasantly aromatic. Gail hesitated, and the woman nodded, and Gail took a suspicious sip. It wasn't tea, it wasn't anything she could name, but it was instantly refreshing and with the fleeting hope that she wasn't due for the 'trip' of her life she drank some and then set the beaker down. Deciding it was time to establish verbal contact, she sat up and pointed to herself and said 'Gail' very distinctly, repeating it three times. Then she pointed to the woman and waited.

For a moment the woman looked at her, then put out a hand and touched her lightly. 'Gail...' she said slowly, and smiled as

Gail smiled, then pointed to herself, 'Aumya,' and waited with much the same expression as Gail had worn at the start of the introduction.

'Hello, Aumya,' said Gail happily, and held out her hand. She wasn't quite sure how the handshake was registering, then she saw Aumya making a solemn gesture of touching her fingertips and turning the palms of her hands outwards as she did so. Carefully Gail copied the greeting, and saw that she had interpreted it correctly. Aumya was more animated now and suddenly she turned away, going to the door curtain and reaching outside for something. When she came back she was carrying Gail's clothes, clean and folded on one of the big oval platters that seemed to be used for most carrying purposes.

But it seemed she was not to dress just yet; the platter was taken to the window and placed in the rays of the sun, then Aumya gestured to Gail to follow her. After the trek to the bathing apartment and the return to dress, Gail was beginning to wonder when breakfast was coming. She did her hair and slipped Max's comb into her shirt pocket, then obeyed Aumya's indication to accompany her again.

This time she was led outside, along a terrace outside the building, and through another archway. Aumya stood back, gesturing that Gail was to enter, and then backed away, making it clear that this was as far as she came. After a hesitation Gail walked in and found herself in a large hall. The floor was tiled with small green and blue bricks worn smooth and shiny and stretched away under a long low table that occupied most of the central space. There were wall murals and painted hangings, and a great deal of carving in the supporting columns and stonework of the three entrances. There were niches all down the length of the hall and in them were stools with cushioned tops, all carved from the same dull black wood of the table and intricately worked with silver and gold wire patterns.

The atmosphere was ceremonial as well as functional, thought Gail, wandering round curiously and looking at the platters of fruit and unleavened bread rolls which were set along the table between big pitchers of water and milk. Llama milk, or sheep's milk? she wondered, then heard the voices and saw the men entering.

They strolled in, shaved and spruce, as nonchalantly as though they were entering the dining-room of Don Felipe's villa. There were five of the elders with them and Professor Denning drew her forward and gravely introduced her. Equally grave, and secretly hoping she was doing the right thing, Gail performed the fingertip greeting Aumya had taught her, receiving it in return from each of the tall, dignified elders, and pretended not to notice the varying degrees of surprise on the faces of her companions.

She then sat down to the strangest breakfast in which she had ever partaken. Young serving boys attended the men and only one serving maid was present, to hover behind Gail and bring her fruit, strange brittle biscuits and honey to dip them in, then a kind of baked fish stuffed with herbs, and lastly beakers of the herbal tea which Gail had already sampled. But it was not the unfamiliar food which made the meal so strange an occasion; it was the silence with which it was taken. No one spoke, not once, and at the end of the meal the five elders stood up. The team also rose, and the elders filed out, leaving the team alone.

Gail looked at Max and her uncle, saw the slight shake of his head, then followed the general move outside on to the terrace.

'Well, can we breathe now?' said Harmon, giving an uneasy laugh.

'Yes, of course,' said the Professor, 'it's simply a case of acknowledging their customs.'

'I say, Gail, old girl,' Roger came to her side, 'your little greeting went down well. How did you know that?'

'Show me—is this right?' said Jonathan. 'I vaguely noticed them making signs like this yesterday, but it didn't register. It must be the equivalent of——'

'That's right. Aumya showed me.' Gail turned to Max. 'Do you think we could smoke? I'm in need of something to settle my nerves.'

'Try willpower,' Clive jeered.

But Max took the worn silver case from his breast pocket and handed it to her. 'It was all a bit alien, I'll admit. And you'd better have these as well—and take them. We don't know how these people prepare their food.'

She looked at the pack of Entero-vioform and murmured, 'Thanks, that thought occurred to me over the fish,' as she returned his cigarettes. 'Anybody know what kind of fish it was?'

They shook their heads and Clive murmured, 'I think I'd rather not know—it was what one might call an acquired taste.'

Someone suggested poached piranha, and Max touched Gail's shoulder. 'About your moving ... I eventually succeeded in——' He stopped as Clive turned to them again and shook his head as Gail looked at him enquiringly, waiting for him to finish. When he remained silent she raised her brows and responded to Clive's teasing enquiry as to how she had slept, then said to no one in particular, 'Well, what's the programme for today?'

It looked like being quite a full programme.

The Professor wanted to collect samples. Roger wanted to find out more about the social structure of the valley's community. Max wanted to see the two journals which the German scientist had kept during his life in the valley. Harmon, surprisingly, wanted to visit the temple, and Clive wanted to wander around and look at things. Obviously they all wanted to do all these things, and obviously they could not be accomplished in the space of one day. However, despite his own natural curiosity, Max was doubtful when the ring of enquiring gazes turned on him. 'I don't think we should attempt to wander around too freely, not for a little while,' he told them, 'and there is also the possibility of us being summoned to see Zarco himself. Until then, and we've established friendly relations with the Leader, I think we'd better restrain our activities. Remember,' he added warningly, 'we're very much at their mercy at present, until we know more about the terrain of the valley and how we're going to leave it.'

There was silence and faces sobered.

'Where does the river go?' asked Gail. 'It must lead out somewhere.'

'Good question, girl,' Clive bowed. 'Where?'

After a moment of reflection she said, 'I think we should have a conference, decide how long we're going to stay and'—she shrugged—'not just leave things to chance.'

This suggestion was adopted. They adjourned to the riverside, made sure the canoes were still safely moored, and it was not until later in the day that Gail found herself with an opportunity to ask Max what he wanted to tell her earlier that morning.

'Oh yes.' A smile she distrusted caught the corners of his mouth. 'About moving your quarters. In case you haven't grasped the layout: we're in residence with what one might term the administrative section of this strange community, and those who serve the Leader. The men make the rules, and the women have their appointed tasks, and the two just don't mix.'

'So I'm beginning to gather,' she said dryly.

'Your uncle endeavoured to convey that you were his niece, and a close member of the team,' Max went on, the same smile not completely suppressed, 'but it didn't quite get over, not the way he intended. You see, here, children have to take their place in the community scheme as soon as they reach adolescence, and if that entails leaving their family surroundings it has to be accepted. So, outside the fabric of actual family life, they just don't grasp our idea of a cosy, unrelated group that works and plays and socializes, and——'

'Integrates?'

'Integrates—as closely as we do. However,' his face was now expressionless, 'remembering your plea of last night, I put in the request on your behalf, and I'm glad to tell you that you now have permission to join your masters whenever you wish. Or rather, whenever *I* wish.'

'What!' The light of amusement was dying from Gail's eyes. 'Masters! You mean . . . do they think I'm some kind of a slave, or something?' She glared at him. 'You'd better tell me the rest of this interesting conversation.'

'That's all there is to tell. They immediately decided that you were my woman, and that carried rather more weight. In fact they were quite understanding.'

'Oh, were they! Well, you'd better—— Oh golly!' she shut her eyes with dismay. 'I'll never be able to face the others. I'll never live it down.'

'What about me?' he said with some amusement.

'You've got to be joking. Oh, Master, clap your hands and bring on the dancing girls.' She tried to laugh, but it wasn't completely convincing.

'All right, you can relax. They don't know—unless they've mastered a lingo it took me two years to get a smattering of. So, unless you like to share the joke, I won't. Anyway, if you like to follow the master he'll show you the layout so that you know where to find us all if a dire emergency crops up. And in the meantime, I think you'd better stay in the quarters you've been allotted.'

'Yes, I think I'd better,' she said tartly, aware that it seemed to be affording him a great deal of amusement. Unsmiling, she fell into step with him along the brick paved terrace outside the hall where they had eaten. As they walked he began to explain the layout of the place.

'If you think of a capital E without the centre bar . . . the main upright stroke is this part'—he gestured to his right—'where the elders meet in council and conduct the affairs of the Valley. The wing where you are at present staying holds the women's living and working quarters, their spinning and sewing rooms where they care for the vestments used in the temple ceremonies, and the opposite wing has the living quarters for the elders. All those in service of the Leader, the elders and the temple priests do not marry, which explains the segregation. The caste system seems to be strongly in force here. Those thatched adobe houses we saw on the outskirts are those of the agricultural workers. The next ring within the periphery is that of the builders, then the craftsmen, and so on, until we reach the heart, over there,' he pointed to the pyramidal shape that rose from the gardens in the centre of the huge area, 'where the Ruler lives. Now, we turn down here, and if you walked far enough you'd come to the gate that leads into the inner quadrangle, and ultimately the main gate to the avenue, the plaza and the river. Got it?'

'I think so,' she passed through the entrance he indicated and found herself in a long passage identical to the one leading to her own quarters, 'if I want to reach you I come in the back way. No bother at all.' She laughed bitterly. 'It's typical.'

He drew aside the now familiar painted hanging and gestured. She walked into a large room similar to her own, except that the divan and stools were strewn with skins and furs, and there was a great deal more colourful ornamentation decorating the walls.

'Quite the sybarite, aren't you, Master? Whatever's this?'

He looked over her shoulder at the carved wood bowl holding what looked like papery leaves and small sticky-looking pellets.

'It's a herbal extract for chewing, relative to the Indian coca. Don't worry,' he added as he saw the face of repugnance she made, 'I've no intention of sampling it.' He took the bowl from her and set it down. 'Your uncle's next door, but the others are farther away—round the angle of the corridor. And your kit's here.'

'Good.' She was still wandering curiously round the apartment, noting the incongruity of Max's few personal possessions against the bizarre setting. Then she spotted the long robe thrown over a stool in one corner. 'You've got one too. Oh, I'd love to see you lot lined up wearing these.'

'Yes, I'm afraid we lack the dignity to wear them with aplomb,' he admitted wryly, 'maybe if we——'

'A little practice—it could grow on you, this kind of life, if one stayed here very long.' She giggled and swooped on a large fly whisk made of radiantly hued feathers and a long carved bone handle. A surge of gaiety possessed her and she advanced, waving the whisk mockingly before his face. 'I'm sure I'd make a perfect slave—with a little practice.'

He ducked back out of range. 'Until the novelty wore off. Be careful what you practise—you might regret it.'

'Oh yes—Master! Oh!—the thing's moulting or something.' She sneezed and rubbed her nose, dropping the feathery whisk which was responsible and dissolving into laughter.

Max rescued the whisk. 'I'm not surprised. It's not intended for amateur fan-dancers.'

She sneezed again and he laughed, and suddenly they were both infected with amusement. She took a deep breath, not quite sure what she was laughing at, not yet aware that this was the first time she had shared laughter with Max, but vaguely conscious of a sense of release. She started to say something trite, and was struck completely sober by the entrance of Roger.

He halted, then saw her and stared. 'Gail, what on earth are you doing here? I thought——'

'I thought it was time to make sure you're all keeping out of mischief,' she said airily. 'Are you?'

Roger appeared taken aback. 'Of course. What was the joke?'

'Nothing,' she said, on the point of succumbing again. 'We just——'

'What is it, Roger?' Max broke in.

'Oh yes...' Roger blinked. 'Uncle Phil asked me to pass the word round. We're going to see Zarco. Now. But I can't find——'

'The Leader!' Gail exclaimed. 'But I'm not changed. I want a clean shirt on and——'

'Sorry, Gail, I don't think you're included.' Roger shook his head. 'Uncle said if I saw you to let you know where we'd gone and he'll see you later and tell you all about it.'

'Well, of all the... !' Gail said indignantly. 'Just like that!'

'Safer.' Max glanced at her. 'Zarco might need another slave girl.'

'Very funny.' She caught the glint in his eye and looked away. 'Where did you say my gear was?'

'Here.' Max paused. 'Have you told the others, Roger?'

'Yes, except Harmon. I couldn't find him. Is that Gail's stuff? I'll help her round with it.'

'I'll see to it,' Max said. 'You'd better root out Harmon and I'll join you by then.'

Rather unwillingly Roger backed. Gail gave him a pert wave and said, 'Enjoy yourself,' and watched Max go to the pile of stuff at one end of the apartment. He looked over his shoulder.

'You might as well leave your sleeping bag and groundsheet here. You won't need them until we leave.'

She nodded, still conscious of this strange sense of exhilaration. 'I just want my pack and my bush jacket, Max, please.'

He bent over the heap of gear and in that moment something happened to Gail. Everything seemed to blur around her and she saw only a vivid outline of him; the broad muscular shoulders making the jungle green shirt taut across them, the dark line of shadow down his throat where the open lapels fell away, strong chin, bronzed features cleanly etched in their intentness, expressive of a character that was honest, forceful and at times uncompromising. It was as though she was seeing him for the first time and yet had known him for ever, before the moment he entered this new dimension, a magnetic centre that had drawn her into its field.

He straightened. Only a second had elapsed, but it could have been an eternity. He looked straight into her stunned face and said casually, 'Right, I'll see you back,' and she knew what had happened to her.

Max Christiern, of all men, had made her fall in love with him.

* * *

So this was how it happened!

Gail watched the tall figure until it had passed out of her sight and wandered into the shadows of her apartment. This was the magic alchemy that quickened perception, sharpened every sense to new acute awareness, brought an unbelievable joy in merely being alive and a breathless, almost unbearable suspense of anticipation that waited on the next meeting with...

Max... She whispered the name aloud, her eyes puzzled and not a little curious. It was so short a name, a careless kind of name, one she would have said she didn't particularly care for if she had been asked to opine on favourite male names. But now it wasn't a name, it was a person who could make it into something special, one certain man who in the space of a few moments had become a part of her existence ... a part she couldn't visualize being without.

But why? How? Why at that particular moment? Why her? Why *him*? Nothing had happened. She hadn't been drawn to him at first meeting. Secretly, though she'd have died rather than admit it, she'd been a little scared of him those first few days, instinctively knowing that authority-wise he was a different proposition altogether from her own easy-going crowd. He'd never singled her out, never flirted, encouraged, teased, even touched her. On the contrary, until the last couple of days he'd given a distinct impression of regarding her as a baggage he'd have travelled more happily without. So why this catastrophic effect?

She tried to open her pack and discovered that during the past few moments of intense thought she had undone all the buckles and then fastened them again. Heavens! Had she tossed off all that side-chat about slave girls, and flipped that whisk over his face, and pranced about like an idiot? An amateur fan-dancer! She'd subconsciously tried to flirt with him, because it was in her heart without her knowing...

Slowly she began to take her things out of the pack, spreading them over the divan and shifting them from one place to another with aimless movements while the warm colour heated her face and she wondered if he liked her more now than when he first gave his disapproving verdict. How did a girl tell if a man liked her? What were the signs—beyond the blatant passes some men made, passes they would make at anything that was female and reasonably attractive? Gail sat down and experienced the sudden plummeting of the spirits that was to become frequent and very familiar very soon. There just weren't any indications she could think of that showed Max noticed her as feminine and—well, not completely unattractive, and—and a girl who waited for and longed for love as much as any other girl.

Coming at last to the item she sought, the little waterproof pack that held her toiletries and personal treasures, she tried to remember why she wanted it at this very moment. Oh yes ... she wanted to give Aumya some small token. But what? She had no jewellery with her ... jewellery ... She turned the silver ring over in her hand and then put it back in the zipped compartment. Now she knew why she hadn't been able to give Roger the answer he wanted. To think she had imagined that she might marry him some day, for affection and because they'd been close since they were children, and people did drift into marriage for those reasons, because everyone took it for granted they would. She had wondered if she loved him without knowing it ... Gail closed her eyes, making no attempt to stem the way her thoughts were going. She only needed to remember Roger's kisses and then imagine a kiss she had never experienced to know the answer...

Her heartbeats pounding, she zipped the ring out of sight and took out her make-up mirror. They didn't seem to have mirrors here, except for polished metal surfaces, and she could manage with the tiny mirror in her compact. She had nothing else that remotely resembled a suitable gift, except a couple of spare pens, cheap ballpoints, and she couldn't recall seeing any writing among the Secret People. Hastily she polished the mirror and unclipped the little support at the back and then stood it on one of the low tables. She would try Aumya's reaction when she ... come to that, where was Aumya?

Still aimless and unable to keep her thoughts from one certain magnetic object, she sorted out her belongings, tried to make the place look like home and decided to take a bath.

When she returned from the bathing-room the sun had set and there was no sign of Aumya. Gail lit the torches in her apartment, smoked a cigarette, resisted the constant urge to go and see if the men had returned from their audience with Zarco, and with a feeling of guilt remembered Azzuni.

She stubbed out her cigarette and made her way along to Azzuni's apartment. The outer room was deserted, and after a moment's hesitation she called softly, 'Aumya?' and waited.

There was no response. She turned away slowly, afraid to intrude, and was walking away when she heard her name called. Aumya stood there and beckoned, and Gail returned, anxiously searching Aumya's face for indication of how the sick girl was faring. But Aumya did not appear distressed. She drew back the hanging and motioned Gail to enter, and pointed proudly.

Azzuni was sitting up on the edge of the great couch. Her long hair had been bound back from her face, and although she still looked very ill she did not seem restless and feverish now. Two of the attendants were speaking to her, seeming to request something of her, but Azzuni looked down and did not respond. The attendants put a robe round her, lifting her arms and putting them into the sleeves, then they knelt down and slipped soft painted leather sandals on her feet. Firmly they took her hands and raised her to her feet, and guided her, half-supporting, half-carrying her, down the steps of the dais. One on either side of her, they began to walk her slowly round the apartment.

The torches flared and sputtered, and the scent of incense was wafted by the silent women who sat round the perimeter of shadows slowly and monotonously waving ornamented feather fans similar to the one Gail had found in Max's apartment.

There was a sense of breathlessness in the great chamber, and Gail found that she was tending to hold her own as she watched the slow, painful progress of the small, pitifully slight figure. Then the dragging steps turned and for the first time Gail saw Azzuni's face unshadowed and she gasped. The beautiful satin brown features were pale and haggard round the fever spots that burned over the high cheekbones, and the dark eyes had lost even the unnatural brilliance of the previous day and dulled to unseeing apathy.

'Oh no!' Gail whispered aloud, 'she shouldn't be up. She's——' Before she could finish her shocked exclamation Azzuni faltered, uttered a low moan and crumpled to the floor.

A wail rose from the women and a frantic cry from Aumya. She rushed forward and flung herself down beside the prostrate girl and tried to rouse her.

Suddenly angry impatience overcame Gail and she broke out of her shocked trance. How could they be so inhumane? These strange people showed many signs of advanced civilization, but their methods of treating the sick seemed little short of insane. Heedless that she would not be understood, she thrust through the cluster of women and seized Aumya's shoulder.

'Get them out,' she cried. 'Make them leave her alone.' Her forceful gestures seemed to convey her meaning, for Aumya looked up and spread her hands helplessly. 'Go on,' Gail repeated, 'make them go away.'

The women fell back, their expressions bewildered, before her vehemence and retreated to one end of the chamber, seeming to be looking to Aumya for guidance. Gail bent over Azzuni and motioned to Aumya to help her. Between them they lifted the frail girl and laid her back on her couch, and Gail looked down at her anxiously, almost afraid that her worst fears might be real.

But Azzuni was still breathing, light shallow breaths that barely stirred the thin white robe over her breast, and Gail sighed with relief. Quickly she covered the girl and looked round for a container holding water.

Aumya saw the glance and interpreted it, but the vessel she passed to Gail held the strange cloudy fluid which was obviously the elixir, and Gail shook her head; if this was the fabled elixir it held no miracle curative powers for Azzuni.

She said, 'Water,' and saw Aumya's puzzlement and gesture towards the elixir. Gail frowned, then mimed pouring water over herself as in bathing, then held the vessel to her lips as though to drink. Thankfully she saw that Aumya comprehended. The woman went to one of the niches and came back with a large pitcher of water. In gestures similar to Gail's she conveyed that the water was for bathing but not for drinking. She then pointed to the pitcher, showed that she would bring fresh water, waited for Gail's nod of understanding and hurried away.

Gail waited in a fever of impatience. There was little she could do for Azzuni—except one thing, and she intended to do that if she could gain Aumya's confidence.

The women still clustered near the doorway to the outer room and Gail decided to stretch her luck a little further. She picked up the nearest bowl of incense and thrust it at one of the women, then gently nudged the woman towards the door. The woman looked blankly at the bowl, then at Gail, and hesitated. Gail pointed at Azzuni, then at the incense, and shook her head, making a gesture of repudiation. For a moment Gail thought she had failed, then the woman turned meekly and moved out of the room. It was only a minute's work to get rid of the rest of the burners and their sickly sweet fumes, and by then Aumya had returned with a pitcher of cool, crystal-clear water.

Together they bathed Azzuni's hot face and hands, then Gail raised her head gently and tried to persuade her to take a sip of the water. At first Azzuni lay inert, making no response, then her eyes flickered open and she made a feeble movement to avert her lips from the vessel. 'Please try,' whispered Gail, and talked soothingly in murmurs that conveyed the same meaning in any tongue. Weakly the sick girl took a sip, and then drank greedily, long fervid draughts, and sank back with a sigh. Gail straigh-tened. The most difficult part lay ahead. Somehow she had to convey hope and evoke trust, a tremendous task in face of the language barrier. Too worried now to care if what she was doing might seem ridiculous, she began a careful mine play in which she herself was sick and recovered, and then pointed to Azzuni.

Aumya's tired face lit with such hope and longing that a lump rose in Gail's throat and she motioned Aumya to sit by Azzuni's side and wait there.

As she hurried out into the cool night and ran on silent feet through the darkness she prayed that she would find Max alone. There was too much to explain to a crowd; too little time for arguments. She heard voices ahead of her, saw the shapes of figures, and the laughter was unmistakably Clive's. She slowed, waiting until they verged to one of the paths leading through the gardens, and knew that three of them were accounted for. There was no sign of the others and she did not hesitate before slipping into the shadow of the archway and drawing aside the heavy material that curtained the entrance to Max's room.

He was lying prone on the divan, one hand behind his head, the other relaxed across his chest, a thin column of blue smoke rose from the cigarette between his fingers. She must have en-tered too silently, for the movement of his head was startled as she said softly, 'Max...'

'Gail!' he jerked upright. 'Good God! What brings——?'

'Sorry to creep up like that, but—— Max, we've got to do something about Azzuni...' She went to his side and sat down, looking anxiously at him, and began quickly to recount what had happened. His expression sobered as he listened and his mouth grew grimmer as she concluded the sad little account. 'What can we do, Max?' she said pleadingly. 'Can't you think of something?'

He sighed. 'You've already thought of it, haven't you?'

She looked down. 'I wondered if I could persuade Aumya to move her into my room, and then . . .'

'No, Gail, not like that,' he said gently. 'I know you're only thinking of Azzuni's welfare, but you've forgotten something.' He regarded her steadily. 'I have a code to follow. It applies here exactly the same as anywhere in our own world.'

'Yes, I know,' she said sadly. 'Will you talk to Aumya? Because I can't. Please . . . and then take it from there?'

'Yes, I'll try to talk with Aumya—and take it from there,' he said quietly.

'Now?'

'Now.' He stood up.

'And bring the medical kit—just in case?'

He glanced at her, a trace of a smile touching his mouth. 'You never give up, do you?'

'It doesn't achieve much,' she returned, 'that's why.'

There was nothing more to say. In silence he walked back with her and she left him to wait in her apartment while she went to bring Aumya.

Aumya was still sitting exactly as Gail had left her. Azzuni appeared to have fallen into a troubled sleep, there was no sign of the other women and already the atmosphere seemed less heady and oppressive. At first Aumya was reluctant to leave the sick girl and was obviously uneasy as Gail tried to urge her into understanding. At last, with many backward glances, Aumya came and Gail heaved a sigh of relief when they finally reached her room and Max.

'Tell her,' she said urgently, 'tell her we want to help Azzuni to get well.' And pray that Max can communicate with her, she breathed to herself.

For a moment Aumya stared, almost as though she was frightened of the big man getting to his feet, then Max spoke slowly, carefully, and before the strange-sounding words were echoes Aumya began to speak. A torrent broke from her and she gestured wildly, towards the direction where Azzuni lay, towards Max and towards Gail herself.

Gail watched, only able to guess wildly at the gist, and watched Max trying to stem the spate. She broke in, 'Do you understand, Max?' and when he said, 'Some of it,' she said, 'Can you tell her I'll go and sit by Azzuni? Unless you think I should stay here?'

He shook his head. 'This may take a little time—you'd better go back if she's alone.'

Aware now of doubt as to the wisdom of her action, Gail

withdrew and made her way back to the sickroom. Supposing Aumya refused their help? Supposing she was too afraid of breaking the taboos, even though she seemed to love the girl devotedly and Azzuni seemed vital to the fulfilling of the Secret People's rites and tradition?

Gail sat down beside the sleeping girl and faced the possibility that her action could plunge the entire party into danger. So far the Secret People had treated them with courtesy and a strange primitive dignity, but they were still an unknown quantity and there was no means of knowing what their reaction would be if their beliefs and taboos were flouted. And yet how could she stand back and watch Azzuni grow weaker when Max might have the power to save her?

Azzuni stirred and moaned, tossing restlessly and crying out as though besieged by pain, and Gail bent over her, trying to soothe while she despaired over her inability to help. She gave her a drink, tried to settle her comfortably, and gently sponged the dry, burning forehead.

Azzuni subsided again, but not to sleep. The wide eyes stared dully up at Gail and switched their gaze round the shadowed room as though seeking something. Gail glanced at her watch. What was happening? Should she go back and see? Or wait . . . ?

The minutes ticked by, the torches burned lower and one flared fitfully on the point of extinction, and Gail had reached the fever pitch of suspense when at last she heard a movement outside. She looked round and stood up, and a sigh escaped her as steps crossed the outer room. Her hope plunged to zero as Aumya drew back the curtain and entered and then rose wildly as the woman glanced round and turned back. A moment later Max entered.

He looked round briefly. 'We'll need more light. Where's the torch I gave you?'

'I'll fetch it. Anything else?'

'No.' He turned to Aumya, his voice softening. 'Will you tell Azzuni that I mean her no harm? That I want to take her pain away, and that she need have no fear?'

Gail hurried to get the torch and quickly sorted out her own small flashlight, then as an afterthought added her cleanest towel; it might be useful.

When she got back Max had moved a stool up on to the dais and was unlocking his medical case. She propped the torches beside it and asked if there was anything she could do to help.

'You can tuck that under her armpit—no, not in the mouth,' he added as she looked questioningly at him over the thermometer.

Immediately she realized that he foresaw the risk of Azzuni resisting and obeyed, wisely remaining silent and carefully carrying out the occasional instructions he issued as he made the first routine examination.

There were many questions she longed to ask regarding Aumya's conversation with him, but they could wait...

Presently he straightened and raised rueful brows. 'A case like this makes me realize how much we take the lab for granted these days.' Gently he turned Azzuni and probed under the dark flowing hair. 'There's a slight glandular swelling which could mean the first stage of Oroya Fever—the type that leaves severe anaemia.' His mouth compressed. 'But she's certainly got a massive infection.'

'Could it be from this?' Gail pointed to the lobes of Azzuni's ears which had been—to her mind—brutally pierced to take the insertion of heavy jewelled ornaments.

'I doubt it. They've healed cleanly.' He turned away to prepare a syringe. 'I hope to God she's not sensitive to penicillin. Can you steady her, Gail? The poor kid's never known injections.'

Gail did as he instructed, knowing a sudden surge of love as she watched the expert hands give the injection so smoothly that it was over before Azzuni realized what was happening.

Max took a phial of Penbritin from the case and handed it to Gail. 'I want you to watch her and carry out checks every four hours, which I'll show you how to do. She's to have two of these four times daily and in the meantime I'll give her some codeine to relieve the aches and pains she'll have. Would you like to give her one now so that she gets used to you dosing her?'

But Gail need not have worried. Obedience seemed to have been instilled in the sick girl and she swallowed the tablets without protest, then lay back weakly and stared up at Max with a strange expression in her eyes.

He smiled down at her and put his hand on her hair, ruffling it lightly as he would a child's. A slight sigh whispered through the girl on the couch and very slowly she raised her hand in a tentative, searching gesture.

Max met it, and tucked the thin questing hand under the covers, and the ghostly little sigh whispered again. Gail watched his face and the tiny compassionate interlude evoked a strangely painful emotion in her. So, behind that strength and assurance, and that quite definite air of arrogance he could betray, he was capable of compassion and tenderness. Would she ever glimpse the infinite love he could bestow—and the wonder of being the object of that love?

CHAPTER VII

BY the following afternoon the first sign of improvement showed in Azzuni. Her temperature dropped slightly and she was less restless. Gail sat up very late with her, then left Aumya to continue the vigil while she took a few hours' sleep. She still did not know the extent of Aumya's authority, but it seemed to carry some weight because the women did not return to crowd the sickroom and the incense burners did not reappear, to Gail's relief.

It was not until later that evening when she saw Max for a few minutes that she learned the relationship of Aumya and the frail child who was to be the Bride of the Sun. Azzuni was Aumya's daughter.

'It's hard to comprehend,' he said, shaking his head, 'the way they discourage undue lavishing of affection on their children. It does make one wonder if they are, after all, the last of the Incas. They followed a similar tradition, this lack of demonstrative love in their relationships; even with their babies they suckled them without any of the warm mother love we accept as a natural fundamental. Inca babies had to learn not to cry, and to be reared into hardy young individuals without any sentiment, according to the few accounts we have to go by.'

'Yet Aumya loves her devotedly,' Gail said.

'Yes, which proves that it's a basic instinct which even centuries of brainwashing can't eradicate. If you'd heard and seen that woman...' he said slowly. 'All the years of suppression breaking its bonds.'

'Maybe that's why she trusted us.' Gail's eyes were sombre. 'She was scared stiff all the time you were there. When will you check on Azzuni again?' she asked.

'Not any more than necessary, unless she fails to respond to the antibiotics.' He frowned. 'You've realized that Aumya took a great risk? That she's kept our interference a secret?'

'Yes, there hasn't been a soul near Azzuni all day,' Gail paused, 'that's why I wondered if you...'

'I don't want to risk Aumya's safety any more than I can help,' Max said grimly. 'As I said yesterday: it's all very peaceful at present, but we don't know how these people deal with those who flout their laws—their own wrongdoers as well as strangers.'

She fell silent, his words reminding her again of how isolated they were here in this strange valley, and how defenceless.

She said, 'I'd better get back.'

As he had done the previous day he walked her back, in silence, and she could not help but reflect wryly on the emptiness of these small spells of time. Away from Max she longed to be with him; with him she became increasingly conscious of how casual his manner towards herself—and how unaware he seemed of his own potent attraction. At least he had accepted her, she thought sadly, and now talked to her as he would to other members of the team. The acceptance she wanted so badly at the beginning, and now it wasn't enough.

But at least he did say, as though with afterthought, before he bade her goodnight, 'I bet you didn't bargain on having to turn nurse to the most important personage of the moment. I'm afraid you're not going to see much of the valley during the next few days.'

'I don't mind,' she said.

It was true, in spite of the fact that she saw little of the others and their activities in the days that followed. As Azzuni continued to recover she and Gail became drawn to one another and it was impossible not to experience a sense of satisfaction in being partly responsible for the way things had turned out. By the third day Azzuni's fever had lessened considerably and she was beginning to take an interest in the newcomer who seemed to be a new part of her life. The incense remained banished, sunshine poured into the airy apartment all day, and the mosquito netting which Max had sent over from the team's supplies amused Azzuni when Gail carefully arranged it over her couch as soon as sundown came. But Gail could not help noticing that Azzuni seemed to be looking for someone else. Each time she or Aumya entered, Azzuni's gaze would remain on the door, hover there a few moments and then close in sadly in a way that was rather puzzling. Probably one of the attendants to whom she was particularly attached, Gail decided, getting out the black and red capsules and preparing for the four-hourly routine.

Each evening she reported to Max on the patient's progress and she came to look forward to these times with a mingling of bliss and dread. Now that the crisis point of Azzuni's illness had passed Gail came in for a certain amount of ribbing from Clive, and this only served to heighten her awareness of the change that had come over her. When he remarked that no doctor was complete without his faithful nurse she felt certain her colour must scream her secret to the world, and if Clive ever suspected, after being the recipient of her early unguarded confidences of what she thought of Max Christiern...

Luckily, that day the team had gone to reconnoitre the unknown reaches of the river and the moment passed, she hoped, unnoticed, as expressions became serious. They had set off in the canoes, to find that several miles past the reaches of the city the river ran into a canyon that narrowed into a high, sheer-walled chasm. The flow became violent, hazardous with rapids, and ended in a series of cataracts that plunged down a cliff face into a dense floor of jungle. It was certain that there was no way out in that direction. They could not return the way they had entered, which left only the blocked pass. However, no one yet seemed to be afraid that they might be trapped within the valley...

The Professor was happily tending rows of little polythene bags in which reposed all the plant specimens he had collected. Gail looked curiously at the little clumps of earth from which sprang an insignificant pale pink flower with small, clover-shaped leaves.

'It this it?' she asked.

'That's it,' Clive said, 'that's the famous flower we came six thousand miles to gather. Here,' he broke one from its stem and tucked it behind her ear, 'see what it feels like to wear the most expensive bloom you're ever likely to receive!'

Gail made a face at him. 'It's a change from the dandelions you always send me at home.'

'You'd better not let Lealholme-Crosse hear you say that,' said Jonathan. 'That flower's worth its weight in gold. I mean, add up the air fares, and the cost of supplies——'

'And the cost of transporting your guitar,' said Clive.

But despite the banter they still tended to regard the little pink flower with a certain amount of awe. As Max said, they had every reason to believe that in lab tests it would yield antibiotic content, and most of the team inclined towards his theory that over the years the Secret People had used it so indiscriminately that resistant strains had developed and it was now virtually useless to them.

The following day held two surprises for Gail. One of them proved more of a shock, coming as it did totally without warning.

She had lunched with Azzuni and she was considering that the time had come to take her out of doors for the first tentative airing when Aumya rushed in in a state of considerable agitation. Immediately Azzuni became wildly excited, and although Gail had picked up a few words and phrases of their language she could grasp nothing except that someone was coming. Aumya began a frantic dressing of the girl and a few moments later the women hurried in, and instantly the apartment became like bedlam. The incense burners were brought back, the torches were lit, two small braziers were carried in and placed ceremoniously beside the high domed niche behind the head of Azzuni's dais. Various bowls and vessels and strange carved effigies were placed around the niche, and the women settled themselves in their appointed places round the apartment.

An unnerving silence descended and Gail came out of her bewilderment and wondered: what next? The next moment she knew.

Sounds of approach came from the outer chamber and two women pulled aside the hangings. The women grouped about the apartment fell to their knees and bowed their heads, and a very tall man came in with a slow, stately tread.

He wore a white robe that swept the ground. His head was bare and completely shaven, and over the robe was a gleaming metallic collar on which symbols and leaves were engraved. Inside the doorway, he stopped, looked long at Azzuni, and then at the astonished Gail. The gravity of his expressionless face did not flicker as he studied the slim girl in the blue poplin pants and white shirt worn knotted to reveal a vee of midriff, short sleeves rolled almost to the shoulder, and a wisp of scarlet tying her short dark hair carelessly back from her brow. Finally he moved forward and Gail came out of her stupor. This must be the High Priest.

He stood before Azzuni and slowly the girl rose to her feet and stepped unsteadily from the dais. Gail felt Aumya's hand on her arm, checking her instinctive movement, and she held her breath while Azzuni went unsteadily towards the head of the room. Now it became obvious; the niche was a form of altar and the strange motions the High Priest was now making were a form of blessing and thanksgiving. She watched curiously, caught by the alien spell that gripped the imagination and aware there was an undoubted sense of power emanating from the being who was the cynosure of the awed women.

Presently he turned and faced her, and she felt Aumya gripping her arm and drawing her forward.

Her heart racing despite the common sense she was trying to cling to, Gail went forward slowly, almost hypnotized by the unflickering stare of the curiously pale eyes, and with a hint of desperation brought her hands together in the fingertip greeting.

The High Priest raised one hand and Aumya motioned her towards Azzuni's side. Awkwardly she knelt down, sitting back on her heels and bowing her head as Azzuni had done. Wafts of incense stung her nostrils and the heat from the braziers gradually penetrated the thin cotton of her shirt. She heard the deep sonorous tones, their nuances unvarying, sensed the movements he made, and then felt something hot pressed against her forehead. A moment later cool moistness replaced it, there was a scent that was not unpleasant, and a light touch of hands on her shoulders. Someone nudged her and she took that as her cue to stand up.

Uncertainly, but breathing a little more freely, she looked at Azzuni, then at Aumya, and finally at the tall robed being. Then she saw something glint in his hand, and everything she had ever read about tribal sacrifice scorched through her mind. Then she saw he was turning to Azzuni and handing her something. The glint became a soft golden gleam, and Azzuni was holding one end of a fine plaited wire chain while the High Priest retained the other. They passed it across her throat and linked it at the nape of her neck, and the golden tear-drop pendant lay cool against her throat. He touched it, then raised both hands in a gesture of invocation, and suddenly all the women raised their hands with the same oddly impressive movement.

Gail bowed her head, seeing the pendant and wondering what she was supposed to do now. She took a deep breath, realizing that something was expected of her, and looked at the High Priest. First she touched the pendant, then opened her hands towards him, bowing her head, then repeated the same gesture towards Azzuni. Finally she raised her arms with the same gesture they had all made, and smiled. 'Thank you,' she said simply.

* * *

'How does it feel to be the girl of the moment—anointed by no less a personage than the High Priest himself?' said Clive with a grin.

'I was petrified,' she said, 'I had no idea what was happening, and then this . . .'

Their gazes returned to the pendant, still fascinated and inclined to be sceptical of her story, except that the pendant was undoubtedly real and fastened securely about her neck.

'You do realize it's gold, girl?' Professor Denning still wore his bewildered look. 'Pure, solid gold?'

'Yes. Well, they did give it to me,' she protested, 'and nobody's asked for it back, not so far.'

'They will,' said Clive in sorrowful tones, 'and it'll be far easier for you if they do. That bauble's going to bring you grey hairs and make you bankrupt, my girl.'

'Oh really?' She fingered the silk-smooth surface of the precious drop, still not quite believing in it or the mystical rite she had experienced.

'Yes, really,' Clive waggled a forefinger. 'The grey hairs will come with worrying about how you're going to smuggle *that* through the Customs, and the bankruptcy will follow automatically when you've paid the fine, the duty, the purchase tax and the import tax, and the legal brains you'll require to explain how you came to be in possession of——'

'Get lost!' She aimed a threatening fist at her tormentor and Clive desisted, grinning. 'Anyway,' she assumed a haughty stance, 'how do you know I'm going to need to do any smuggling? I may decide to stay here now, and if I command it you'll all have to stay as well. So you'd better treat me with respect in future.'

Clive raised his brows and looked at Jonathan. 'Shall we spank her?'

Knowing Clive was quite capable of carrying out his threat, Gail retreated hastily. 'I've got to change if we're really going to have a look at the temple tonight.'

Only two days remained now before the ceremony in which Azzuni would become the Bride of the Sun. All along the avenue work was in progress for the great day. Floats were being prepared, hung with flowers and painted symbols. Vines woven into intricate designs trailed from them and archways were being constructed at intervals along the route to the temple. There were enormous baskets to hold the torches, bonfires were rising in every open space, drums lined the avenue, the approach to the temple, and were massed in the well of the amphitheatre, and the whole atmosphere was charged with muted excitement.

It took them well over an hour to climb the long winding road to the temple, and the journey might well have taken longer had they paused to explore the gardens that rose terrace upon terrace all the way up to the great building in the shape of an elongated pyramid. The air was bright with the flashes of exotic birds whose vivid hues were only equalled by the flowers that carpeted the terraces and entwined in every rock crevice.

A maze of low walls and shrubs surrounded the temple itself, and a broad flight of some eighty steps led up to its elaborately carved portals. The party broke up into pairs. The Professor and Jonathan examining the way the stonework was constructed, Harmon levelling his camera, Clive drawing Roger aside to point out something, and Gail found herself alone with Max for the first time that day. She did not waste time in making her confession.

'Max,' she said, when she was sure the others were out of earshot, 'I can't go on taking the credit like this.'

'What credit? Stand still,' he directed, 'I'll take you against the steps.'

Impatiently she remained still while he clicked the camera. 'The credit for restoring Azzuni to health,' she said firmly.

'But you did—with the help of a little Penbritin,' he said lightly.

'I didn't, and you know it. But they're treating me as though I'd worked a miracle or something.'

'And it's going to go on that way.' He perched on a low wall and gave her a direct look. 'It's so happy a solution I never dared dream of it. And I don't want any credit, I'm just glad she's better.'

'That's how I feel.' Instinctively her hand went to the pendant, and his glance followed the movement.

'You know exactly what that is, don't you?'

'It—it's a very beautiful piece of jewellery, isn't it?' she said slowly. 'With a certain symbolic significance about it because of Azzuni.'

'They've given you the most precious token they could give you.' He reached forward and took the pendant lightly, letting it lie against his finger. 'It's tear-shaped and gold. They've given you a Tear of the Sun.'

She stayed silent, held by his steady gaze, and the warmth of his hand against her throat moved her more at that moment than the symbol of the sun. At last she said, 'I thought it might be something like that, but—but it shouldn't have been given to me.'

'Who, then?' His hand dropped away and the golden tear, still warm from his touch, fell back against her skin.

She gave a shrug, suddenly aware of a dangerous weakening she had to control, and he smiled slightly. 'What would *I* do with a sunny teardrop? One day you——'

'Max, are you there?'

The Professor's shout came from the terrace below and Max stood up. With a murmured excuse he moved away and Gail sat down on the wall, twisting the strap of her camera with restless fingers. What had he been about to say? One day ... She smiled wryly. It would have been some trite, teasing little remark. Probably about saving the pendant for her grandchildren. Grandchildren! Except that Max rarely made trite, pointless little remarks.

She got to her feet and wandered along the terrace, looking

over the panorama of the valley spread below, and came face to face with Roger as he climbed from the lower level. His face lit up and he seized her arm.

'Come and see this. I've been looking for you.' He led her along to where a narrow flight of steep stone steps curved up the hillside near the temple. 'You know, these people could build.'

She had heard the distant sound of rushing water without consciously defining it as such, and now she saw the source. In the rock face, high above her head, a spring gushed. Around and beneath it, the rock had been chiselled and carved into a miniature shrine over which the crystal cascade fell like a living rainbow curtain to the large, rough-hewn pool by which Gail was now standing. The sound and sight were strangely satisfying, but the beauty was wasted on Roger. What interested him most was the arrangement of ducts which drained the water and directed it into a maze of branching irrigation channels to feed the terraces beneath.

When he had enlarged at some length on the subject and she made no response he stopped suddenly. 'Are you listening?'

'Of course.'

'You're very quiet.'

'Can't I be quiet if I want to?' she asked wearily.

'I suppose so, except that it's usually with me these days,' he said with a resigned tilt of his head.

A twinge of guilt stabbed her. 'I'm sorry, Roger. I don't mean to be. It's just . . . I was thinking of something else.'

'Supposing you think about me for a change.' His arm went round her shoulder and he drew her to the shadow of the temple wall and looked down at her with whimsical eyes. 'You do remember me, don't you?'

This sounded so much like the Roger she remembered that she relaxed, even though experience should have told her that when he adopted that rather wheedling tone and expression he wanted something. 'Considering I've known you since I was three I should do.'

'Yes, you should.' His attention moved to the teardrop pendant where the sun glinted as though illuminating its own tear. 'You know, that's a beautiful piece. It could be worth a small fortune. There are six separate strands woven into the chain. Pity it isn't a chain of fine links instead of that plaited way. I've never seen a chain made like that.'

'I've never seen *anything* like it,' she said, moving uneasily within the circle of his arm. His touch was on the verge of becoming a liberty, one she was not inclined to permit, but he forestalled her move to free herself and clipped his hands round her waist.

'What's the matter? Can't I even touch you now?'

Coldness ran through her and she sighed. 'No, it isn't that. Oh, Roger, don't start that again.'

'Why not?' His tone was aggrieved and tinged with anger. 'You know I'm in love with you. Do you think our relationship can stand still for ever? What's got into you? You never used to be like this.'

Her mouth tightened. 'You never used to want to paw me like this. You've changed and you——'

His grip tightened painfully and anger whitened his mouth. 'So that's how you see it! I think you're the one who's changed. You used to be a warm, affectionate person. Now . . . you're just as cold as——'

'If I'm as cold as that then you don't want to waste your time over me,' she said bitterly. 'Oh, Roger, I don't want to hurt you. It's just— I don't know myself. Why do we end up quarrelling like this?' she ended despairingly.

'Ask me another,' he said bitterly. 'All I did was ask you to marry me.'

'And I asked you to wait until all this was over and we were home.' She turned away and now he made no effort to stop her. 'You said yourself we'd have to wait, so why this urgency?'

'I want to be sure of you.'

'But I'm not sure of myself.' Suddenly she swung round, determined to end something that could only result in unhappiness for both of them. 'It's no use, Roger,' she said quietly. 'I can't promise to marry you in two years' time. I'm sorry I ever accepted that ring and let you believe I—I just wanted time to be sure. It wasn't fair to you, and it's my fault for not telling you right at the start.'

There was a cold, unhappy silence after she stopped speaking. Roger stared at her, his expression plainly disbelieving, before he spread his hands and exclaimed, 'But what do you mean? Right at the start? You've always loved me. You've always been closer to me than anyone else. We've always come back to each other, even after we've quarrelled, and I've never thought of marrying any other girl when the time came.'

It was Gail's turn to stare at him. 'But we've never been in—we've never——' She stopped, not knowing how to put it into words. 'We've never looked upon each other as lovers,' she said at last. 'At least I haven't,' she added helplessly.

'That's pretty obvious.'

'I'm sorry,' she began again, wishing with all her heart she could break this impasse without hurting him. 'I—I don't know what to say.'

He was silent again, frowning moodily at his feet. He said suddenly, 'There isn't anybody else, is there?' He looked up, his expression suspicious. 'Somebody I don't know.'

She hesitated over the instinctive denial, hating the lie, then said unsteadily, 'No, of course there isn't anybody else.'

'Are you sure?'

'Sure,' she said more firmly.

He hesitated. 'You were a bit put out when Tony Millsom couldn't come out with us. And you went out with him a few times while I——'

'It isn't Tony Millsom,' she cried. 'It isn't anybody!' Even as the words left her lips they seemed like a betrayal, but they had to be spoken. Once Roger's possessiveness gained ascendancy he would probe and eliminate until he eventually reached ... And no one, least of all Roger or anyone in the team, had to know her secret. If they did, the atmosphere would become unbearable ... knowing they knew, wondering if the one person who must not know had guessed ...

'Oh, come on,' she said desperately, 'they'll be wondering where we've——' The exclamation died as the accompanying movements brought her out of the shadows and round the angle of the corner buttress. Only three steps away Max was sitting on the terrace wall, looking directly towards her and Roger.

Her heart missed a beat and gave that peculiar tremor it always gave the moment when she first glimpsed him. How much had he heard?

All the way down she tried to read his expression, seeking some indication in his demeanour that would tell her if he had noticed or heard that painful conversation, or if he had heard it and *cared.* But there was nothing she could remotely define and seize at, and gradually she convinced herself that she was exaggerating the incident beyond all proportion.

It wasn't easy to dismiss, though, no matter how much she tried to concentrate on the thought of the ceremony that was now so near. Roger's moody silence and avoidance of her was a perpetual reminder the rest of that day and she was thankful when the time came to return to her own apartment. Did Roger feel the same way about her as she felt about Max? It didn't seem possible, but if he did she might well experience guilty regret and a hopeless wish that somehow it might work out for him. She wouldn't curse her worst enemy with the anguish of a love not returned ... It was only one step to another aspect which had not yet occurred to her—the nature of Max Christiern's own love. How many women had passed through his life? Who was the one who stayed? For all she knew he could be married.

For the first time she cast her mind back over the past few months, trying to garner every single thing she had heard spoken of him, and was left with the empty knowledge that she couldn't recall a single mention concerning his personal life. She examined the little she did know; that he'd spent the last two or three years in Lima, working in medical research, that before that he'd been in San Francisco, and before that he'd done a three year stint in Boston. Before that ... a blank. He'd made a study of the conditions under which the jungle tribes existed, and he'd travelled extensively in Peru and Ecuador, and he'd campaigned vigorously to relieve the appalling conditions in which slum children were forced to work in some parts of South America ... someone had said he'd been too outspoken, turning over too many stones ... she could well imagine that, if he took on the role of reformer. And yet he had hesitated over Azzuni, almost as though he was reluctant to interfere. She couldn't imagine him being afraid of anyone or anything for his own sake. Surely it couldn't be that he was afraid for herself and the rest of the team ... or imagined they were afraid for themselves ...

On this thought she fell asleep with a vague sense of depression.

It still persisted when she awoke and lingered for quite a long time, in odd contrast to the excitement which stirred everyone else that day, and centred round Azzuni.

The preparations for the marriage began early that day. Azzuni's hair was washed and scented and oiled and polished by a chattering bevy of women. She was bathed and her body rubbed with unguents, not once but three times, and finally her robes were brought and tried on with great ceremony, while at least thirty women and girls crowded their way into the apartment, all trying to help and mostly getting in the way as Aumya adjusted the white robe, the headdress of jewels and thousands of tiny interwoven feathers, and the adornments with which the bride was to be decked. Certainly Azzuni was going to look magnificent, Gail reflected, when at last it seemed that every preparation that could be made had been seen to and the women had drifted away reluctantly, leaving the bridal panoply spread over every available space.

Azzuni looked tired, tensed up with strain, and Gail felt worried. Azzuni was not yet completely recovered and the ceremony tomorrow could not be anything less than an ordeal.

Impulsively, she took Azzuni along to her own apartment, to rest there while she started on her own personal preparations for the great day. Not that there were many she could make, apart from washing her hair and attending to her nails. She had no finery to don, very little make-up with her, and her limited wardrobe was, to say the least, practical to the point of austerity. Still, even a shampoo fulfilled the psychological need to do something.

Azzuni lay on Gail's divan and watched curiously while Gail towelled her hair roughly dry and pinned up the damp ends. When she had finished she reached for her compact and automatically applied a quick skimming of lipstick. About to drop them back in her cosmetic bag, she saw Azzuni hold out her hand. Smiling, Gail handed them over and Azzuni studied the swivel lipstick for a moment, then cautiously applied it to her own well-shaped little mouth. After a moment of consideration of her reflection she looked uncertainly at Gail.

'Good?' she said wonderingly.

'Beautiful,' said Gail, 'but I've a suspicion the High Priest wouldn't think so.'

Azzuni looked puzzled and licked her lips, and Gail, deciding that the cosmetic might be distasteful to her, handed over a tissue to remove it. But Azzuni had no intention of removing it. She handed back the tissue, murmured, 'Thank you,' and regarded herself again with such evident satisfaction that Gail could not repress a smile.

'Beautiful,' said Azzuni, closing the compact and handing them back, 'like you, Gail.'

'I wish I was!' Gail laughed ruefully, then saw the solemn little face and the expression that tried earnestly to convey the compliment. Her own expression sobered and she said impulsively, 'You're very sweet, Azzuni. I wish I knew more of your lingo and you knew more of mine, and I wish we'd had more time to exchange ideas and find out about each other.'

'What is sweet?' Azzuni said slowly.

'It's—oh——' Gail gestured helplessly. 'It's good, and beautiful.' With another impulse she stooped and kissed Azzuni's cheek.

Azzuni put her head on one side and said nothing, and Gail turned away, aware of the slight awkwardness when sentiment is not completely understood. Suddenly she felt that this was the moment for a cup of tea—if only they had the makings of that infallible beverage. But they hadn't, unfortunately, having left half of their supplies back at the mission in reserve for the return journey.

Gail went in search of the girl who seemed to be 'tea wallah' in the women's part of this little world and when the tray came with the strangely shaped cups and the tall pitcher of the steaming scented brew that was almost, but not quite, as good as tea, she sat down beside Azzuni and wondered what lay ahead. Somehow, during the past week, she had ceased to think of the future. It lay no further ahead than the ceremony tomorrow, and everything that had happened led to the mystical ceremony that they had all taken for granted they would remain to see. Now, once the next twenty-four hours were over, their own affairs would have to start moving again.

Beside her, Azzuni moved sharply and stood up. She seemed to be listening, and Gail, who couldn't hear anything, looked at her with some surprise. Then Azzuni took a step forward and Max's voice outside came as a shock a moment later. How had Azzuni sensed his approach?

'Yes—I'm here.' Gail hurried to the door. 'Is anything wrong?'

'Not that I know of. I just came to see if all was well with you.' He gave her a rather disconcerting glance. 'Is Azzuni all right?'

'Yes, she's fine—she's here. We—we were just having a cup of tea,' she said rather wildly.

'Oh,' he stayed where he was, resting one hand against the stonework of the doorway, 'I'd better leave you to it, then.'

'Tea,' said Azzuni softly from behind Gail's shoulder. 'Tea—yes?'

With an expression in her dark eyes that made a universal language unnecessary Azzuni came forward and held out a cup towards Max.

'Thank you, that would be very nice,' he said in the tongue of which Gail still couldn't grasp more than a few isolated words, and took the cup from Azzuni.

'Well, you can't stand there and drink it,' said Gail, suddenly feeling as though things had been taken out of her hands and not sure how she should regain control.

He sat down gravely, Azzuni sat down on one of the stools not far from him, and Gail poured herself another cup of the brew and sat down on the divan feeling very much like a bystander.

There was a silence, then Gail said uneasily, 'I think she remembers and knows. I—I think she wants to thank you.'

He raised his brows, but said nothing, and Azzuni sat, apparently quite content to stay silent and regard Max with a wide, innocent gaze that suddenly made clear the answer to a small question that had puzzled Gail several times before she had dismissed it as unanswerable. This was the reason for all those odd little searching glances Azzuni had betrayed during her illness, that rather sad expectancy each time Gail had entered the sickroom, and the resignation that had followed and lingered for quite a while.

Max said something to her, and Azzuni nodded, then she got up and gravely took his cup, taking it to the tray and refilling it, then moving with the lithe graceful walk that was so alien to the average European girl's brisk purposeful step to stand before him and proffer it with both hands.

An incredulous sigh ran through Gail and something like despair stabbed at her as she comprehended at last. Azzuni had all the symptoms of a girl who had found the end of the rainbow. If she wasn't in love at first sight she was well on the way to it. The Bride of the Sun was as frail and vulnerable and feminine as the weakest of womankind, and of course it would be Max!

Suddenly Gail didn't know whether to laugh or cry, sure she was imagining it all out of her own hopeless weakness, and then conscious of a deep pity for a girl whose life had been ordained and arranged for her with complete disregard for the secret hopes or dreams she might herself cherish. Poor little Azzuni, a prisoner of fate, who had never set eyes on the man who would claim her tomorrow.

Max got up and replaced the cup on the tray. He said uneasily, 'Is something worrying her?'

Yes, Gail wanted to say sarcastically, *yes, something's worrying her, all right!* Instead she said slowly, 'I think she just wants to thank you and—and have your blessing.'

Max still looked puzzled. He turned back to Azzuni and said something slowly and carefully, which Gail would have dearly loved to understand, and ended it with a smile.

Azzuni sighed, nodded and smiled, then looked up at him and said clearly, 'Sweet.'

Gail closed her eyes. Now she knew what Azzuni wanted. When she opened them Azzuni was still looking up at him and he was betraying the first signs of awkwardness Gail had ever seen from him. She turned away and said in a flat tone, 'She wants you to kiss her.'

'Are you sure?' The exclamation was astounded.

'Sure.'

There was a silence. Gail turned her head and Max looked down at the wide innocent eyes upturned so trustfully. He said quietly, 'Azzuni, I hope you're going to be very happy. You're a very sweet little girl and you deserve to be happy.' Calmly he tipped up her chin, kissed her with slow deliberacy on each cheek, and then, lightly and tenderly, on the soft rouged mouth. He stepped back, smiled at her, said, 'Bless you,' and then, in a rather changed voice, 'I think I'd better go.'

'Yes, I think you'd better.'

Gail sat down weakly and reached for a cigarette. A disturbing suspicion had just occurred and filled her with a dismay that had nothing to do with Azzuni. She would have given a great deal if she could be certain her own eyes never spoke with the crystal clarity of Azzuni's when she looked at Max Christiern.

CHAPTER VIII

THE day that Azzuni became the Bride of the Sun was one that Gail would never forget, even though it was not until many days later that she was able to look back and isolate the vivid impressions within the kaleidoscope of colour and events with which it passed.

The sun himself, as though lending majesty to the ritual being played out below, blazed down all that day with radiant, triumphant force and bathed the valley in shimmering gold splendour. From the first glimmers of dawn the trek began, emptying the city and its environs, and wending its way up the steep curving ribbon of road to the temple, until the vast natural amphitheatre before it became a living bowl of humanity.

The men from the outside world had all tended in varying degrees to look on the ritual with some scepticism, although none of them, with the exception of Harmon, would have dreamed of expressing detraction of the beliefs held by a people of strange culture, but as the ceremony progressed a silence of intent gripped them all.

At noon a hush descended on that great throng. On the forecourt in front of the temple lay a large octagonal of stone with carved symbols around its perimeter and a raised flange that wasn't quite central. Gail had noticed this previously and now she realised it was a big sundial. When the shadow ceased and it was noon Azzuni and her bridegroom were led up the wide steps till they faced the tall commanding figure of the High Priest. At some prearranged signal two women and two of the elders stepped forward and removed the long, cloak-like robes worn by the couple. In the utter hush the two cloaks were spread on the ground and Zarco took a handful of sand from a shallow gold bowl which the High Priest held and slowly sprinkled sand across the cloaks. Four more attendants came from the temple bearing fresh raiment of white which was solemnly placed round the two central figures, then the High Priest began to speak in a slow, toneless chant. Gradually the crowd took up the chant while the elders formed a processional into the temple, to be followed by the bridegroom and lastly Azzuni.

The ceremony took almost an hour, after which Azzuni and the tall, stern-faced young man were borne shoulder-high to one of the decorated floats for the return to the city. That was the last the crowd saw of them as they were taken to the palace where, according to custom, they would feast with Zarco and receive his blessing.

And now the crowd threw off solemnity. The drums thudded, people shouted, children ran and gambolled, and everyone headed for the esplanade by the river and the feasting and dancing that continued all the rest of the day and far into the night.

If the day had been impressive the carnival air that took over at darkness was even more exhausting. The torches were lit, the leaping flames of the bonfires turned the sky to smoky scarlet and bathed the river with vermilion sparks. Dancers, their bodies gleaming under the flares as though coated with liquid bronze, donned strange masks and whirled to a frenzy to the increasing rhythm of the drums.

Gail had lost all track of time when someone suggested they take to the flower-strewn boat on the river and cool off. No one noticed them as they climbed aboard and flopped down thankfully to watch the festivities, and the sigh she gave was echoed by Clive and Max and Jonathan.

Clive rarely smoked but now he lit one and said wryly: 'At last I know what women feel like when they slip their shoes off under the table.'

'I'm bushed,' said Jonathan. 'I can take heat as a rule, but today...' He mopped at his face and slumped back, closing his eyes. 'I'll have a lager, iced, somebody, please.'

'No lager, sonny, but there's plenty of river,' said Clive. 'Where would you like it? Down your neck?'

For once Jonathan did not rise to the challenge and Gail smiled to herself, content to relax back in the hollow of the big curved prow and watch Max's profile silhouetted against the night sky and the diffused glow of the flares. She thought of

Azzuni, of the bizarre unreality of the day's events, and from there it was only a thought away from the memory of the previous night and that tenderness she had glimpsed briefly in Max. His unsuspected gentleness in the way he had kissed Azzuni had surprised her, and yet was it so surprising? If Max had proved as hard and invulnerable as she had believed when first she met him would she have fallen in love with him? It was difficult to tell, but somehow she doubted it, recognizing with a flash of self-knowledge her own particular desire for a man who was strong enough and honest enough to be unashamed of compassion and unafraid to own to it.

The profile moved and she sensed immediately his gaze turning towards her even though his features were in shadow. The need to move and break the silence seemed urgent. She said in too bright a tone, 'I was nearly asleep—what time is it? My watch seems to have stopped.'

'Nearly three—you probably forgot to wind it.'

She had. Carefully resetting the hands, she said, 'Do you know where the others got to?'

There was no response from Clive or Jonathan, but Max answered: 'I don't know where Roger got to—the last I saw of him he was filming those dancers—and I haven't seen Harmon since the bunfight started.' He paused. 'I should imagine your uncle went to bed long ago.'

'Bed,' said Clive sleepily, 'wish I was there without the bother of getting there.' He yawned widely and closed his eyes. 'Call me when the Cross turns over.'

She looked up at the Southern Cross, knowing exactly how he felt. The thought of stirring, waking up enough to go ashore and walk back to her quarters, and starting to clean teeth and ... It was too mundane and too much effort, and as long as no one else moved and the boat rose and fell softly on the current, and she knew Max still sat there, the outline of his shoulders faintly luminous, his dark head unmoving, safe, reassuring ...

She would never have allowed sleep to overtake her if she had known they would let her sleep on, or that nightmare would reign, so that when she opened her eyes to blinding sun through a clinging stifling veil and a sense of such disaster she struggled wildly, still unsure what was happening.

'Some people can sleep all right, I must say.' Clive's face loomed above, momentarily disembodied. 'Wakey-wakey!'

She groaned, stirring stiffly and struggling out of the blanket and net somebody had put over her. 'Who put this over me?—good grief! Is that the right time? And I'm still ...' She looked at the placid sun-rippled river and put her hand to her head.

'Why didn't somebody wake me?'

'Orders,' said Clive, grinning. 'You beat Jonathan by exactly forty minutes.' He bent and grasped her arm to help her up. 'Children have to have their beauty sleep.'

She shuddered. 'I've got the daddy of all headaches. Thanks for saving me from being bitten alive.'

'Don't thank me—it was my night off from responsibility.' He helped her to climb over the side and down the little gangway on to the steps and returned to collect the blanket and net while she stood there trying to clear her head of the daze from too heavy sleep. But there was a warm little thought that was perfectly clear as she walked across the esplanade with Clive: it could only have been Max who had thought of her and issued Clive with his 'orders'...

If she hadn't been bemused still she might have noticed the deserted stillness of the avenue, unusual at this time of day, and the strange glances of the women as she returned to her room, glances that held shock, unfriendliness and something very like hatred. But these did not register, except as a vague awareness that everybody seemed remarkably subdued, which wasn't surprising after the festivities—she was feeling pretty much under the weather herself.

There was no sign of Aumya, and the immediately sensed lack of Azzuni's presence brought Gail to the realization of change. The turning point was over and they would have to start making plans for their return, she thought listlessly as she took a couple of aspirins and adjourned to the bathing place.

By the time she had bathed and dressed the aspirin was taking effect and she was feeling more human. It was time to go in search of grub and see if her team-mates had recovered from their hangovers, she thought with a return of briskness.

The same silence was still abroad and there was no sign of the men when she crossed the terrace and looked into the great dining hall. Shrugging, still not alarmed, she made her way to Max's room and found it deserted, as was her uncle's room next door. Strange, there was usually one of them around, and it couldn't be more than an hour at the most since she'd left Clive. Puzzled, she turned back, scanning the wide vista of gardens between the terrace and the distant palace of the Leader. Could they be over there? Or had they taken off on some exploration without telling her? If they had...! Indignant at the thought, she swung back into the building and rushed down the passageway calling each name in turn. No response. She reached the gate that barred her way, pushed at it, not expecting it to give, and fell back before the two elders who stood there.

She exclaimed, but before she could move one of them grasped her arm and rapped something in his sharp, guttural tones.

Gail shook her head and stepped back, gesturing that she did not understand. For the first time she noticed that the deep-set eyes were inimical above the high lean planes of the cheek-bones and the thin mouth could set in cruel lines. The other man looked equally unfriendly and Gail wondered what on earth she'd done. He spoke, and there could be no mistaking the accusation even though the linguistic gist was beyond her. She said slowly, 'Professor Denning? Dr Christiern? Uncle Phil...? Clive...?' hoping they would understand that she was seeking her own people, and unconsciously her hand went to her throat, touching the golden pendant.

The grip fell away from her arm and, encouraged, she tried again to convey whom she sought. One of them glanced at the other, then shook his head and motioned her to follow.

Now what? she thought resignedly, turning to obey. Then she realized they were leading her to a part of the building entirely strange to her. She stopped and a thrust between her shoulder blades sent her forward. The place seemed a warren of stone-bricked passages and archways, despite what Max had told her about the layout being quite simple. At last they stopped before a recess with the usual heavy curtain, and real fear came to Gail as one of the men drew it aside. Instead of the familiar arched opening behind it there was a massive grille of solid timber. A baulk rested horizontally across, fitting into deep stone sockets, and when this was slid out the door swung outwards revealing a large bare room within. Gail turned round, tensed by warning instinct, and the next moment she was thrust forward and the door thudded shut.

'No! What are you——? Let me out!' She whirled round and hammered desperately against the heavy grille. 'What's happening? Why have——? Let me out!'

There were small interstices in the grille through which she glimpsed the movement of the grey robes, heard the grating of the baulk slide into the stone sockets, then silence, Her fingers clutched at the rough grooves in the timber, then slackened despairingly as her shock and bewilderment gave way to realization. She was a prisoner. But why?'

In sudden anger she began to pummel at the grille, and seized at the finger-holds in the chinks, trying to shake her way free. The grille did not move by a fraction and at last, her knuckles painful and skinned, she desisted and turned to inspect her prison. It was some twenty feet square, obviously intended to cater for quite a large number if the gaolers weren't fussy about overcrowding, she thought with grim humour, and it was unfurnished except for a pile of skins in one corner and the inevitable baskets set in the walls to hold the torches. High up in one wall there was a small opening but too narrow to permit even the slimmest of prisoners to escape, even if she had means of reaching it. The thin grey light in the cell came from it, and she suspected it merely opened out into a ventilation well as no sunlight crept in to lighten the gloom.

Not knowing what to think she paced round several times, hammered on the grille again, paced again, then flopped down despairingly on the heap of skins, only to spring up immediately with the instinct of preservation newly developed during the past few weeks. She picked the top one up cautiously and shook it, half prepared to recoil from a loathsome shower of insects. However, to her surprise, there was nothing, and she sank down and gave herself up to contemplation of why and where and how...

* * *

What seemed an eternity later she looked at her watch for the hundredth time and discovered that barely ten minutes had elapsed since the last time she had peered at the dial. The light was fading rapidly and she was very near the verge of panic.

As near as she could tell she had been imprisoned for nearly six hours. It had been almost eleven when she awakened on the boat that morning, and about an hour after that when she had set off in search of the men. It would soon be night and the darkness, when it came, would be rapid; surely they weren't going to leave her there all night, without food and water.

Gail got up and resumed her pacing, trying not to panic, trying not to dwell on the fact that she was hungering to the point of sickness, that she had not eaten since the previous night or drunk since noon, and that another natural urge was causing discomfort. A surge of anger sent her hammering at the grille, impervious to the bruising darkening her knuckles. She yelled, kicked, yelled, hammered, and then the anger spent itself and her mouth quivered. She pressed her hands to her face, willing back the disintegration into tears, and made herself take several slow, deep breaths. *Don't panic,* she whispered aloud. Somebody's got to come. There are six of them somewhere. One of them is going to miss you, wonder and start to search. Unless...

Her cheeks blanched. What if they were in the same plight as herself? Shoved in some hidden cell, without food and water, to worry and wonder about her. Or . . .

The last of the light dimmed. Gail raised her hands before her face and could barely discern their outline. The walls were dark and they seemed to be closing in. She turned wildly, groped to the door and tried to peer through the chinks, listened for the sound of anything, anything that would denote she wasn't entirely alone in the world, and there was only the silence pressing against her eardrums, and the fear that would not be kept at bay. Something dreadful had happened. Something . . . she would never see them again . . . Clive . . . Roger . . . Uncle Phil . . . *Max* . . . Where were they?

Icy coldness numbed her limbs. She stumbled blindly into the darkness, caught her foot against the heap of skins and fell forward. She crouched there, heedless of the tears coming unchecked, of the trembling that would not be stayed. It had to be a dream—a dreadful nightmare. It couldn't be real. Nothing made sense. If only she——

There was a grating sound and her head came up sharply. She heard muffled voices, nearer, and her heart beats began to pound. Someone was coming, the voices were nearing, the thud was the baulk flung down outside and suddenly light was flooding into her eyes. Blinding, but it couldn't blind her to the man bursting in behind that powerful beam, the man she wanted more than anyone else in the world at that moment.

'*Max* . . .' she whispered brokenly. 'Is it you?'

She almost fell into his arms, her relief so great it brought a wave of faintness and she would have fallen had he not held her tightly, his own breathing almost as ragged as her own. For a little while she was oblivious to the figures of Clive and Jonathan behind him and other figures clustered beyond the doorway. Max's exclamations were violent with anger even as he brought tenderness and the sanctuary of his strength.

'How long have you been here?' He was disengaging himself, keeping his hands on her shoulders to hold her away and look down at her with angered concern.

'Since noon. I—I—— Oh, I thought no one would ever come. I——' Conscious now of the others, she tried to regain composure and turned her head to dab at her eyes. 'I—— Max —what happened? Why——'

'Here,' he pushed a hankie into her hand, 'it's all right. You're quite safe. We had no idea that they——' He was flashing the torch round the bare cell and his mouth tightened grimly even as he tried to comfort her. 'I'm afraid we've bad news, Gail. Harmon's gone.'

'Harmon?' She stared.

'He's missing,' said Clive.

'And he's sacked the temple,' said Jonathan.

'What?' She stiffened. 'Harmon?'

'I'm afraid so,' said Max. 'Several of their sacred relics. Gold and silver stuff. It's irreplaceable. And I'm afraid that's not all. Gail,' his hand touched her shoulder, 'your uncle's been hurt. He——'

'Oh no! Not Uncle Phil! How? Is he——'

'No, it's not serious. But let's get out of here.'

He took her arm, shouldering past the others and the two elders who stood silently outside and made no effort to impede their way.

'Where is Uncle Phil?' she asked in a frightened voice, the appalling news about Harmon already taking second place to her concern for her uncle.

'In my place.' Max was hurrying, exclaiming impatiently as he sought the way through the maze of passages. 'You see, when we heard about the theft our first thought was to search. Your uncle insisted on coming as well. He missed his footing up among the terraces by the temple and fell. We had to carry him back. I'm afraid he's fractured a bone in his foot.'

She gave an exclamation of distress, and he said, 'Now don't worry, I've seen to it and he's quite comfortable, but unfortunately I didn't have a——'

'But if it's broken...' She stopped and her eyes were dismayed. 'He won't be able to walk. Max, how are we going to get back? How is he going to——?'

'Let's worry about that when we come to it,' he said sharply. 'Are you all right?'

He was looking at her with worry in his expression, and she said hastily, 'Yes, I'm all right now. I was just scared, not knowing what——'

'Did they bring you food?' He pulled the hanging aside and motioned her through.

'No, but it doesn't matter ... oh, Uncle!' She ran to the divan where Professor Denning lay, his sunburnt features drawn and his injured foot supported on a folded blanket. 'Is it very bad?' She dropped to her knees and looked at the still wet plaster drying round his foot.

'No, my dear,' he raised himself on one elbow and his expression was anxious for her, 'but what happened to you? We——'

'I'm all right, now that I've found you all. I didn't know where you all were and——'

'All right, talk later.' Max loomed up with a cup and a packet in his hands. 'Get this into you or we'll have another casualty on our hands. If I'm right, you haven't eaten since last night.'

He had reverted to the authoritative, practical demeanour she knew best, and now she was thankful simply to comply with whatever orders he issued. She drank the water and finished the pack of biscuits he had taken from the supplies while he checked on her uncle, dispatched Roger and Clive on a mission to the elders, and organized a meal for everyone. By the time they had eaten and the elders arrived for the conference Gail was feeling recovered and had been able to piece together the missing links of the day's events. When he had left the boat that morning Max had returned to find, not a sleepily waking Professor but a distraught man facing the accusations of the Secret People. At dawn the discovery had been made, that among other things a small, beautifully sculpted gold figurine of the Rain Goddess had disappeared and an intruder had been seen hurrying from the vicinity of the temple. More telling was the discovery that some of the compressed food packs from the emergency stores were missing and Harmon's personal kit from the apartment he shared with Jonathan. The elders had been furious, demanding the return of their sacred relics, and it had been obvious that the atmosphere was sullen with danger as the word passed from lip to lip through the city. When Clive left Gail at noon he had searched, puzzled, much as she had done, and encountered Jonathan, who imparted the latest news: one of the wiry little mares was missing from the stable. Clive had immediately gone with Jonathan to join in the search and Gail had been forgotten.

'But why did they pitch me into their prison?' she demanded.

'Anger, my dear,' said the Professor. 'They were afraid we might all try to escape before their belongings were restored. They felt that we must return for you.'

'But where could we escape? There's no way out of the valley,' said Roger. 'If there is they're keeping pretty quiet about it. Heavens,' he gestured, 'they must know we're practically dependent on their guidance to get away ourselves—if we ever do.'

'So Harmon must be hiding out somewhere,' said Clive.

Max frowned. 'We can't be sure. We know there is a pass, supposed to be blocked by a landslide, but it may not be impassable from this side. From what I've gathered the landslide was not nearly so great as Father Lorenzo believed. It served to disguise the outside entrance to the pass and prevent the passage of mule transport. Which suited these people. They have no desire to leave this valley. They have everything they need, and a peaceful way of life free of intruders.'

'Until we came,' said Clive dryly.

As though Clive had not spoken Max went on thoughtfully: 'I'm inclined to believe that Harmon has attempted to find his way over the hills. I doubt if he could hide for very long anywhere in the valley without the people finding him. He hasn't a great deal of food, and only he could have taken the mare.' He paused and turned to greet the four elders who entered.

They gathered round the Professor's divan and the conclave began. Now, more than ever, Gail wished she could comprehend their tongue. The elders were cold and implacable and the atmosphere grew more tense as the discussion became argument. Max seemed to be trying to persuade the elders to agree to some course they flatly refused to adopt and his face grew more worried as he tried to reason with them. At last they withdrew and in a state of trepidation Gail waited for Max to speak.

'Well,' he sighed at last, lighting a cigarette and drawing deeply on it,' 'we can be thankful for your intervention in the Azzuni business. But for that and my reminding them of it I doubt if they'd have agreed to let any of us leave at all.'

'Could they stop us?' said Jonathan with a show of belligerence. 'I'm game any time.'

'You forget something.' Max glanced at the Professor and Jonathan subsided into silence.

Max went on: 'They've agreed to provide us with whatever assistance we want for *two* of us to leave, on condition we find the traitor in our party and restore their relics. Until we do, the rest of us must remain here.'

'Hostages,' said Gail flatly.

The Professor sat up, giving no indication that he had heard her. He said calmly: 'It's understandable. We have accepted these people's hospitality and grossly abused it. Harmon must be found.'

There was a long silence, then Clive looked at Max. 'It had better be us.'

Max nodded, his mouth tense. 'We'd better pack what we need—only the absolute essentials—and be ready to leave at first light. They're providing us with mules and guides to take us up the valley and into the foothills. After that we'll have to climb on foot and probably spend at least one night in the mountains.' He turned to Roger. 'We'll get help back to you as soon as humanly possible. In the meantime, look after them. Gail, you'll have to look after your uncle, and stay near. Keep together and don't roam abroad. The situation is ugly. Don't provoke it. And try not to worry too much.'

'How long?' she asked.

'At the very least . . . a week,' he said flatly. 'There's no radio contact before we get back to Huamano.'

She nodded, her eyes shadowed with worry as she looked at her uncle. There was no other way but the way Max had planned. But a week . . . possibly longer . . . and her uncle injured . . . She straightened her shoulders with an unconscious gesture of resolution. Max couldn't do everything; they would have to assure him that they wouldn't be another source of worry to add to the burden he already carried. She said: 'Is there anything I can do to help?'

'No, just watch over your uncle.'

'Just a moment.' The Professor's tone was so strange they all turned to him. He said, 'Clive must stay here. You go, Max, and take Gail with you.'

Max started. 'That's impossible,' he exclaimed. 'You can't be serious. She'll never make it. We don't know what conditions we'll have to face. We——'

The Professor raised his hand. 'She'll have to face them sooner or later—we all will, or resign ourselves to staying here like von Schaumel. No, I want you to take Gail. Please do this for me. If I were able to I'd go myself and take her with me. But I can't. Max'—his voice dropped—'get her out of here while we've got the chance.'

The argument for and against broke out while Gail sat silent, torn between longing to take the chance her uncle had suddenly provided and the instinct to stay and protect him. But he remained impervious to all reasoning, and at last Max agreed unwillingly. With grim resolution he supervised the packing of what they would need, food rations from their rapidly diminishing stocks and extra clothing with their sleeping bags to protect against the cold of the mountain night.

There was a tightness in Gail's throat the following dawn when she bent to embrace her uncle. Suddenly his resemblance to her father became poignantly pronounced, and with a demonstrativeness not usual in his nature he held her close for a moment before he whispered, 'God speed—you'll be all right, girl.'

No one, not even Max, knew that hidden at the bottom of her pack were two of the films, a small sealed package of the flower, and a closely written pad of his notes. He looked frail and ill as he sank back on the divan and her determination was strengthened; she and Max had to get through: not for the sake of finding Harmon but to bring help so desperately needed.

'Look after him, Clive,' she whispered, thankful that it was

Clive who would be staying behind. Her uncle would be safer with Clive; somehow, the past weeks had gradually betrayed the immaturity of Roger and Jonathan.

Only Roger was sulky when the moment of departure came. She said pleadingly, 'Help Clive to look after him, please,' and he nodded unsmilingly, his eyes cold. Sighing, she mounted the small cream mare and waved, wanting to keep them in sight for as long as possible. For who knew how long it might be before she saw them again?

At noon they were still winding their way upwards, above the temple and the maze of terraces, the fields of maize, the grazing lands where the llamas and vicuñas roamed, and above that to the hills where the fertile soil became thinner and the green gave way to scrub and thorn, and finally to barren rock.

They made camp at sundown, under the scant shelter of an overhanging outcrop, and at first light they resumed the journey. They had covered little over a mile before they came upon the missing mare, riderless, and the traces of lather dried on its flanks.

The two guides stopped and it seemed the reproach and accusation in their unfriendly faces were directed at Max. Silently, one of them attached a leading rein from the mare to his own mount and slowly the little procession moved on.

With the discovery of the animal Gail's hopes had flared. Harmon must have come this way, and even though he had had twenty-four hours' start he would now be on foot and so it could be only a short while before they overtook him. She looked at the grim set of Max's shoulders as he jogged ahead and reflected that she would not care to be in Harmon's shoes when the moment of retribution came. But her moment of hope was brief. The path was narrowing and becoming increasingly steep. A little farther on it curved round an apron of rock and passed beneath a precipice that seemed to rise sheer to the sky. Ahead, a second peak reared, closing in on a fissure that disappeared into the heart of the mountains. Obviously this was the end of the first stage; this was the beginning of the pass.

On the apron the guides stopped and their gestures were quite clear. Max dismounted and came to help her down. The guides looked on impassively as he unloaded the two packs and helped her to fasten the straps with the old grim courtesy that made her heart heavy. He hadn't wanted to bring her. All the hard-won sense of understanding that had grown during their time in the valley had vanished: once again she was with him on sufferance.

He faced her for a moment and she saw the doubt in his eyes.

She raised her head defiantly. 'Don't worry. I know I know we're on our own now, and—and I'll die before I let you down,' she added bitterly.

'That shouldn't be necessary,' he said grimly, and waited.

She gave a final shrug into her pack straps, touched the satiny cream of the mare's neck, and gravely thanked the guides, even though she doubted if they understood her words, then turned towards the unknown.

Gradually the sounds of hooves diminished to faint echoes, until they faded in the still, clear mountain air and there was only the light grating crunch of her own footsteps and the steady, heavier treads of Max.

The valley was gone; only the lonely, inimical mountains waited.

CHAPTER IX

GAIL knew she was tiring long before they reached the point where the landslide had blocked the pass.

They had been climbing steadily for several hours when they came to the first fall of boulders barring their way. She halted, thankful for the respite, and watched Max's practised eyes surveying the blockage for the easiest and safest way past. After a few moments he turned.

'Stay put for a while.'

For a big man he was remarkably agile and light-footed, she thought, watching while he tested footholds on the rockface to the right. Slowly he began to edge along some six feet above her eye level and dropped out of sight on the far side. A minute or so later he reappeared and made his way back. With a brief, 'Wait here,' he took her pack, shouldered it and set off again, to return empty-handed and hold out his hand to her. 'Just watch where I step and don't think.' Somehow, she followed in his steps and completed the detour he was making for the third time.

This was the pattern to be repeated, slowly and painfully, many times during the hours that followed, and each time she wondered anew at the grim, patient determination of him to accomplish the apparent impossible. Once, when the gaunt slashes of rock and jagged needles of shale seemed beyond passage of humans, she turned away and pressed her hands against the chill rockface. Max might make it, but she wouldn't.

None of them had had the vaguest notion of what it would be like in reality—except Max.

She closed her eyes against the frightening picture; the uneven ledge on which she stood, the point a little way farther on where it tapered to a wavering thread over a dark drop to infinity below, and the great jutting spur barring the way to the broader ledge visible beyond. A sigh shuddered through her and she bowed her head.

Max moved behind her, brushing past, and silently she willed him not to speak. The knowledge of her failing courage was sufficiently humiliating; to face his patient, unsmiling strength and summon a further reserve of her own in response was beyond her at the moment. She sensed his hesitation, his moving on, and she looked up.

He was standing on the lip of the far ledge, under the overhanging spur, and the thin sunlight etched his shadow darkly against the slate hues of the rock. His eyes were narrowed against the glare and his mouth a thin taut line as he stared across the chasm and waited for her to make the steps that would bring her to his side.

Again the sickness of fear rose in her, the fear of her inadequacy to meet the demands which still lay ahead. The way would not get easier, but it was quite likely to get harder. His voice came: 'It isn't as bad as it looks. Take your time.'

With an effort, she shouldered away from the rockface and hitched her pack more firmly into place; this was the wrong time and place to admit her kind of fear. It was not a fear but a senseless, twisted vanity that was making her hate the thought of betraying weakness in his presence. She must recognize it as such, even though to be a hindrance would be the most galling humility of all. Then she saw he was watching her with that narrowed intent look and an echo of something he once said flashed into her memory: *I don't expect you to disown your sex—I loathe swaggering young Amazons—but God help you if you act the helpless female. You'll get no sympathy from me!*

The thought was enough to put new strength into her limbs and a resolve that a helpless female was the last thing she'd be. It was enough to make her pretend not to see the hand he stretched out as she moved those last cautious steps, and it was enough to keep her going through the next few hours, through the sudden onslaught of icy mountain rain that came with the sun's decline and the thin curling tendrils of mist that brought fresh worry into Max's eyes though he did not voice it, until the moment when he stopped on a broad, overhanging lip and gestured.

'Cheer up. Look!'

From the vantage point she peered through the drifting curls of mist and saw what she had almost despaired of seeing: a clear, if thinly marked, path leading down into the darkening chasm, and far beyond it a blurred dark bed of green—the beginning of the rain forest.

The sight brought a tremulous curve to her mouth and a sigh of thankfulness. It vested her limbs with unsuspected reserves of strength and her spirit with sudden exhilaration, so that without thinking she caught at his arm as though they could run all the way down that thin thread to the formless green blur that spelt their goal.

He moved a few steps with her before he disengaged his arm and slowed. 'It's a hell of a lot farther than it looks, you know, but we might make it by tomorrow afternoon.'

'Tomorrow? Why not tonight?'

'Through the dark? Are you crazy?'

The brief flare of vitality ebbed and the cold encroach of night struck through her, instantly reviving the ache and the weariness. She said flatly, 'No, of course we couldn't,' and resumed the steady, determined plodding.

She had gone only a few paces when he stopped again. Without speaking she waited for him to go on, and he said abruptly, 'Are you all right?'

'Of course I'm all right,' she said with a flash of irritability.

He glanced at his watch. 'Take a rest. I'm going to scout round for shelter.'

'Why? We could go on for another hour. It isn't dark.'

'We're stopping all the same.'

'Not for me,' she said stubbornly, and brushed past him. 'You're not tired, are you?'

'Tired? No! I'm just ready to crawl into the nearest hole and tell the world to go to hell.' With a roughness she wasn't expecting he caught her shoulder and yanked her round to face him. Hard-eyed, he surveyed her grimly, his mouth a tight line in the cold shadowed hollows of his features. 'Seeing things misty?' he demanded.

'No.' She stared. 'Should I be?'

'Still cold?'

'Of course I'm cold, standing round here—I haven't dried out after that last shower. Oh, come on,' she broke free of his grip and stumbled a little, caught off balance, 'and stop fussing or we'll never get there.'

'Is that how you feel?'

The penetrating stare was unnerving. She fumbled with the

straps of her pack and flexed her aching shoulders, suddenly wishing he would get on with it and leave her alone. He did move then, and she gave a start of surprise as the weight eased suddenly across her shoulders and he said, 'Let go.'

'No—why? You can't——'

He thrust her cold fingers away and unclipped the buckle, sliding the pack free. 'Don't argue. You've had enough. Now *sit down*!'

The tone brooked no argument and stifled her weakening protest. Not very graciously, she dropped down on the pack and wondered why she had ever fallen in love with Max Christiern.

He was rummaging in his own pack and pulled out a crumpled dark green jerkin. 'Here, put this on—it's dry—and keep your hands in the sleeves.' He waited impatiently, ignoring her startled expression, until she fumbled out of her damp jerkin and donned the green one. 'Now wait here. I'm going to check on that cleft down there—it might be deep enough for a shelter.'

Without waiting for any response he loped down the track, his tall figure diminishing with distance, and then seemed to vanish into the rockface. Now she had the answer to her question: the sudden blankness where he had been and the intense silence were enough to invoke a pang of loss. No matter how hurtful and infuriating he could be it was preferable to his absence. She stared at the blank, cruel landscape and uttered a sigh as he reappeared and began to make his way back.

'It'll do to make camp. No, I'll take that. Come on.' The two packs looped and bumping clumsily over his shoulder, he put out his free arm and drew her into a close supporting grip. Not hurrying, he piloted her down the narrow track until they reached the cleft in the rock.

It widened inside into a high cavernous space with a floor sloping upward and a cold unfriendly damp smell. Max moved deftly, with a speedy economy of movement. He opened out the packs, shook out the sleeping bags and one of the soft vicuña wool blankets belonging to the Secret People, and sorted out the two cans of self-heating soup and the packets of nut and honey bars. He didn't seem to require her help and she wandered back to the opening, to stand and stare at the jagged purple and crimson planes of the peaks across the chasm.

The sky was deepening to heavy violet slashed with rose and greeny-blue streaks. She began to shed the jerkin and held it out to him, her gaze still on the savage beauty of those peaks as she said, 'Here, you'd better have this back now.'

'Keep it on—I don't need it. And forget about the glories of nature. Come out of the wind.'

He had propped the torch on a ledge. He switched it on and adjusted the ray to its broadest focus. The light outlined her as she stood at the mouth of the cave, still holding the garment at arm's length.

He said sharply, 'Gail!'

'What?' She turned blankly. 'What did you say?'

'I said keep that on and come in out of the wind.'

'Oh.' Shrugging, she obeyed, groping her arms back into the overlong sleeves and struggling impatiently as one hand encountered a cuff turned inside out when she had taken off the garment. She swore softly and he swung round, then came to help.

A wave of irritation rose in her. Why did he fuss? Making her feel like an inadequate child, and—— She twisted away, ramming her hand through and bending to pick up the groundsheet he had dropped.

But it slipped out of her grasp and she gave another impatient exclamation, more born of resentment than clumsiness, as she bent to it a second time. Suddenly it was snatched out of her hand. He spread it flat, laid one of the sleeping bags on it, and held out the other one. He said sharply: 'Get into it—I think the cold's got you.'

'What?' She stared at the green quilted bag as though he had gone mad. 'Now? What for? I don't——'

'Gail...' his voice had gone dangerously quiet, 'haven't you heard of mountain exposure? I don't want to frighten you, but I don't want a casualty on my hands.'

'Casualty? I don't understand. What are you talking about? I'm not——'

'Maybe not, but do as I say and argue afterwards.'

'But...' She shook her head. 'I'm not ready to settle down. I want something to eat, and—and comb my hair and—and have a cigarette, and——'

'Will you listen?' He dropped the sleeping bag and put his hands on her shoulders. 'You're tired and cold, and you've been in damp clothes for the last few hours. You——'

'But so are you. We're both tired and we both got wet. So what? When we've had a hot drink and——'

'No, it isn't just that. For the past hour you've shown signs that I read as danger signals. Twice you've gone into a daze and not heard what I said to you. You've alternated between lagging for rests and violent spurts of energy. You're unreasonably bad-tempered and your lips have lost their colour. That's enough for me.'

'But that's ridiculous,' she said at last. 'We're bound to be tired. We've been climbing since dawn, and it's always colder on mountains at night. It's ridiculous,' she repeated, 'you're just trying to frighten me, making me——'

'Why the devil should I want to frighten you?'

Her mouth tightened. 'You're making me feel like the nuisance you've thought I am ever since the day we set off. Well, I'm all right, it's probably *soroche* or something. And if—if you can't be human, then—then'—her voice rose angrily—'then leave me alone.'

'Just a minute,' he exclaimed grimly, 'if you must bring personalities into it ... I suggest you calm down and forget the resentment *you've* nursed against me right from the start—why, God only knows. All right, so we've been out of step, but you're going to have to forget it and trust me. I assure you,' he shook his head, 'I'm not trying to scare you or *make* you feel like a nuisance, but I *am* trying to make you understand that you could crack, and I can't stand by and wait for it to happen.'

She fell back a pace, silenced by his force and a memory that suddenly stirred, bringing a tremor of disquiet. It had been all of three years ago, almost forgotten yet now vividly clear. It had been the only occasion when Roger had figured in press headlines, and how he had hated it. But his courageousness could not be denied; they said the boy would have died but for Roger. Died from exposure if Roger had not carried him to shelter, looked after him until the rescue party arrived. But that had been in England. On the lonely fells when Roger and a friend had been on a walking holiday. It had been cold, misty and damp ... but it never got cold like that here ... it couldn't happen to her, not here, even though she was tired and a bit shivery, and the air did seem chill after the warmth of the valley and the stifling humidity of the forest. Of course it couldn't happen here...

She became aware of her icy hands and tried not to shiver. What if Max's suspicion was right? Neither of them was equipped with windproof clothing; climbing had not been part of the programme. Certainly they had not expected to spend the night in the open on a mountainside.

She said uncertainly, 'I'm okay, I'm sure.'

'Probably you are,' he said dryly, 'but that's the danger of it. By the time you realize that something's wrong it's too late. And help is too far away.'

For a long moment he looked at her, his eyes narrowed, then he shook his head. 'I can't take any chances. There's too much at stake. Your uncle's lying injured back there—he needs medical attention I couldn't give him. And there're the others, they're depending on us. To say nothing of our moral obligation to the Secret People.'

He paused and his gaze willed her to heed him. 'Remember this instead of trying to provoke me into letting you take your chance and saying to hell with it all.'

So the concern wasn't for her, after all. As always, he was considering the entire picture, each component only in its ultimate effect on the others. He had said he would find Harmon. He had said he would restore the missing things. He had told her uncle he would get her back to safety. She had no doubt that he would do all these things, and accept no interference in the way he did them. Her shoulders drooped wearily and she conceded defeat to exhaustion—and the man who was too strong to fight against.

She said dully, 'Whatever you say. Those cans should be heated by now.'

'In a moment. You need insulating against chill first.'

Her heart bitter, she submitted to his orders, keeping on everything she was wearing, including his jerkin, and taking off only her shoes before she crawled into the sleeping bag. He put the blanket on top, even though she was sure she would melt to a grease-spot long before morning, whether the bottom fell out of the thermometer or not. Then he sat down on the corner of the groundsheet and spread out their rations.

When she instinctively cupped her hands closely round the can of hot soup he stopped her brusquely. To her puzzled reaction he said curtly, 'It's bad to increase surface circulation by applying local heat. Drink it instead of nursing it.'

She obeyed silently, aware again of unease and that the expected combustion was not taking place. The cocoon in which she lay showed no signs of melting her bones—all they were doing was to ache intolerably. She sighed and reached out for her pack, seeking and finding her last packet of cigarettes, only to have them taken out of her hand. Her resigned lack of protest seemed a potent reminder of the depression undermining her spirit.

'We're both better without them,' he said quietly, dropping the packet into his pocket. 'You can smoke yourself sick tomorrow if you feel so inclined, but not tonight.'

She huddled down, remembering vaguely that nicotine affected the circulation, as well as a lot of other things, and wondered that he didn't deliver her a lecture about *that* as well. She sighed and closed her eyes, contemplating the long night that lay ahead. She would never sleep. Certainly she was tired physically, achingly so, but her brain seemed charged with a frantic energy. Then she remembered something and she sat up sharply, the loose folds of the sleeping bag falling away from her shoulders.

'I have to get out,' she said, impatient of his glance. 'It's underneath. Remember?'

'The other sleeping bag,' she went on when he frowned. 'You put it on top of the groundsheet. Anyway, I'm in the wrong one. This one is yours.'

'I know,' he said calmly, reaching out and checking her movement. 'I did it on purpose.'

'On purpose? But——'

'Yes,' his calm tone did not change as he reached up to take the torch from the ledge, 'I'm coming in with you.'

'You're——!'

'Now don't fly off the handle or jump to the most obvious conclusion. I thought you had more sense.'

For a moment she thought she must be delirious—really ill. She stared at him and her lips formed soundless words.

He was packing away the remains of their meal. 'I said don't jump to conclusions. It's a case of improvising to fit the circumstances. Living warmth is the best warmth of all, and make no mistake,' he added grimly, 'it's going to be very cold before the dawn comes. Even in the tropics it can be cold at night, if you happen to be in the desert—or stuck up on a mountain pass.'

Shocked into silence by this totally unforeseen bombshell and the inevitable train of thought it engendered, she could only stare at him helplessly.

'Listen,' he sat back on his heels, 'do you think I'd suggest it if there was any other alternative, or if I didn't care a damn about your welfare? You don't have to look at me as though you think——'

'What do you expect me to think? When you ...' Her voice trailed off into silence and her glance fell before the scorn in his shadowed features. Suddenly she felt shame at her suspicion, and shame because it should instantly spring to her mind. It warred violently with every impression she had formed of Max since she came to know him, and the picture she had built up of him—and fallen in love with. No, it didn't fit—except with the ability he possessed for always knowing what was right. She turned her head away and mumbled, 'I'm sorry, I didn't mean that at all. You know best.'

There was a brief silence, then he said coolly, 'I do.'

At first she was tense, almost rigid, conscious of the awkwardness of him wriggling in beside her and tugging and pummelling the corner of his pack into a pillow under his head.

At last the movements ceased. 'Are you all right?'

'Yes.'

'I know it's not very comfortable, but try to get some sleep.'

'Yes.'

She felt his breath waft against her hair, heard it steady and slow to an unhurried rhythm, and was immediately conscious of how loud her own breathing seemed in the confined space within her curled-in arms. Her heart was beating at twice its normal speed and suddenly she felt a fresh surge of unease. She wanted to relax the rigidity of her body, but her limbs refused to obey her will, threatening to tremble when she moved them, threatening to communicate that trembling to the lean hard contours cradling her own.

'Try to relax and sleep,' he said. 'The shivers will go off soon.'

She swallowed hard. 'It feels as though the bottom fell out of the barometer.'

'You'd just got used to an extreme of heat after England,' he said calmly. 'Now you've forgotten what a bit of cold's like.'

'Extreme is the word.' Suddenly she remembered something that seemed the funniest thing in the world. Hysterical mirth bubbled up in her and she giggled, 'It's only three weeks since the barometer blew its top and you had to cure me then. Remember?'

'Not barometer. Yes, very funny.' There was no trace of amusement in his voice. 'Now calm down. The laugh's over. Okay?'

She wondered if she was imagining a rough tenderness in the words, and the tendency to hysteria faded as quickly as it had come. The pendulum swung full tilt and she remembered her ill-temper, her suspicion, her unspoken but implicit accusation. That had been a bitter misjudgement, she thought sadly, like several more she had made about him. So much had happened during the last few weeks that it all seemed a crazy fantasy when reviewed in retrospect. And during it all Max stood out sane and steady, dependable as a rock. Rock! Word association made her want to giggle as she became aware of the solid, unfeather-bed quality of the cave floor making its solidness felt against her hip and shoulder. She choked back the giggle; she had to make her peace with Max.

She turned cautiously, her movements restricted in the confined space, and twisted her head to try to make out his face.

'What's the matter?' The question was brusque and alert, before she could frame what she wanted to say. 'For heaven's sake, keep still.'

'I can't. Not until I—— Max, I'm sorry.'

'What for?'

'For—for saying that—— For——, I didn't mean——'

'Forget it. Go to sleep.'

'I can't!' A constricting fold gave suddenly and she wriggled her elbow under her, raising herself on it and trying to see his face in the gloom. 'Max, I'm not really ill, am I?'

'I don't think so.' He seemed very slow in replying. 'But it's as well not to take chances.'

'I don't feel ill,' she said after a long pause. 'I don't feel cold any more.'

She sensed his stare through the darkness before he said, 'Probably not. But we've been over all that. The sufferer often thinks he or she is merely cold and exhausted.'

She sighed. 'That wasn't what I was talking about. But we could have gone on. I—I'm not even tired now.'

'Good,' he said dryly. 'You don't feel ill, you don't feel tired, and you don't feel cold any more.' With an impatient movement he huddled down again. 'Do you think you could feel less talkative now, and then we might both get some sleep?'

Sleep! She closed her eyes against the conflict of emotion that surged with the curt words and the movement that brushed her limbs. Suddenly she knew he was willing himself remote from her, even though physical distance could not be attained. A shuddering sigh caught her breath and she wished she *was* freezing out on the mountainside, instead of here, in this new agony that lay on the borderland of ecstasy. How could she sleep and ignore the living breathing nearness of him? Sleep and subdue the turmoil that his nearness was starting to wreak? For a moment she came near to hating him for forcing her into this impossible situation, hating him because she loved him and he could look on her as a responsibility he had to deal with in a cold concerned manner that was...

She choked, 'I'm sorry—I never could sleep on a feather mattress,' fighting to cling to the last frail defence of humour, then dropped her face to her arm.

There was a slight movement, arrested abruptly, then, 'Turn over.'

She stiffened and despair voiced the wild, unspoken plea: couldn't he even let her stay where she was, where she could make out the outline of his head, where she knew she could reach out through the darkness and touch the reassurance of his living warmth, even if her hand remained curled tight to herself, instead of facing the cold rock wall behind, the unknown chill of this crevice in nowhere? But he couldn't even spare her that small comfort, let alone love...

The hot ache closed her throat and burned behind her eyelids, and she drew into herself, huddling away from him, then abruptly he moved. Hard fingers groped for and seized her shoulder as he struggled up, and with the awkward movement his elbow pinned into the soft flesh of her arm.

A small cry of pain escaped her as he began to speak, and the words stopped as he groaned aloud. The painful pressure eased and he sank back.

'Gail, for God's sake! Must you make it so impossible for me? I'm not made of stone.'

'Aren't you?' She twisted frantically, striving to fight free of a tangle of blanket. 'Neither am I! So I'll get out and leave you to sleep in——'

'Don't be so damned stupid! Just—— What did you say?'

'I'm getting out. I—I'm not—— Don't touch me!' She lashed out at the vice on her wrist. 'You——'

'Will you calm down?' he hissed. 'Listen, I undertook to get you back safely, and get you back safely I'm going to do. Now make up your mind. Are you going to calm down and go to sleep or do I have to tie you down?'

She recoiled in horror and he said grimly, 'It's no use crying. I'm not going to comfort you.'

'I didn't think you would,' she gulped, the flare of fight already consumed in his strength, leaving her drained and weary. She knuckled the clinging strands of hair out of her eyes and twisted away, as far away as she could, uncaring that her pillowing arm now rested on ice-cold bumpy rock from which a damp chill emanated immediately.

She could see the jagged vee of sky framed in the opening of the cave and the frosty pinpoints of silver out in the zero of space. and the vista of cold, lonely infinity evoked instant awareness of her own frailty against the immensity of nature. She felt spiritless and afraid, not of the night but of her own weakness and the unspent force of the emotion one man had invoked in her. Why? Why did it have to be the one man whose single-mindedness of purpose would never waver, least of all for a woman, and least of all for herself?

'Gail...'

There was warning in the tone, and sensing that further recrimination was imminent she reluctantly settled back into a stiff, uncomfortable posture that avoided contact and pulled the folds of the blanket over her head. She wouldn't sleep, but she must pretend to, let him sleep, try to summon pride and face reality. That the comfort she craved, that he withheld, would not prove the balm she sought; that it could only precipitate a betrayal of the emotion she dreaded his discovering.

He moved, and she stiffened, freezing even her breathing into stillness until he settled again. Then she heard him sigh. There was despair in it, and a tremor of resignation, and his arm stirred and found its way clumsily across her body.

Unbelieving, she felt its warmth settle and curl round her waist, drawing her into that other warmth within the curve of his body. His breath whispered against her hair and there was a gruff note in his voice as he said softly:

'All right. I know. You've had about as much as you can take.'

Her sigh was almost a convulsion. Words would not come and became a chokiness in her throat. Then the impact of his total reversal brought about the betrayal she had feared. Blind response and a wave of longing too long pent broke down the bonds of pride and resistance, everything, so that she murmured his name and turned to the haven her entire being craved.

She was hardly conscious of his sigh, of the murmured phrases of conventional comfort—or that they were merely conventional—as he drew her close and settled her head into the warm crook of his shoulder, until suddenly he was silent, his hand stilled against her hair, and through that silence the drum of her heart beat was echoed by a stronger rhythm.

'Gail...' He moved uneasily. 'Gail, you ... I think you should...'

She looked up, impatient of the fall of her hair across her face, and felt his face against her brow. Then somehow her mouth was moving across his cheek and his was moving across hers until their mouths touched, hesitated, then clung with a fierceness almost painful.

The sweet intensity brought an ecstasy beyond all reason. His arms bound her closer and she merged into them, her own curving her response as she gave herself into the magic world he had created out of darkness and despair. His touch, his kiss, his nearness sparked to blazing life an undreamed-of fire within her. This was what she had waited for all her life, merely existed for until this moment of magic awakening.

Lost in the wonder of him, triumph came as instinct told her that Max could be hers now, if she so wished. No man's control was unlimited, and Max was no exception, even though he was breaking the kiss, pressing her face into his shoulder, only the iron hardness of his arms and the quickened rise and fall of his breathing against her breast betraying his own awakened senses.

He muttered, 'Gail ...' and she moved convulsively against his shoulder, not wanting him to speak, even as she knew her movement was denying his effort at control.

His mouth burrowed into her hair and his hand dragged across her breast, clung for a moment as she quivered, probed at her throat, then caught at her face and stayed the movement of her head, forcing her to face him. He whispered, 'Gail, I don't want you to regret anything ... if you ...'

She sighed, seeking and imprisoning his hand against her, and he groaned softly. 'Is this the way you want it? I'm as human as the next man, you know. If you ...'

She wanted to cry out exultantly: *Yes, and I'm glad!* and silence his lips, but the cold little word *regret* was already implanted in her subconscious and she stayed silent, fighting the overwhelming desire to make the eternal ploys of a woman to the man who has taken possession of her heart, knowing full well what the outcome must be, even while she realized the unfairness of waiting for Max to make the next move.

He moved slightly and she took a deep shuddering breath, forcing herself to stay quiescent in his arms, her face buried against his chest, and presently his breathing steadied, the fierce tension in the hard body slackened against her, and he gently disengaged his hand from her clasp. She felt the sigh shiver through him, then she drew back and whispered shakily, 'I don't think we intended that to happen.'

'We?'

She sensed his stare and felt his slight start.

'Well ...' She dared not look up. 'You—you know what I mean.'

'Yes, I know what you mean.'

The response was brusque, and utterly unhelpful to the terminating of a situation literally unterminable now—until the hour of dawn. Before then, many hours waited, to be existed through, as effective a barrier to escape as the great chasm yawning below the brink exactly six feet from the mouth of the niche wherein they lay.

Gail felt a chill heaviness pervade her spirit with the despair of renunciation. It was her fault they had had to rest here; alone, Max would have travelled faster and farther. She had proved a hindrance, forcing him into a situation it was plain he hadn't wanted, and then ... On this train of thought, she whispered, 'It's my fault—I'm sorry.'

'What for, for God's sake?'

'For being weak—and idiotic,' she said bitterly.

He shifted impatiently. 'What the devil did you expect? A

gentle pat on the head to soothe away your fears?'

She recoiled from the harshness of his tone. 'No,' she said tautly, 'I didn't mean idiotic in that respect. You forget—it takes two for—for that. I meant—before. If I hadn't——'

'Oh, forget it,' he said bitterly. 'At least you're honest. But the next time you decide to be idiotic you'd better pick your partner with care. You might find you've started something you can't stop.'

With that he turned his back on her and burrowed down into a withdrawn, unfriendly heap. It was as well for Gail's peace of mind that he did so: weakness, love and idiocy might yet have won.

CHAPTER X

GAIL wakened, stiff and cramped, to a sunrise that should have delighted her aesthetic eye and filled her heart with promise for the new day of hope. It didn't. It merely brought surprise that she had actually found sleep at some time during that miserable night and reminded her that she had to face Max in broad daylight and go on facing him for many more hours before she could find refuge from his eyes and her bitter memories.

He was sorting out the remains of their food when she crawled out the sleeping bag and went to the mouth of the cave. She stared out at the topaz and tender young blue opening across the heavens, and the distant peaks under snow caps tinted with apricot and pale silvery streaks. The mountains are eternal, she thought sadly, and we are so transient. They stand alone, impervious and majestic, but they seem nothing against the power of human joys and fears and love, and against the barrier of despair that now separated her from Max Christiern. *Why* had she been such a fool?

Sighing, she walked a little way along the ledge, feeling the cool clear air driving away the dull sleep feeling from her skin and creased clothes. Without thinking she thrust her hands into her pockets, to encounter unfamiliar oddments and remember that it wasn't her own jerkin. Slowly she took them out, knowing it was an invasion but unable to stop herself.

There was a clean folded handkerchief with a blue and grey criss-cross border, a small, black-handled pocket-knife with three blades, a book of airline matches, a stub of blue and grey mottled pencil with a white top, three coins and a folded slip of paper. She opened the slip of paper and smiled wryly: one dry-cleaner's check. What had she expected? A love letter?

Slowly she dropped them back into the pockets in which she had found them and returned to the cave.

He looked up. 'If you're thinking of washing there's no water, I've already looked.'

'It doesn't matter,' she said dully, seeking her comb and wandering out on to the ledge while she rough-combed her hair into some semblance of tidiness. Her shoes were scuffed and her clothes creased and grubby, but one couldn't rough it and turn out like a newly polished pin. The thought occurred that he was unlikely to notice in any case, and at the moment appearances ceased to be important—a preoccupation with feminine frivolities in the glamour line would doubtless earn her only a scornful glance that would express clearly justification for the already low opinion he seemed to have of her.

'Is there anything I can do to help?' she asked, not looking at him.

'It's done, such as it is. The sooner we get away the better.'

In silence they ate the remains of their food and began to pack up the gear. She folded the blanket with slow, deliberate movements and started to stuff it into her pack on top of the rolled up sleeping bag. He said, 'I'll take that.'

She took no notice, continuing to ram it down, and said flatly, 'No, you've got more than your share already. All the heavy stuff...'

'I said I'll take it.'

'It's packed now.'

'Unpack it.' He turned unexpectedly and the brush of his bare arm against her made her flinch as though from fire. She started back, and he straightened slowly and looked at her.

For the first time that morning she encountered his direct glance and the chill in it started the turmoil of regret anew. He said, 'What's the matter now?'

'Nothing.' She bent fiercely and snatched the blanket. 'Here.'

He ignored it and she saw his chest heave with his indrawn breath. 'Listen,' he took a step forward, 'you don't need to shy at my touch like a scalded cat. Oh yes, you know very well there's something the matter. Now let's get this straight. If you're still worrying about last night, I can assure you that you needn't. So what? You shared a sleeping bag with a man because it was the only sensible thing to do. And felt a bit bushed and wanted comforting.' His mouth tightened. 'And the comfort turned to natural chemistry that you weren't expecting. Well, you needn't worry. Still less feel ashamed.'

He took the blanket from her trembling hand and stuffed it

savagely into his pack. 'If I'd had any sense I'd have looked for another solution to wrapping you up for the night. But I was certain my own reactions would remain sane and practical. Unfortunately, I forgot to take yours into consideration. I should have remembered that women are unpredictable, and that you're far from being the tough-shelled girl you'd have me believe. I should have also remembered that women rarely play fair,' he added bitterly.

In the pause that followed she stared at him with horror in her eyes. 'So it's all *my* fault!'

A sardonic smile turned the corners of his mouth downward. 'Not entirely. Once nature reminds us of the man–woman business the chain reaction can start up pretty fast. And it could get out of hand with any man and woman in the circumstances we landed in last night. I could have taken you quite easily last night, and that's what's eating you, isn't it?'

She stared at him, her face drawn with shock at the cold raw statements.

'But I didn't,' he said coldly, 'so forget it. It's over.'

'Just like that?' She found her voice and turned away, unable to bear the gaze of those cool grey eyes any longer. Forget it! *How blind could a man get*? And the hardest thing of all to bear was the bitter voice of self-knowledge: that if his voice softened, if he showed a glimpse of tenderness, if he made one gesture of revocation, her defences would cave in no matter how she tried to harden herself against him. She picked up her pack and slung it over her shoulder.

'All right, forget it,' she said tightly. 'It all seems very silly in cold daylight, doesn't it?'

'Doesn't it!' He also turned away and gave a searching glance round as though to ensure they had left nothing behind. Obviously the whole matter was already leaving his mind.

They reached the mission early that afternoon and entered wearily to a startled Father Lorenzo.

Max checked the priest's spate of concerned questions and asked if Harmon had been seen near the mission.

The old man shook his head. 'We've seen no one since you left. But tell me; what has happened? Did you——?'

'Gail will tell you everything.' Max frowned towards the river. 'I want to get on. Harmon must be found and he can't have got so far ahead. I——'

'Yes, my friend, but you look weary,' Father Lorenzo interrupted, his kindly features bewildered. 'You must rest first and eat. What is this great urgency?'

'This man, he deserted our party after stealing gold from the temple,' Gail broke in. 'They call their precious things the Tears of the Sun—they're sacred to the Secret People—and we have to get them back. We have to stop him leaving the country. And my uncle is hurt—they're all still in the Valley. We have to get help to them.'

'Tell me what I can do, my child,' the old priest said simply.

Before she could respond, Max spoke. 'I want to reach Huamano as quickly as possible and inform the authorities. And arrange to have a helicopter pick up the Professor and get him to hospital. Speed is vital.'

Father Lorenzo nodded, and Max went on: 'Will you give me food for the journey and keep Gail in your care until I return?'

'Of course, my son. But I have a better idea. I will ask Tapibos to send your message. They know the forest far better than we do and they will cover the journey in half the time it will take you, courageous as you are. As for this man who has betrayed you . . .' the old man's eyes clouded and he sighed, 'I fear you will not find him easily in there.'

Gail followed his glance towards the dark mass of the forest and knew he voiced her own fear. But they must make the effort; so much was at stake, not least, faith and integrity.

The priest turned. 'Your mules are all here still, well fed and watered. I will have them brought in readiness and I will seek Tapibos immediately. But this will take a little time, so will you not avail yourselves of what I have here? Surely I do not have to remind you that a man does not enter the forest without making sensible preparation for the journey.'

'I suppose he's right,' said Max unwillingly, watching the rotund figure in black cross the compound and make towards the village.

'Of course he's right!' For a moment Gail forgot herself and the barrier that was shutting her away from Max. She said sharply: 'At any other time *you* would be the first one to insist on the right way.'

'It's different now.'

'Maybe, but that doesn't mean you've got to be foolhardy and plunge into danger without——'

'All right, I get the message.' He gave her a sidelong glance. 'I presume you've forgiven me?'

'Oh! Well, do as Father Lorenzo says.' Abruptly she avoided his eyes. 'I'm going to wash—then I'll make something to eat while you wash.'

She half expected to find him gone when she emerged from the hut which housed the primitive washing facilities, but he was in the living room, ill-concealed impatience making his movements jerky as he stowed corn bread and canned meat into a haversack.

With a brief, 'I won't be long,' he went out carrying his towel and Gail lit the ancient stove and set about preparing a quickly cooked meal.

Max was having his second helping of richly spiced corned beef stew and marble-sized potatoes liberally garnished with *ajis*, a fierce, eye-watering pickle, when Father Lorenzo returned.

He said, 'It is all arranged. Two men are now waiting. If you will write out your message it will be delivered at Huamano within two and a half days' time.'

Two and a half days, thought Gail despairingly. But it had taken the team nearly a week to traverse the forest.

'I have also arranged for you to have a guide,' Father Lorenzo continued. 'He is an expert tracker and if a white man has gone before you he will know.'

'Thank you.' Max searched his pockets for writing material and, failing to find what he sought, barely repressed an expletive. Gail was about to offer the spare pages from her diary when Father Lorenzo smiled and produced some lined notepaper and an envelope.

'Thanks,' Max said again, 'some day I might be able to repay you for all this.'

The priest shook his head. 'Do not repay *me*, my son.'

The tautness of Max's face softened for a moment. 'I'll remember that,' he said quietly.

Within a short time the message had been written and dispatched, and Max had loaded one of the mules with the essentials for the journey. Near by, the guide waited, already mounted, a machete thrust into the broad skin belt about his hips and an ancient shotgun slung from one shoulder.

Max gave a final tug to the straps, patted the mule's neck, said something to Father Lorenzo and at last turned to Gail. He looked at the slight droop to her mouth of which she wasn't aware, and his own mouth compressed at the corners.

'Not suited at being left behind, are you?'

'Would you? If you faced the prospect of nearly a week of—of waiting and worrying, and not being able to do a thing?'

'Worrying won't help.'

'How can I help worrying? Not knowing if the message gets through, wondering what's happening in the Valley, and what is happening to——' She bit her lip. 'Max, for heaven's sake watch out. If you do find Harmon...'

His brows flickered slightly. 'I reckon I can take care of myself, if that's worrying you. Keep out of mischief yourself—if you can. So long.'

She watched him take the halters of the two mules and follow the guide across the compound and down the long winding track towards the forest. The sun blazed down, etching a sharp outline of the compound rail across the dust, but where the forest edged the clearing the brilliant glaze was lost abruptly in the dense dark viridescence that closed round the three plodding animals and the silent riders.

Gail did not feel the light touch on her shoulder or hear the priest's murmur. A wave of unease was verging very near panic as she stared down at the silent forest. For no reason at all she remembered the shotgun and could not explain why it should worry her. Nor could she explain why that transition of sun into black shadow should appear as an omen of evil. All she was conscious of was a terrifying premonition that she would never see Max again.

Without stopping to reason with the overwhelming instinct she whirled suddenly and ran into the mission. Feverishly she threw her belongings back into the pack, sorted out some food-stuff and essentials, snatched up her jerkin and emerged into the sunlight to face the startled gaze of Father Lorenzo.

'It's no use,' she cried. 'I can't stay. I've got to go with him. Please understand. I must!'

Before he could form protests she had rushed to the rear of the mission and found her own mule. A few minutes later she was urging the animal down towards those dense dark shadows from whence came the fear now driving her into their depths.

* * *

The Indian must have sensed her pursuit long before she caught up with them, for when she eventually sighted them she experienced a mild degree of shock. Expecting to catch up and append herself quietly to the tail of the little procession, instead she found two mounted men facing her, barring the track and obviously prepared to take the offensive initiative.

'Good God!' said Max, when she halted her mule's plodding gait and looked at him defiantly.

His expression could not be described as welcoming, even by the longest stretch of wishful thinking, but at least it was satisfactorily shaken!

She raised her hands with a gesture that carried admirable aplomb and ventured a smile. 'It's all right, I'm unarmed.'

'Are you?' he said grimly. 'What the devil do you think

you're doing?'

'Nothing. I've done it.'

'Well, you can turn round and do it again. Go on, back the way you came.'

'I'm coming with you.'

Abruptly he got down and strode towards her. 'You can't. For heaven's sake, stop being a little fool.'

She looked into his angry face and said stubbornly, 'Thanks—I like being a fool, sometimes. Having got this far I'm going to see it through and nobody, not even you, is going to stop me. So, if you like, I'll go back, but only to find myself a guide.' Her eyes, bright now with the light of the obsession to which she had surrendered, did not waver. 'Don't try to make me go back, please. Listen, I know how you must feel. I should never have set out on this trip in the first place—none of us knew it was going to work out like this—but it's too late now. I have to go on. You see—I forgot to tell you—but Uncle gave me the films and a couple of the specimens. They won't keep for ever.'

'Hand them over. That's easily settled.'

'No. Please—after this I'll never ask anything of you again, if you'll be patient just this once more.'

The Indian watched, his face impassive, his dark eyes remote, while Max searched the young, eloquent features upturned to his own. For once the struggle of decision was visible in his tired eyes, and she wavered, knowing in her heart she was being stupid and unreasonable, and adding to his burden of responsibility. Momentarily the two loves battled within her, the love that said follow and protect, the love that said be sane and unselfish. She opened her lips, on the point of conceding defeat, and at the same moment he raised his hands with a gesture of despair and turned away.

'All right. You never would see reason. Come on, let's not waste any more time.'

The set of his shoulders as he returned to his mount was not exactly warming, but for the moment the victory was enough. Wisely, she remained silent and contented herself with following in the rear as inconspicuously as possible. But inwardly she sighed for the Valley days, for their sweet brief rapport found with him during Azzuni's sickness. Now that was over. The night on the mountain had destroyed his hard won acceptance of her, and friendship was out of the question—impossible. Her awakened responses to Max as a man ruled that out; what other relationship remained? Guilty warmth flooded over her with the memory and pain came with the echo of his words that morning. It was true; she had all but offered herself to him.

She stared ahead. She had to forget; the admission of the truth, even to herself, was a sweet form of torture. But the moist green fastness of the forest evoked more memories, and soon she found she was striving to recognize the place where they had camped the last night before reaching the mission. Impatient with her sentimentality, she made herself concentrate on the present, knowing that to her tenderfoot eyes the forest lacked landmarks. It was an endless tangle of creeper and bush and towering trunks, each one a centre of its own clustering colony of vine and fungi and parasites, a continuous barrier of green density to be hacked and trampled and overcome. Any small landmark left of that overnight camp with Max would be as transient as his few moments of tenderness.

She thought of Harmon, and once ventured to ask if there was any trace of his penetrating the forest ahead of them, but Max's response was grim and non-committal, and she did not ask again. The guide rode on impassively, giving no indication if he noted anything out of the ordinary, and at sundown he left them, going silently on some mission of his own.

When he returned, two small limp carcasses were slung from his shoulder. He made a small fire, some little distance away, and deftly prepared his kill. Suddenly Gail's appetite left her and she put down her portion of greasy cold chicken and began to peel a hardboiled egg with a noticeable lack of enthusiasm.

'Don't watch him if you're squeamish,' Max said. 'Believe me, hunger soon banishes squeamishness. Now eat that. We'll be reduced to mashed bananas and tinned meat by tomorrow night.'

She knew this made sense and obeyed, trying to pretend that the brusqueness of his attitude didn't hurt, that it didn't matter as long as she could draw together the tatters of her pride and believe he did not suspect the torment he had invoked.

But it did hurt, and it did matter.

After he bade her a cool goodnight and she settled down under the dark starless canopy there was nothing but the thoughts and memories that would not stay imprisoned. How could one man bring about this change in her, without the smallest careless effort, transforming her pride and determination into this hopeless longing, making her so weak she could implore him to let her follow? Gail looked into her heart and did not like what she read there. For it was true; she had deluded herself from the start. All along she had fought and begged every inch of the way, deluding herself that it was only the expedition that mattered and her part in it. Instead, he had brought her to full awareness of herself and the treachery of a woman's senses.

Despising herself, she lay sleepless all that hot humid night trying to escape the bitter truth. No matter what he did to her, she still loved Max Christiern, for everything he was, exactly as he was, and no matter what happened she would go on loving him till the end of time...

She must have dozed off some time before the pale misted green dawn filtered through the curtains of the forest, for suddenly she was lying there, her eyes wide open and seeking to find the cause of her wakeful alertness. Then she saw the shadowy form of the Indian bending over Max's sleeping form and she sat up sharply, the alarm bell of protective instinct bringing instant unease. What was the Indian doing?

But Max was sitting up, listening, saying something, then he was scrambling out of his sleeping bag, reaching for his jerkin and thrusting his arms into the sleeves. Without even a glance at her he was walking away, following the Indian into the green gloom.

Gail hesitated only for a moment before she also enacted the same movements as those of Max. Without a thought of the wisdom or otherwise of her action she obeyed the instinct that sent her silently in the wake of the two stealthy figures ahead.

They had not gone very far before they paused. Gail also stopped, watching their wary glances about them, their brief whispered exchange and the Indian's gestures. Then they moved on a few paces, paused again, and Max bent down to examine something on the ground to which the Indian was pointing.

Max straightened, and even from this distance she could see the grim set of his jaw and the stiffening of his shoulders. He took a step forward, then halted, turning to the Indian, and after a moment the Indian nodded and loped back the way they had come.

Again instinct prompted Gail to step into cover, to wait motionless while the Indian passed within a few feet of her and disappeared along the thin track. When she judged he was out of hearing range she slipped out of cover and hurried with small noiseless steps after Max.

The track had given way to a barely discernible path that was more like a tunnel beaten through the undergrowth. Creepers snaked to ensnare her feet and catch at her face, and for a moment she hesitated breathlessly, unable to see or hear Max and wondering if she had lost him already in this featureless maze. Why had he sent the Indian back? To bring her? To break the camp? To tell her to stay there? Maybe she should turn back. This was a foolish move, venturing alone into the forest. So much for the buddy system! Yet Max couldn't be so far ahead.

She looked down at the crushed patches. This was the way he had come. She took a deep breath and plunged on, heedless now of scratches and the awakening clouds of insects that buzzed and tormented every exposed portion of skin. What had Clive said? That the insect population worked two shifts: all day and all night. This lot seemed to be putting in a double shift. They were the worst cloud she'd——

The next moment she forgot the pests. The green mass had opened into a small, roughly hacked clearing, and before she could check her steps she almost ran full tilt into the man who was crouching there.

She gasped, unbelieving, as he sprang to his feet and whirled round, his gaping mouth as incredulous as her own.

'Harmon!'

'What the—— How the devil did you——?'

Suddenly he lunged forward and life came back into her limbs. 'No!' She thrust out her hands and leapt back. '*Max!*' she screamed at the top pitch of her lungs. '*Max!* He's here! He's——'

'Why, you——!' For a moment she thought he was going to fell her, then he turned, his dark features twisted under a three-day shadow of beard, and seized at the pack on the ground. There were traces of his sojourn strewn about; a water filter, a chipped enamel mug, a crumpled groundsheet of the cape variety and an empty tin. He ignored them, kicked viciously at the tin, and staggered across the clearing.

Gail stared. He couldn't run, even though his actions screamed flight. Then she saw the strain in the curiously lopsided gait and she knew its cause. Weight. Gold was heavy. She remembered her father laughing once, at some film he'd seen where a couple of characters lifted a crate of supposed bullion as though it were a crate of feathers. Bad production, he'd commented, they ... She forgot the flashback and any doubts she had as to Harmon's guilt. Why should he run?

She started in pursuit, impervious to her own risk, guessing with wild accuracy at his intention. He would hide the relics, then return later. But if he did it was unlikely that he or anyone else would ever succeed in locating them again. The forest would cover all trace of them in the space of days, so fecund was the rate of growth in its wild depths.

'No! Stop!' She caught up with him, heard the oath he grunted, and tried to snatch at the pack. 'You won't get away with it. You've got to——'

'Leave go, you little fool!' Fury and desperation contorted his unshaven features as he turned on her. 'Let go!'

Suddenly he aimed a blow at her. It caught her across the side of her head and knocked her off balance. He yanked the strap free of her grip and thrust viciously at her with a force that sent her sprawling.

'Now,' he gritted, 'shut up, or you'll really get hurt.' He stood over her, ugly threat patent in his face. 'If you make another sound...'

Still watching her, he began to back away, and she stared at him with fixed intensity, making no move.

'Going to be sensible,' he sneered, bending to heave up the pack. 'Wise girl.' He gave her a mocking smile and turned as Max burst into the clearing.

'You, Christiern!' Harmon fell back, but only for a second.

Gail's thankful cry died to a gasp. Harmon dropped his burden and flung himself at Max. The next moment the two men closed in combat.

The forest responded to the sudden violence. Birds rose shrieking, wings beating and flashing rainbow slashes of colour among the branches, to settle and screech alarm, then rise again like leaves in an eddy.

Gail picked herself up and gasped as the two struggling figures went down. They rolled and flailed before her horrified eyes, fists, knees and feet fighting for supremacy, and every crack against flesh and bone made her flinch. She could see blood on Harmon's mouth and a darkening contusion of Max's cheekbone, and she cried out as he went down, to repel Harmon with a well-aimed kick and scramble up as the other doubled up.

'Stop it!' she screamed. '*Stop it!*'

They were deaf to her cry. She saw the Indian through the trees and darted frantically towards him. 'Stop them!' she begged, then waved her hands frantically as the impassive stare comprehended and he unslung the shotgun. 'No, not that! Oh!'

She closed her eyes as Harmon went down, started to rise, then flopped back into a clump of huge spiked ferns, and Max stood over him for a moment, still tense as a coiled spring, and at last straightened contemptuously.

The Indian lowered the gun and walked over to the vanquished Harmon. Max stood still, his chest heaving, then pushed his hair off his brow and wiped his hands over his face. He turned to the frozen Gail.

'Did he hurt you?'

'No—— Max, are you all right? Are you hurt? Your face...'
Suddenly she was trembling. 'I—I tried to stop him, but he——
Max, are you sure you're——?'

He wasn't listening. He went back to the pack and bent down, unfastening the top and reaching inside. He withdrew his hands and the soft, beautiful mellow gleam of gold was within them. The Indian moved at Gail's side, a startled, wondering light in his dark eyes.

She saw Max take out the jewelled silver figurine of the Moon Goddess and lay it in the gold ritual bowl the High Priest had used for the anointing at the wedding of the Bride of the Sun, then examine the exquisitely formed effigy of the Cat Goddess.

Slowly he put them back and began to fasten the straps. A sigh ran through Gail and she took a deep breath, as though to dispel the reaction of tension pervading her limbs. She glanced at the enrapt Indian and another movement caught at the periphery of her vision. Instantly she was gripped again by tension.

Harmon was stirring, sitting up and staring at Max Christiern with hate in his eyes, and something dull lay in his hand. Gail blinked, not believing in that glint of bluish sheen, and heard the soft metallic click. Almost too late, she knew.

'Max!' she screamed. 'Look out—*he's got a gun!*'

He leapt up. Harmon shouted. The Indian spun noiselessly and a nerve-shattering report exploded the silence. Max keeled back, there was another softer, duller thud, almost obliterated in the crack of the second shot, and bedlam started in the branches above. Gail stood frozen, and through a curious sense of unreality, as though a slow motion sequence had stopped, she saw Max lying motionless on the ground.

It seemed a mile to his side, a stumbling run straight into a nightmare of fear that was turning into a core of physical pain inside her. She dropped to her knees and smelled the acridity that lingered on the moist air, and saw the runnel, so small, just above the breast pocket of his shirt. The voice crying 'Max! Max!' over and over again didn't seem to be her own, and another voice inside her was saying, '*He's dead!*' as she touched his face and saw the terrifying stain edging that scorched little runnel in the material.

She tried to raise his head, then stopped. It might be wrong to move him. 'Oh, God,' she whispered, 'what do I do?'

Some automatic response seemed to guide her hands. Not daring to think what she might see, she undid his shirt and felt for his heartbeat. Her own pulses were drumming in her ears, and for a dreadful moment she couldn't distinguish the other throb under her questing palm. But it was there, and her sobbing breath escaped. She drew the shirt back, away from the place where white hot metal had scored into the flesh, and fumbled for the clean handkerchief in her pocket.

'That's no use,' he said faintly.

The sound of his voice brought a relief so great she felt faint. His eyes flickered open. He stirred and groaned, his hand going to his chest, and she cried, 'Keep still! Don't move. In case ...'

'They say it's like the kick of a mule.' His voice was thin. 'Now I know ...' A groan escaped him and his face twisted. 'In my pocket ... something to pad this mess ...'

'Yes,' she said feverishly. 'Don't try to talk or move.'

She found the handkerchief in his pocket and shook it out to its cleaner inner folds. It was difficult to see the extent of the wound and the agonized thought drummed through her mind: How deep had the bullet penetrated. She pressed the small pad into his hand and shook her head as he held it to the wound. It was hopelessly small protection and it wouldn't be sterile. She had nothing ... Abruptly she slipped off her jerkin and removed her shirt, turning it inside out and improvising a pad from it. She put it across his chest and shouldered back into her jerkin. 'Tell Jimo to bring the mules here—and the medical case. And——' She looked up as the Indian's shadow fell across her. He held something out and she recoiled. It was Harmon's gun.

Max looked at it. He muttered, 'Browning automatic ... how did he keep that out of our sight?' He looked at her. 'What happened?'

His voice sounded stronger, and she said: 'Jimo clubbed him. He's still out—over there.'

Max groaned and said something to the Indian. Jimo shook his head and hurried away. Awkwardly, Max shifted and sat up. She put out a restraining hand. 'Don't—until we're sure——'

'I'm not going to die—yet,' he said grimly. 'I want to see if——'

'Stay there.' Her fear was increasing, despite his return to consciousness. 'Max, the bullet ... will it be lodged inside, or ... ?'

'Still there. He fired from a disabling distance.' His mouth set. 'Check round here,' he turned his chin over his shoulder, 'then you'll know.'

'You mean ... ?' Her cheeks blanched. Fearfully, she moved her hand across his back before she looked at the unmarked, unbroken surface of material over his shoulders. She said, 'There's no sign—no wound. It must be still lodged.'

He ignored her, glancing towards Harmon. 'See if he's still alive, for God's sake.'

She looked at the sprawled figure and said grimly: 'He doesn't deserve to be.'

'Oh, Gail . . .' Max passed his hand over his brow. 'Don't talk like that.'

'He tried to kill you.'

Max said nothing, and she went slowly towards the man whose greed had caused tragedy. She bent over him and a few moments later straightened and returned to Max's side.

'He's all right,' she said bitterly. 'When he comes round all he'll have is a bump and a headache. What are we going to do about him?'

'Do?' Max stared at her. 'We'll have to take him back with us. What else should we do? Leave him here?'

'He would have left you.'

'Maybe. But would it make you feel happier to match his behaviour?'

'I suppose not.' She stared anxiously through the trees. How long before Jimo returned? Not very long, surely. They hadn't come very far from the camp.

She said, 'Is the pain very bad?'

'No.'

She knew he lied, and the unbearable tension tightened its coils. It was the feeling of helplessness, having to wait, wondering how they were going to get back to the mission without further aggravating the injury. Worst of all was the fear she could not keep at bay—how much unseen damage was one small cylinder of metal causing at this very moment . . . ?

CHAPTER XI

HARMON recovered consciousness just in time to solve the problem of transporting an unconscious man by mule-back. To Jimo, however, it presented no problem. About to hoist Harmon's limp form crosswise over the saddle like a sack broken in the middle, the Indian seemed puzzled by Max's instant objection.

Gail, in an agony of impatience and sick with anxiety, had reached the point of desperation where she could have consigned Harmon to the river to get rid of him. If Max should pass out before they got him back ... If Harmon came round fighting mad ... 'Please ...' she begged, 'leave him to Jimo. We've got to get you——'

But Harmon stirred groggily as she spoke and at least one of her fears could be discounted. It was plain that it would be some time before Harmon regained his truculence.

At last they were on their way; Harmon slumped low over his mount, under the untender eye of the Indian; Max riding stiffly, unnaturally erect, and Gail uncomfortably astride the mule with the two packs, riding as close to Max as she could, watching feverishly for the slightest sign of fresh crisis in the set face that had gone pale and drawn under its tan.

The journey seemed to take an eternity, even though it lasted little over three hours. That was the one fact for which she was thankful; they had set off so late the previous afternoon. If it had been morning, or if it had happened a day later, deep in the heart of the forest ... But it hadn't, and at the mission Max would be able to rest, and they could attend to the wound ... stop the bleeding ... Her thoughts revolved frantically, trying to recall everything she had heard or read of bullet wounds, to come round full circle to the despairing realization that she knew nothing of the procedure for dealing with this kind of emergency. And yet, when the actual moment came, a new calm took possession of her and she forgot fear.

She met Father Lorenzo with the brutally simple statement: 'He's been shot,' and wasted no time on explanations.

In the mission, she first filled every container she could find with water and set them to heat. Then she went to Max. 'Tell me what to do.'

He glanced at the priest, then back to her. 'I think you'd better stay out of this. It won't be exactly pretty.'

'I didn't imagine it would be,' she said calmly, 'but it has to be faced. I have water boiling, and I think it would be best if you went into the little room I had. The sun's full on it, so the light will be good. If I may'—she turned to the priest—'I'll take this table in there. We'll need it to put things on.'

'Yes, of course. Anything.'

'A clean cloth? I'll need something clean for a cover. A sheet, tablecloth, anything.'

'Yes, I'll see.' He was flustered. 'I live very simply. Would some clean towels do?'

'Yes, ours are all getting pretty grim now.' She heard the hiss and spat of the pans boiling and hurried to the stove. Quickly she scoured the table top, carried it into the other room, and brought the bowl and two jugs of hot water. She turned to Max.

He had removed his shirt and was standing by the window.

She dragged a chair over for him. 'Is it——? Can you tell?'

'Yes.' He did not turn. 'I've been lucky.'

She caught her breath. 'How?'

'Look.' He gestured towards the shirt he had discarded. 'I never believed it could happen that way in real life.'

The old silver cigarette case which she recognized instantly lay on top of the shirt. She stared, then snatched it up. 'It's had a bash. The corner's all——'

'It deflected the bullet, that's why.'

'You mean'—she leaped instantly to the joyful conclusion—'it's not lodged in you? It's only a flesh wound?'

'No. I'm afraid it's still there. As far as I can tell, it's ploughed along the surface flesh and buried itself in the pectoral muscle. Gail,' he turned his head, 'can you face this?'

'I'll face anything,' she said firmly.

'I'd hoped to be able to do this myself, but it's difficult to see and reach myself, and I'm afraid the padre's eyesight isn't as good as it might be. But you'd better be sure,' he added grimly.

Without speaking she crossed to his side and kept her face expressionless while she deliberately inspected the raw furrow of the wound across the left side of his breast. 'I'll scrub my hands again,' she said, 'then you can tell me exactly what to do.'

Following his directions, she opened the medical kit and got out the things that would be needed. He took the morphia syrette, a tiny tube with a stilette containing the measured dose ready for injection, and shook his head. 'I'll do this myself.'

Only then did she betray her first hint of alarm. 'Not yet,' she begged. 'Tell me again, if you go out before I'm sure of——'

'It won't put me out,' he said patiently, 'it's merely to deaden the pain. I've never experienced surgery from a lady amateur.' He saw her lip whiten as she bit it, and added softly, 'I'm sorry—you're doing your best. Now listen carefully, Gail. The bullet isn't in very deep, but it'll slip away. Make sure you don't dab cautiously. When you spot it dig it out without hesitating. Have you got the right forceps? The ones with the serrated teeth—*not* the dissectors.'

'Yes.' She looked at him steadily. 'What else?'

'You'll have to stitch it. Don't break the ampoule with the needle in till you're ready to use it, and when you tie them off you must use a reef knot.'

'Oh.' Her mouth compressed with dismay. 'I hadn't thought of that. I—I'm not sure how...' She reached for a length of tape and began a hasty experiment. 'It's over like that—an ordinary tie, then over again. Like this?'

'That's a granny. Like this.' He showed her, made sure she'd grasped it, then said, 'Now, if you're sure ... and for heaven's sake, don't be afraid of hurting me.'

She swallowed hard and nodded, and without further ado Max gave himself the intramuscular shot and prepared himself.

If anyone had ever suggested to Gail that one day she would find herself undertaking to remove a bullet from a man's body, in the most primitive of conditions and with only the patient to guide her actions, she would have greeted the suggestion with the ridicule and incredulity it deserved, and certainly with a candid, scornful prophecy as to exactly where she was likely to finish up should such an unlikely contingency ever arise.

But she did not finish up flat out in a faint, at the first sight of blood, or beating an ignominious retreat to the nearest bathroom. That strange ability latent in everyone rose in her and vested her with an icy calmness and a surety she had never known she possessed. It was not until the ghastly little cylinder of metal lay on a piece of gauze and she snapped the ampoule containing the cutting needle ready threaded with the black nylon surgical thread that she hesitated, and became aware again that the stoic man sitting by the window was the man she loved. When she probed for the bullet she was taking away something vile and dangerous to him; now ... she looked at the needle ... she was going to be the means of inflicting further pain.

She took a deep breath and turned back to him. He had not moved, but there was a whiteness at the corners of his mouth and the sheen of moisture glistened on his chest and shoulders. He said in a constricted voice, 'The cavity must be closed completely. Take a deep bite with the suture—no, hold it this way ... I'll try to help ... take it easy ... don't think about hurting me ...'

For a dreadful moment she thought her nerve would fail her, then he said, 'Go on,' and she noticed the slowing of his usual crisp tones. The sense of urgency came back with the thought that she might not finish before the effect of the morphia began to lessen. She took a deep breath and bent over him. 'Yes, keep telling me, please, if you can ... if I ...'

'If it helps ...' He was watching her hands, trying to guide. 'There's a diversity of opinion in field surgery; whether to leave the wound open for two or three days until it's certain it's clean ... steady ... put it down until you tie it ... the scissors ... not too close together ... the bullet itself is sterile when fired, with the heat, but it carries shreds of material as it penetrates the clothing, maybe soiled clothing, and embeds infection...' His voice ebbed away and he closed his eyes.

She reached to take the scissors he held and felt her hands beginning to tremble. The sun was pouring into the room and her shirt was sticking to her back. But she couldn't touch anything ... She looked at him and said in a whisper, 'Are you all right?'

His eyes opened. They had a strange heaviness about them, and his breathing was rapid. He nodded, one small inclination of his head, and she licked dry lips. 'I—can you bear it? This is the last one.'

'Go on.'

He turned his head away and she made the final stitch. Carefully she tied it and snipped the two ends of thread. She took the pack of dry dressing which lay ready and said, 'Do you want to—to check before I put this on?'

'No.' His mouth clamped shut on the negative, and she laid the dressing in place and secured it with strips of adhesive tape. He was bathed now in perspiration and she took a towel and gently wiped at his face and shoulders.

'You'd better lie down,' she said in a thin voice. 'Come on.'

She put an anxious hand under his uninjured arm as he took the two steps to the bed and sank down. She said, 'Can I go in your things to find you a clean shirt?'

He nodded, and she turned to the door, becoming aware for the first time of the silent Father Lorenzo who had remained there motionless.

The priest said, 'You are both very brave—I wish I could do more to help. Stay with him, my child, I will bring anything you want, then perhaps I can be more useful and make you a very strong cup of tea.'

'Oh yes, *please*,' she whispered.

When he had gone she looked worriedly at Max, terrified in case something had gone wrong, that she had made an unholy botch of everything, made him worse instead of...

He must have sensed her approach, for his eyes flickered open and the heaviness and unnatural brightness was still in them. She said, 'Father Lorenzo is bringing some tea.'

He did not respond and she knew a desperate need to hear his voice. She glanced at the untidy array of surgical stuff and gestured. 'What should I do with this? The forceps and things should be sterilized, shouldn't they, before I put them away?'

'Just leave them for the moment.'

'Yes.' She hovered, indecisive, sure that she should cover him, despite the fact that the room was hot. But he was lying on top of the blankets and she did not want to ask him to move. There was nothing to hand except the large worn old towel. After another hesitation she put it over him as a temporary measure, then remembered something else.

She turned to the medical case and opened the drug compartment, seeking the antibiotic capsules. At first she couldn't see them and gave a small exclamation of dismay. They had used quite a lot, for Azzuni, and Jonathan had suffered an insect sting which had turned poisonous, all of which had made inroads into the supplies. Then she found a phial with about a dozen of the familiar red and black capsules. She poured some water into a glass and touched him gently, holding out the tablets.

'I don't know the dosage. How many?'

He said, 'Must I?'

'I think so.' She shook two out into her palm, then remembered something he had once said and withdrew her hand. 'Are you allergic to these?'

'Not as far as I know.'

She returned the one he left to the phial and retrieved the cap. Suddenly it seemed inordinately difficult to replace and he seemed to be taking a long time to drink the water. She put the phial on the table and rested her hands on it, conscious of the onset of reaction now that it was over. Perspiration was breaking out on her brow and a tightness was pressing in her ears. Abruptly she sat down on the edge of the bed, taking a deep breath and trying to ride the sudden wave of clammy weakness. From the corner of her eye she was dimly aware of Max's hand holding out the glass, but if her life depended on it she dared not move to turn and take it from him. Suddenly the glass went down to the floor through a green haze of sparkles and overturned. The water trickled along towards her foot and a hand gripped her arm. From a long way away a voice said, 'Put your head down to your knees.'

Fighting the faintness, she obeyed, only the fingers holding her arm were preventing her toppling down into that smothering, hissing cloud of green cottonwool.

The blurred voice said, 'It's all right. It'll pass.'

Ages later, it seemed, the hissing subsided and the green clamminess dissolved. The room didn't swim so wildly at the slightest movement, and she was able to straighten slowly. She sighed and rubbed her brow. 'Sorry,' she said shakily. 'That isn't much use, is it?'

She made to stand up and his grasp slackened. 'Sit still.'

The realization that he was getting to his feet at the other side of the bed brought alarm that shocked her back to full consciousness. 'No!' she cried. 'You mustn't——'

'I only wanted this.' One arm hanging limp, he flopped back again and applied his teeth to the brandy flask he'd taken from the medical case. 'Here, get some of this down you. I'm not surprised that you feel dicky. That must have been quite an ordeal.'

'It must have been a worse ordeal for you.' She sipped a little of the spirit and was instantly conscious of its reviving warmth. 'Thanks—I would make an idiot of myself.'

He took the flask from her and sought for the cap.

'Here, let me do that. I'm better now.' But she wasn't quite as all right as she assumed. Her hands had lost their steadiness and the thread crossed as she tried to screw on the tightly fitting cap. Impatiently she struggled with it, and he sighed: 'Relax—leave it. Leave everything.' He lay back against the pillow and closed his eyes. 'It's all over.'

She stared at the window and her eyes blurred. 'I know. Oh, that's just it. I'm just waking up from a nightmare and it was awful.' To her dismay the words were bursting from her and the sick shaking was pervading her whole body. 'I don't know how you stood it, how you could let me do all that without—without making a sound. I tried to tell myself I was taking a very large splinter out of you, but it was the stitching,' she cried. 'I didn't even know how to tie the right knot, or—or—and everything felt dirty. Everything should have been sterile and—and I don't know if I scrubbed my hands enough, and—Oh, Max, it was awful, and you might have died. If it hadn't been for that case in your pocket and—— Oh, Max, is it going to be all right? Are you sure you——?'

She put her hands to her face and turned away, overcome by the storm of pent-up emotion and striving to choke it down. 'I'm sorry,' she sobbed, 'I didn't mean to—I'm making it all worse, and you——'

'No. No. Oh, Gail ...' He sighed and held out his arm. 'Come here. What is there to be sorry about? It's over.'

He looked at the downbent head and sighed again, raising himself awkwardly and drawing her towards him. 'Come on, little one,' he drew her head unresistingly against his shoulder and held it there. 'Get it out of your system and you'll feel better.'

'You shouldn't,' she sobbed, 'you shouldn't be moving, in case it—it doesn't heal. In case the——'

'They won't. And tomorrow we'll both be on top of the world. It'll be all right...' He stroked her hair, and touched the trembling shoulders. 'It's all right,' he repeated.

The sudden tenderness was too much. All the frustration and anxiety and strain leading up to that moment had gathered into a great tight lump inside her that clamoured for release and she wept as she had not wept since she was a small child.

Until at last she found release and a strange empty weakness. She stirred and looked at him with troubled eyes, and the tiredness in his face struck fresh sorrow in her heart.

'I'm sorry,' she said in a small ashamed voice.

'Why?' he said gently. 'It's a natural reaction.'

'I suppose so, but ...'

He touched her cheek where it was still moist and made a small negative movement. 'This is the first time you've ever experienced violence at first hand. Meeting it in reality is a far cry from watching it from the comfort of an armchair, where the flick of a switch can restore you instantly to your safe and familiar surroundings. I don't suppose you've ever handled a gun in your life, let alone faced a man armed with one.' He paused, then added quietly, 'I think you've been wonderful.'

There was a sweet sincerity in the words that almost precipitated another breakdown. Praise was the last thing she had ever expected to hear from Max Christiern. But a new humility was being born in her and she shook her head.

'No, I haven't,' she said flatly. 'I've just realized how unthinking and selfish and frivolous I've been all my life, and how much I've taken for granted.'

'Conscience?' He sighed. 'It's a common reaction when danger is past. You've hardly begun to live your life. What are you? Eighteen ... nineteen ... ?'

'Nearly twenty—and you're not going to talk any more.' She drew back and regarded him with a sober gaze. 'I know you're very strong, and very courageous, and the last person you ever worry about is yourself, but there are limits. When the effects of that morphia wear off you're going to feel pretty sore for a while, so you must rest.'

'Must I?'

Faint amusement came into his expression.

'Yes,' she stood up, 'I'm going to see if there's any sign of that tea Father Lorenzo promised us, and then you must sleep.'

He nodded, and she reflected that it was probably the only occasion she was ever likely to see Max Christiern subdued. He said drowsily: 'I don't want any tea or any food, but I wish you'd do something ...'

'Just tell me.'

'See what happened to that bag with the relics ... and see if Harmon's all right.'

'I will,' she promised, and saw his tired eyes close.

She sat for a little while, watching the shallow rise and fall of his breathing become deeper, and turned her head as the priest came into the room. She made soundless motions towards the tray he brought, and he put it down, to come and look over her shoulder at the sleeping man. At last Father Lorenzo touched her shoulder. He said softly, 'I think you have much love in your heart, my child. Why hide it?'

She whispered, 'I must.'

He sighed, his eyes wise and compassionate. 'One of the great sadnesses of human nature. So often we have great love for another and are afraid to show it. Never be afraid to show love, or give it, my dear. It is humanity's greatest gift.'

She looked down on Max and experienced a longing to touch and smooth out the lines of pain in the tired features. She said slowly, 'I know, but sometimes the gift of love is not wanted, Father. Not from a woman to a man.'

'That is not the love I was speaking of, my child, but very often it is difficult to distinguish between the two. But you need not fear with this man. I know he is good.'

'Yes, I know.'

Father Lorenzo sighed. He laid his hand on her head and involuntarily she closed her eyes. She could grasp at his meaning but knew in her heart that she could never betray this love, or bring its gift where it was unasked.

The light touch on her head was raised and there was only the slight rustle of the old priest's soutane as he went from the room, leaving Gail to her lonely vigil.

* * *

Max was still asleep when she returned to him some time later, and she did not disturb him to tell him that everything was under control. The relics were still safe in the haversack under the living-room where their stuff had been thrust when they returned, and Harmon was in the small room off the back of the house. When she went to see how Harmon was recovering he turned away from her enquiry and muttered in a surly voice, 'Leave me alone.'

She frowned, uneasy, and asked, 'Is there anything you want? Some tablets ... if your head aches ... a cup of tea and something to eat ... ?'

'Go to hell.'

She sighed. He could blame only himself for his troubles, but she no longer felt indifferent to his welfare. However, there seemed little she could do while he was in this mood. She looked in again on Max, then went into the living-room, sitting there for a while and talking quietly to Father Lorenzo. The mission house was quiet and peaceful, and gradually her sense of strain began to ease. Presently the priest said he must return to his work and suggested that she should rest for an hour or so.

She shook her head. 'I couldn't rest. And there are several jobs I want to do.'

'As you wish, my child. Would you like me to bring our nurse back with me? If you are worried about your patient, and this other man . . . perhaps she could be of help.'

'Thank you, I'm sure she would, but I think I can manage.' She smiled, unable to tell him that she couldn't bear the thought of anyone but herself caring for Max. 'It's very kind of you,' she added, 'but I think the worst's over.'

'I sincerely hope so.' He put his hand on her head and regarded her with wise old eyes. 'I shall leave Jimo here. You can trust him absolutely, and if anything occurs to worry you, you need only call. But I won't be away very long.'

When he had gone she smoked a cigarette and then cleared away the dishes before she set to work purposefully. The opportunity of washing her hair was too good to miss, and while it dried she carried the relics into the room where Max still slept and quietly concealed them. The Browning was also taken gingerly and concealed, and that done she turned to more personal matters. Limited wardrobes did not permit any let-up in the laundering chore, and there were two somewhat gory shirts in need of attention. When Max awoke he would be hungry—at least she hoped he would be hungry—and Father Lorenzo had said he wouldn't be away a great length of time . . .

It was a full and busy afternoon, and it served to keep her thoughts from dwelling too much on the shock of the morning and worrying vainly round the vicious circle of a message getting through, the rescue of her uncle, and the fear of any ill-effects Max might suffer. It also served to work off a certain surge of restless energy that masked physical tiredness and made it impossible for her to relax.

The violet shadows lengthened across the compound as she stirred and concocted at the stove. Jimo sat stolidly on the veranda steps, his jaws moving steadily and rhythmically while he stared towards the river, and Gail felt strangely happy. For a brief interlude they had ceased to chase events—or events had ceased to chase them—and between herself and Max there was a truce both tender and infinitely heartwarming. For a little while at least she could be near and cherish him, and for a little while he couldn't argue. For the moment she did not want to look ahead...

He was awake when she took him the meal she had prepared so lovingly, and the heaviness was leaving his eyes.

'How do you feel now?' she asked.

'On top of the world, nurse.'

'Oh.' She did not quite believe that, and she was glad she had arranged his food so that it could be eaten with one hand. The left arm was obviously causing him pain when he tried to move it, and at last she said impatiently, 'Listen, for goodness' sake, ask me instead of trying to be independent. That's what I'm here for.'

'I just want my shirt and shaving tackle,' he said, sitting back while she sorted through his kit for the desired articles.

'You could grow a beard—at least until tomorrow.'

'I dislike being unshaven—and there are certain things you can't help with. Shaving is one of them.'

She made a face of derision. 'That's kid's stuff to me now.'

'No doubt—tilt the mirror a bit this way.' Over the top of it he caught her glance and his mouth compressed slightly at the corners. 'Oh yes, I'm well aware the wheel's come full circle.'

'What do you mean by that?'

'This morning you—— Ouch!' He grimaced, and she dropped the mirror.

'What's the matter?' she exclaimed anxiously.

'Nothing—just your knitting work straining at the seams.' He picked up the razor and resumed shaving, more cautiously this time, and she relaxed again. 'There,' he mopped his face and ran testing fingers round his chin, 'that's better, but not much. Now, as you once announced rashly that you'd make a very good slave girl, could you get those lamps going? Before the light vanishes?'

'Yes, of course—Master.' Secretly delighted, she investigated the two oil lamps which stood on the old-fashioned chest in a corner of the room. 'I think they want filling. I'll ask Father——' She stopped as Father Lorenzo tapped briefly and pushed open the door. Her smile died as she saw his face.

He said, 'Forgive me, but I think you'd better come—this man Harmon, I think he is very ill.'

'Oh no!' Gail's hand went to her throat. 'I was talking to him less than an hour ago—just before you came back—and he was quite lucid. I took him some food and he ate some. I thought——'

'I'll take a look.' Max brushed past, and after a momentary hesitation she followed.

At first sight Harmon frightened. His teeth chattered, he shivered so violently from head to foot it was difficult to steady him long enough to check his temperature, and his pulse raced like a millstream.

'It's malaria,' Max said.

They heaped blankets over him and got the chloroquine tablets into him, then Max sat down, his expression uneasy.

Gail said, 'Is it very dangerous?'

He did not reply immediately, then he shrugged. 'You can't lay down any hard and fast rule in medicine. There are too many factors to consider. If it runs to course he'll turn feverish—high temperature, sweating, maybe delirium—then it'll settle for a day, maybe two, and the cycle starts again, shivering, and so on, until the attack passes. But that blow on the head worries me...'

After a long while she looked up. 'You should be resting.'

'I'm okay.'

She sighed, privately of the opinion he was anything but 'okay' but knowing it was useless to say so. She made tea, and rejoined him. Some time later Max said, 'The shivering's passing. Can you keep his head steady? I want to examine his eyes.'

She did as he instructed and waited expectantly when he straightened, but he made no comment, except to sit down again and say, 'Why don't you turn in? There's little you can do.'

'No. I'll stay here.'

'It's very late.'

'It doesn't matter.'

He glanced at her. 'Why, for heaven's sake? You must be tired.'

She shrugged, turning away from a certain intentness in his gaze. 'Shall we say—the old buddy system.'

There was no reply, and when she eventually looked up he was watching Harmon...

All that night they alternated between long silences and spells of desultory conversation. They talked of the Valley, the Secret People, the invasion that would be inevitable now...

'They'll come from all over the world,' she said sadly. 'They'll bring their cameras, their scientists, their historians and archaeologists, and they'll probe and analyse. There'll be no end to it, and the Valley won't be secret any more.'

'Time can't stand still, Gail,' he said quietly.

'Sometimes I wish it could.' She shivered a little, was silent, staring at the soft glow of the lamp. 'Max, will you go back to the Valley, later, when it's all different?'

'I may...' He shifted, groping awkwardly for cigarettes and

lighting one. 'What are you going to do with yourself when it's all over?'

'I don't know.' She considered the question seriously, even though she knew it had been idly uttered. 'I feel torn. As though I'd lived a lifetime during these last few weeks. Now'—she sighed—'I can't imagine going home and settling down to some job, and—— Even though I desperately want to see my father again, I don't want to go back. I'—she shook her head—'I don't know . . .'

'It feels like that now; it'll be different later.'

'Maybe . . . I can't imagine it.'

'It will,' he said flatly. 'You'll have so much to remember, to tell your father. You'll soon settle down—and put Roger out of his misery.'

'Roger?' She was startled out of the half-asleep musing state. 'Yes, Roger . . . I've done that already. It isn't just that. It's the dreadful feeling that I'll never come back, never see the Valley again. There's been something about this journey, something about it all . . . nothing will ever be the same again,' she said sadly.

'How can it?' He touched her shoulder. 'Go to bed, there's a good girl.'

Too weary now to argue, she went, to stretch out and close her eyes and fall into a deep dreamless sleep as the first rays of the morning sunrise stole across the skies.

She missed the ugly, panic-stricken outburst of Harmon when he returned to lucidity during that morning, and perhaps it was just as well she was not present when a weary Max Christiern was able to reassure a frightened, impenitent man that he wasn't going to die.

When she awakened at noon Harmon was dozing peacefully and the Indian woman who helped Father Lorenzo had arrived. The priest said: 'Do not worry—she knows what to do when his fever flares again, and soon we will hear from the authorities. Then all your worries will be over, my child.'

She smiled, but it was without joy. The hours were running out now; it was difficult to believe that the three days since they sent the message were almost past. Yes, it was almost over. It was only a matter of waiting, waiting for the arrival of the 'chopper' Max had requested, then a brief return to the Valley to restore their belongings to the Secret People and bring out the anxious men who waited there. Then back to Lima, treatment for her uncle and retribution for Harmon . . . and then there would be nothing, except to say goodbye . . .

Like a lost soul she wandered around during the long hours

of that hot, airless afternoon, her glance constantly returning to the sky in search of a distant speck, wanting, yet not wanting to see it gradually enlarge and take shape.

But it did not appear and at sundown, guiltily aware of a sense of reprieve, she was leaning on the rail of the compound, staring at the waters and that dark cavern under the hill that engorged them. Here she had fought one of her many battles with Max Christiern, and believed she had won. Her mouth curved bitterly; maybe she had, but it had been a small victory compared to the one he had finally won, unknowingly. She turned away and saw Father Lorenzo hurrying across the compound.

She went to meet him, instantly wary with the unease that had become second nature during the past few days. 'Is anything wrong?' she asked. 'Is——'

'All right, my dear,' he said hastily, 'all is well, but I must go to the village. I'm needed there.'

'Is it anything we can help with?' she asked. 'We still have drugs, medicine some dressings ... if it's sickness.'

'It is beyond the need for that, my child, but bless you for your thought.'

Suddenly the weariness dragged at her spirit and she went slowly back to the mission. It was silent within and she began to fill the lamps ready for the long night. She wondered if Max had wakened and gone out and was tempted to find out, but she resisted the desire; through Harmon he had gone almost twenty-four hours without sleep, at a time when he was least fitted to spare it, and for a man who had almost cost him his life.

The Indian woman came into the living-room and began to busy herself at the stove. Although she greeted Gail with the withdrawn, almost wary politeness Gail had noticed in several of Father Lorenzo's 'flock' there was a certain possessiveness in the way she moved about the mission house. So long as Gail remained a guest all was well, but if Gail stepped over that invisible boundary on to the Indian woman's reserve ...

Gail withdrew and hovered indecisively for a moment before she tapped very softly on the half-open door of the little side room. There was no response and she pushed the door open and looked in. Max was still asleep, one arm curved over the wound, and she wondered if it still caused a great deal of pain. She opened her lips to call him, then closed them without making the sound. He had asked to be called at sundown, or the moment anything untoward occurred, but she was reluctant to stir him. On silent steps she let compulsion take her to his side to look down on the features on which sleep had softened the stern lines and left them curiously vulnerable.

The longing for a small physical contact was suddenly overwhelming. She watched the slow, even rise and fall of his breathing and very slowly stooped over him until she could almost touch his brow with her lips. Abruptly sanity returned and she jerked upright, aghast at her foolish tenderness, then she saw to her horror that his eyes were open, unblinking, watching her put her hand to her face. His expression did not flicker.

'Well, go on. Finish what you started.'

'F-finish what? I—I just came to wake you. You said you——' She could not sustain meeting that gaze and turned, making a pretence of adjusting the lamp. 'Shall I light it?'

'No.' He reached out and his hand closed round her wrist. 'You were going to kiss me. Was it just the eternal nurse that's in all women? A little gentle comfort during the dark hours?'

'N-no, of course not. I told you——'

'Then what was it, if not the desire to comfort? Or do you always deny your desires?'

'Most of us have to in this life,' she said with a trace of bitterness, 'or haven't you discovered that yet?' The alarm bells were ringing now and she desperately wanted to pull away, but some instinct was warning her not to try. She made an attempt to be casual and glanced at him. 'You must have been dreaming.'

'I never dream.'

'Well, the dark hours are over now—I hope.'

'And one thing I have discovered,' he went on as though she had not spoken, 'you didn't have so many reservations the night you first discovered how dark and lonely the hours can be.'

She gasped, and her mouth worked tremulously. She said in a choked whisper, 'Do you have to remind me of that? If I remember rightly, you didn't have so many reservations yourself.'

'Why should I?' He turned his head away as though weary and the grip slackened on her wrist. 'I'm not immune to darkness and loneliness and weariness any more than the next man. You're young and warm and vital, and there's a certain ardent quality about you in everything you do that would evoke response in less vulnerable men than me. Even though you're still groping and experimenting with human relationships, and as stubborn and self-willed as a child.'

She took a deep breath. 'You mean, don't you, that any woman would evoke response in you, given the same set of circumstances, as long as she was young and warm and—and foolish enough.'

'I didn't say that.' His voice hardened. 'But I don't like being played with by sentimental little girls who start something

they're frightened to finish.'

He moved suddenly, and with deceptive speed his hand shot out and fastened round her arm, pulling her off-balance so that she sprawled across him. He twisted over, pinning her down, and bent over her, surveying her with dark-shadowed eyes.

'I never cared for half measures,' he said, then brought his mouth down on hers, hard.

Gail had no standard of experience by which to measure a man's passion. There had been tentative adolescent kisses, as clumsy as her own, and Roger's boyish efforts to rouse her to acknowledgement of his affection, and the only other kiss she had known from Max, a kiss that had been tender even as it was fierce with despair and exasperation, but none of them had taken her mouth with the sheer male demand Max was making at this moment, and none of them had prepared her for the hard bruising strength of a man's body when he chooses to dominate.

She cried silently against his mouth, and struggled, because she wanted tenderness and words of love, and it seemed he had no tenderness or words of love to give her, and suddenly, with almost brutal repulsion, she was freed. He twisted away.

'Forget it,' he said thickly. 'Go on, go back to England with your tame little crew of men, and your anaemic little yes-no affair with Roger. And then grow up.'

The silence which followed was fraught with bitterness and the painful hurt of disillusion. Her head throbbed with the emotion of shocked senses and it seemed that all the misery of a lifetime was concentrated in the space between herself and the man who sat with hunched shoulders turned coldly towards her. The last of the day's light was fading from the room and the outline of his head dimmed to a dark shadow.

And then the darkness became a blessing, cloaking her distress and the tremulous effort to regain control before she could say vehemently, 'Oh yes, I will. *I most certainly will*!' and rush from the room, as though in headlong flight she could leave not only his presence but all the heartbreak he had brought into her world.

CHAPTER XII

Lima,
Thursday 14th

'...just a postscript to the letter I started last night. Uncle Phil has decided to leave on the Sunday flight—his foot is mending nicely—so we may be home before this letter. So it is all over now. We've been back in Lima a week and already the expedition seems like a dream—but poor Don Felipe doesn't think so! His phone never stops ringing. Two historians have just flown in from New York this morning, and some film people landed as well. I'm sure Don Felipe will heave a sigh of relief when he sees the back of us!

'By the way, I forgot to say thank you for your letters—it was so comforting to find them waiting when we got back—it suddenly made me homesick. Oh, Daddy, I'm longing to see you again, it's all been tremendously exciting and I wouldn't have missed it for the world, but...

'Yes, the men all got along very well with Max C.

'This p.s. is turning into another letter. I keep remembering things I've missed out. We still haven't got over the biggest shock of all; finding that Harmon wasn't Harmon at all. When the helicopter arrived at the mission that morning and this tall man got out with the pilot and the police chief and said he'd caught up with us at last we thought he was joking. But no. His cable had chased us as far as Huamano and stuck there. It seems that the crooked Harmon knew him years ago, and came to him with a hard luck story a couple of weeks before the expedition started. I'd better explain that the real Harmon is tall and husky and Texan, with a lopsided smile and a handshake that leaves you paralysed for a couple of hours, and everybody calls him Tex. Anyway, Tex took pity on the bogus Harmon and gave him a couple of assignments, after which Harmon just lighted out, and about the same time Lealholme-Crosse shifted another job on to Tex and he had to postpone his schedule on our job. So he sent us a cable, but it didn't reach us in time—missed us by a few hours—and of course when the other Harmon met us at the airport none of us had ever met him or Tex and we just took him as genuine. And to think I was the only one who had a hunch he was shady, and nobody would listen to me. Especially Max C.

'So we found the Flower, and the Valley, and the Secret People, and——'

'Gail! are you still scribbling? We're going to the beach. Coming?'

'No, thanks.' She shook her head. 'Count me out.'

'But why not?' Jonathan squatted at one side of her deck chair and Clive squatted by the other. 'What's the matter? You've just mooned around the villa all this week. What's the attraction?'

'There isn't any attraction.' Her mouth set and she stared unblinkingly at the placid blue of the pool. 'I just don't want to go to the beach this afternoon, that's all.'

'Yes, but . . .' Jonathan rested his arms across her knees and peered up into her face, his head tilted on one side. 'You didn't want to go for English tea yesterday at the Hotel Bolivar, and you didn't want to go to Pachacamac on Tuesday, and we just managed to drag you to the Country Club on Monday and you sat all night glowering at us, and then wanted to come home the minute Max turned up with that professor from the University. Isn't that right, Clive?'

'That's right,' Clive said solemnly.

'Well'—Jonathan gestured—'we've only got another couple of days to paint Lima red.'

'You can paint it red or any colour you like—without me,' she said stubbornly.

'But we're all going,' Jonathan persisted. 'We're going to try our hand at surfing. Max and Tex are going to meet us there. It'll be super.'

'No.'

Jonathan looked at Clive, and Clive shook his head. 'Never argue with a lady, sonny boy. You can't win.'

Jonathan stood up, looked puzzled, then said, 'Have you got a headache, or something?'

'No, but I will have soon,' she said pointedly.

He flushed, and she felt a pang as he turned away. She sighed when they had gone and wondered despondently how she was going to fill in the afternoon. She would have liked to try her skill—or lack of it—at the exciting Hawaiian surfing down at the beach club, but not if Max Christiern was going to be there. The memories of Max were too raw still to allow indulgence in sociality in his company. And judging by the coldness of his manner the two occasions she hadn't been able to avoid being in the same room with him he had no more desire for any resumption of friendly relations than she had.

She finished the letter to her father and decided to go for an hour of so of window shopping. For a little while she found forgetfulness and made an impulse buy of a lemon voile dress, then admired the real baby llama at the shop which sold skins and pottery and silver work, and sat for a little while watching the people go by on the San Martin Plaza before she made her way back to the villa.

The others had not returned and there was no sign of their host. She tried on the new dress, and turned away impatiently from the sad-eyed girl who contrasted unfavourably with the fresh cool attractiveness of pale lemon voile. Despondently she took it off and donned her bikini.

She was climbing out of the pool when they returned, tousle-haired and full of noisy animation over their afternoon of sea sport. Jonathan and Clive turned and came across the terrace the moment they saw her, while Professor Denning, jovial despite his limp, called jokingly that he'd caught an anchovy as he moved indoors with Roger at his side.

Only Max remained standing at the end of the terrace, and for a heart-stopping moment she thought he was going to follow Clive and Jonathan. He did take a step forward, then glanced at his watch and hesitated, his unsmiling glance on her, and swung round abruptly to follow her uncle into the villa.

For a moment she was back in time to that morning a week ago, the morning after the bitter scene in which her tender dreams and illusions had finally withered, looking at Max Christiern as he prepared to board the small reconnaissance helicopter to return to the Valley. Neither of them had faced one another that miserable morning, until that moment when the sudden commotion came as they finished breakfast and Max's chair went back with a clatter. There had been a lot to say, to the pilot who had searched for their location all the previous afternoon, and to the man who had proved to be Tex Harmon.

It had been easy to avoid direct confrontation with him during the excitement, to withdraw as he said, 'Well, shall we get going?' and they moved towards the great metal insect that dwarfed the compound. And then, then she least expected it, he had turned at the last moment, when the rotor blades were beginning to spin, and called, 'Well, aren't you coming with us?'

She had shaken her head and walked, chin high, into the mission, to wait. Less than five hours later she was reunited with the men, and at sundown that evening, unbelievably, they were walking into the villa, to the triumphal celebration Don Felipe had prepared.

'Gail! Are you asleep or something?'

The face before her eyes dissolved, from the one unforgettable unity of eyes and mouth and nose and chin, into the youthful face on which life had not yet printed its full maturity, and she saw Jonathan's teasing grin widen as he snapped his fingers.

'She's in one of her trances, Clive.'

'Better wake her, then.' Clive strolled away, whistling, and Gail forced herself back to the present. 'Sorry, I was miles—Oh! *No*——!'

She ducked away from the shower of water Jonathan had scooped up and over her. Jonathan, ready as ever for horseplay, assumed this was the cue for pursuit and seized her round the waist, with the obvious intention of depositing her in the pool.

'No—leave me alone!' There was a very brief skirmish and a resounding slap, and Jonathan raised his hand to his face, his laughter transformed abruptly into bewilderment.

Gail took a step back and her face crumpled with anguish. She hadn't meant ... An incoherent murmur escaped her and suddenly she couldn't bear Jonathan's hurt, accusing gaze. 'I—I'm sorry, I——' she mumbled. 'I didn't mean to——' The blue sparkles on the water swam in a haze, and she ran with down-bent head along the terrace, full tilt into Clive.

'Steady. Steady!' He caught her by the shoulders and held her firmly. 'What's all this——?'

'But I didn't do anything. I just ... and she——' Jonathan loomed indignantly, his voice tailing off as he met Clive's glance over Gail's head.

'She's having one of her off days.' Clive enfolded her close and added warningly, 'It's time you learned not to tease girls when the storm signals fly. Now run along.' He patted her shoulder while poor Jonathan retreated in bewilderment, and presently she sniffed and took her woebegone face away from Clive's shoulder.

'I'm sorry. I—I don't know what came over me. I—I didn't mean to——'

'These things happen.' Clive kept one arm round her shoulders and led her along the terrace to the little curved part overlooking the arbour. 'But it isn't poor old Jonny's fault that you've fallen out with our mettlesome Max.'

'Oh no!' She couldn't repress the exclamation.

'Oh yes,' he said softly. 'You've been too quiet this week. It doesn't take much adding up. You left us in the Valley and in spite of everything that had happened there were stars in your eyes. But I had a feeling you might come to blows, all the same. You were on your own with him for the best part of a week, without a referee.' He leaned over the parapet and pulled at a big pink blossom, turning and tucking it into her hair. His eyes whimsical, he said slowly: 'I suppose it was inevitable. To any woman, Max Christiern must present an irresistible challenge. Why couldn't you pick a ready tamed one, like one of us?'

Clive could not know how poignantly ill-chosen was his choice of words. She said in a choked voice, 'You've got it all wrong, you know.'

'I wish I had. Then why did the temperature drop at least ten degrees when he walked into the club on Monday night? And why did you dodge him yesterday morning, and this afternoon? Gail, honey, let me tell you something.' He paused and took the flower her restless fingers were shredding to bruised tendrils. 'There are four ages of weeping in a woman's life. They begin by weeping for their mothers when four-year-old Tommy down the street pulls their hair. Later, they weep for their own children. Later still, they weep for their lost youth. But at your age, honey-girl, they weep for a man when he hurts them. Is it as bad as all that?'

She nodded, and he squeezed her shoulder gently. 'It won't always hurt, my pet, even though it seems like the end of the world just now. Men don't consciously try to hurt a girl, but sometimes it's inevitable. You in your turn didn't want to hurt Roger, but it was impossible to avoid doing so. You can't make another person happy at the expense of your own happiness. That way it ends in misery all round. But it's harder for a woman because convention says she shouldn't ask a man for his love, as the man is free to ask a woman. So the man remains in ignorance, unaware of how she feels, while the woman has to wait and wonder and long for him in silence. Until eventually it dawns on the brute,' he added wryly.

'If it ever does.'

'If it ever does,' he said sadly. 'It doesn't seem fair, somehow.'

She sighed and stayed silent. There was warmth and comfort within Clive's protective arm, and his understanding was bringing the first grain of healing to her sore heart. Somehow, it made it easier to know that there was at least one person with whom she didn't have to go on pretending that she hadn't a care in the world. Most of all, she was thankful it was Clive.

'Now'—he turned her gently and tweaked her shin—'it's time you went in and got some clothes on—you'll turn chilly now the sun's gone. And this evening we'll——'

He broke off, giving a small exclamation, and his glance went upwards, over her head.

Max Christiern said, 'Excuse me. I—— No, Gail, don't go away. It's you I want to see.'

Her face shuttered and unfriendly, she turned round, backing close to Clive as she said, 'Well . . . ?'

He said coldly, 'I can see this isn't the right moment for surprises. Your father's coming.'

'*What?*' Shock wiped away the careful composing of her expression. 'My father?'

'He's arriving tonight.' Max gave a brusque gesture. 'It was to be a surprise, but the explanations will have to wait. Do you want to meet him at the airport?'

'Yes, of course.' She was still flabbergasted. 'But how . . . when . . . Clive'—she spun round—'you didn't tell me. Why didn't——'

'But, honey,' he began, 'I'm as foxed as——'

'When?' she demanded, swinging to face Max again. 'What time?'

'Almost immediately. You'd better hurry.'

'Yes—oh help, I'm still—— Clive, are you coming to the airport?'

'Sure thing. This is wonderful news. We'd better round up the others and——'

'Give me ten minutes,' she begged, 'and don't dare go without me, do you hear?'

Her thoughts in a whirl, she rushed into the villa and took the stairs two at a time. After the quickest shower on record she put on the new voile dress and feverishly dabbed on a touch of make-up. She couldn't believe it. Her father coming. Tonight. It was the most wonderful news ever. But why hadn't he told her? Nobody had breathed a word. Had they known? A surprise, Max had said . . . It certainly was a surprise.

It would have to be Max . . . She checked quickly at the mirror, the thought momentarily dimming the wild rose of exhilaration the news had induced. Then she thought of the other most obvious angle; if her father was flying out it meant he must be greatly recovered. It meant . . . but she had to hurry.

Her uncle was in the *sala* talking to Don Felipe when she went downstairs. At her enquiry, he shook his head. 'Someone must remain to make the welcome here. Now hurry, my dear, I think they're waiting for you outside.'

Don Felipe's big saloon stood out on the wide curving driveway, and in front of it was the long gleaming white Oldsmobile which belonged to Max. He stepped out of the shadows so silently she jumped.

'Where's Clive?' she asked. 'And Jonny?'

'They're coming.' His tone was cool. He opened the passenger door, and after a momentary hesitation she slid into the cool, leathery-smelling interior. He closed the door and walked round the front of the car and got into the driving seat. The lights sprang out across the bank of oleanders and the engine purred to deep-throated life at the touch of the starter.

She sat up sharply. 'Aren't you waiting for them?'

'No.' The car swished softly down the slight incline and out of the gateway. 'They can follow.'

Gail sank back uneasily. This wasn't how she had planned it. She said, 'I don't understand. Why didn't somebody tell me this was being arranged? It is true, isn't it? My father *is* arriving tonight?'

'Do you think I'm lying to you?'

'No, but...' she gestured helplessly, 'it seems so——' Another thought occurred and she turned in alarm. 'But we're going back on Sunday! Uncle Phil arranged it all today. Surely Daddy isn't coming just for two——'

'It was your father's idea,' Max interrupted calmly. 'I telephoned your father the night we got back. I wanted to——'

'Why didn't you tell me? I——'

'I was going to tell you. Will you hear me out?' A hint of the impatience with which she was all too familiar crept into his tone. 'I decided to telephone him because I thought he should be told the moment we'd got back and were able to contact him. After all, he of all people was entitled to hear our news. I had planned to book a call for you, so that you could talk to him yourself, but during the course of our conversation a somewhat different plan transpired. Your father, feeling completely recovered from the heart attack which prevented him coming with us at the start, suddenly decided to fly out as soon as he could make the necessary arrangements. I am beginning to see who you take after, incidentally,' Max interjected. 'He asked me to keep quiet about the plan, in case anything prevented him fulfilling it, and then give you a surprise when it was all fixed. I merely carried out his orders, and I didn't tell the others as I had a hunch they wouldn't be able to resist telling you.'

'I see,' she said bitterly, 'so you waited until the very last minute. If I'd known a bit sooner I could have arranged to borrow a projector so that he could see the films straight away, and——'

'It's all in hand,' he said, his tone calm again. 'We're taking your father to the Valley next week. We'll probably stay there for two or three weeks, possibly longer. Then——'

'But...' Gail was trying to comprehend all this and dovetail it into the line of action to which she was geared. 'What's going to happen? We can't go home and leave him here,' she said wildly. 'We're booked on the flight, and—and my visa's almost up.'

'Your uncle and Roger and Jonathan are going home as planned,' Max told her. 'Clive is staying here. As for your visa, that can be arranged without undue difficulty. That is, presuming you wish to stay on, and go back to the Valley.'

Go back to the Valley! Gail stared unseeingly at the highway racing to meet the headlights and did not know whether it was ecstasy or dismay making her head spin. To see her father, and show him all their discoveries, meet Azzuni and Aumya again, explore those fabulous garden terraces by the temple, see the harvest of the Flower and the Secret People at work in the vast hall where they processed the plant by their ancient recipes. But could she bear it all if Max was so near . . . ?

A sudden slewing of the car brought her out of the daydream. She turned sharply. 'Is this the way to the airport? You've passed it, Max. This is the coast——'

'Don't panic. We'll be there on time.'

'I hope so.' Another thought occurred. 'What time is his flight due in?'

'Not for another hour.'

'Another hour?' she echoed. 'Then we could have waited for Clive and——' The car jerked to a halt so abruptly she was thrown forward. Max switched off the engine and slewed to face her.

He said, 'I want to know what all that was about, back at the villa.'

'What all what was about?' She would not turn her head.

'Why were you weeping?'

'I—I wasn't weeping. And if I was, I don't see what it has to do with you—if I wept the Pacific, it's no——'

'Yes,' his mouth tightened, 'you might well say that, after . . . But I want to know what's been eating you for the past three weeks, since long before I lost my temper last week,' he glanced at his watch, 'almost at this exact hour.'

He rested his elbow along the back of the seat and met her glance squarely. 'I want to know who it is that makes you lie like a trooper and weep like a perishing willow. Oh yes, you've wept in my arms, and you've wept in Clive Logan's. In how many more men's arms am I going to find you weeping?'

His tone held the same old impatience, the trace of harshness, and in spite of herself and all her resolution her eyes filled and she turned away.

'Oh God—no! Not again!' he groaned. 'I knew it would be hopeless. Come on. Forget I ever . . .' With the words he reached out to the starter, then exclaimed as she scrabbled wildly for the right handle which would open the door.

She was out of the car, stumbling off the road and on to the soft dry sand of the dunes. The great Pacific rollers roared down on the fringe of the beach, but she could think of nothing but escape and the agony of knowing she couldn't take another moment of the torture it meant to be near Max Christiern. The thuds of his steps overtook her and his hand shot out.

'Can't you leave me alone?' she sobbed, striving to evade him as he barred her path.

'No, I can't! That's just the trouble,' he almost shouted. 'I thought I could let you go out of my life. But I can't. Not till we straighten this thing out once and for all.'

'There's nothing to straighten out. Now take me back. We'll miss——'

'We'll miss nothing.' He caught her by the shoulders and stared down at the distracted face she was trying to hide. 'Will you tell me just who you *do* love?'

'I—I don't love anybody.'

'No?'

'No,' she said stubbornly.

'What about this business with Roger? Are you still waffling about over him, like a ship without a rudder?'

'I don't. I didn't want to hurt him. And it's no business of yours.' Her head came up, and anger sparked in her eyes. 'You told me to——'

'Yes.' His mouth came down with angry force and effectively stifled the accusation. The hard grip on her shoulders shifted to enclose her like a small stiff wand within his embrace, and he broke the kiss long enough to exclaim softly: 'Please stop fighting me for half a minute—until I can take back those words I didn't mean.' His arms gathered her closer and his kiss stilled her mouth again, deepening and demanding her response.

At last he raised his head. 'Don't dare tell me you didn't mean *that*.'

The shadowed eyes searched her face, and she looked back at the grim, unsmiling mouth as it said, 'Or that I don't mean *this*!'

When at last he did give her the chance to answer those two forceful statements she swayed unsteadily and looked fixedly at a bright cluster of stars just to the right of his shoulder. Suddenly they seemed to take on the form of a small twinkling flower, and she watched them with feverish desperation while she whispered, 'What *does* it mean, Max?'

'It means that I love you—God help me—and you, *I think*,

love me, if you only knew it.'

The five little star petals seemed to wink, then twinkle frantically, and suddenly it became of vital importance that they stayed in the flower-like illusion. She said in a low voice, 'I don't *think* I love you ...'

'Think?'

'I know.'

She bowed her head and he said with remarkable calm, 'You're sure this on–off business with Roger is really over?'

'It never really started.' Her face was now against his chest and the small shiny roundness of a shirt button was pressing into her cheek. She moved a little and touched the pearly button with her lips, aware that the world was gradually becoming a happier place than she had ever believed possible. 'Max, did you say ... that you love me?'

'I did. But I have to warn you; loving me will have to be different from the milk and water business with Roger. There's to be no not being sure of yourself or me. You either love me with all your heart or nothing. I'd rather have nothing than half measures.'

She stirred and looked at him. 'Max, please ... just for a moment ... you've always been so angry, so—so impatient. Will you try to be tender, just for a moment, till I start believing it, and——'

'My darling!' He touched her face, her brow, and his touch was the balm of ecstasy. 'I want to be tender. I want to love you. I'll give you all the gentling in the world, as long as you promise to love me for ever—and promise not to weep in anyone else's arms.'

At last she believed, could surrender to a mouth that now had the tenderness she craved, and the caresses that made everything else cease to exist outside their ardour and the man who was taking her into his sweet possession.

'Oh, Max,' she said weakly, when he let her speak, 'why, *why* didn't you tell me all this—do all this—weeks ago? At the mission, that night in the cave ... ?'

'I know. If it's any consolation I suffered just as much as you did. I suppose, compared to your own little gang, I must have seemed pretty brusque, but I kept thinking of all the things I had to weigh in the balance. You had that poor youth on a string, the entire team under your thumb, doting on you, and you didn't appear to think tuppence of me. And yet you stuck to me like a leech, and thank God you did.'

His breathing quickened against her as he cradled her head to his shoulder. 'This last week has been hell. Looking for you at every turn, listening for your voice, and then finding you weeping in Logan's arms.'

'But, my darling'—she looked up at him—'that's why I wept. Because of you, because I wanted you so much and I thought you didn't care. Half measures!' she cried. 'Are *you* sure? Don't you know I was trying to stay away from you? That sometimes I thought it must be shrieking out loud to the world, the way I felt about you. That night in the cave ... I thought you despised me, thought I was cheap.'

'No, never.' He sighed. 'I have to tell you, I did begin to wonder that night if you were attracted to me, until I thought it over and decided the circumstances were so rough they would knock any girl off balance. How could I be sure it wasn't just stress, and the fact that you'd become dependent on me? But that night was torture. I was just beginning to realize the effect you were having on me and wondering how I was going to keep my sanity until I got you back to safety. Believe me, I'd rather take on the Amazon and a tribe of head-shrinkers than go through all that again. Oh yes, I was well aware of your misery, but I was in no mood to offer the baby comfort I thought you wanted, nor'—his mouth curved wryly with recollection—'when it began to seem that baby comfort wasn't quite what you had in mind, was I prepared to offer mere sexual comfort.'

He paused. 'You can't blame me, darling. You did your best to keep that hoyden schoolgirl act going convincingly. That canoe business...' He groaned softly. 'Then, when we reached the Valley, it seemed that at last you were admitting me into the privileged circle and treating me like you treated the rest of your crew. You're quite a demonstrative girl with those you trust and who have your affection. It just didn't occur to me that you might be falling in love with me.'

The sudden glimpse of unashamed tender humility in him moved her deeply. She held him more closely and said softly, 'If only I'd known. That was the most heartbreaking part of all. Being so close to you, and that ghastly shooting ... everything conspired to make us forget the petty little pretences of civilization. There wasn't room for the ordinary conventions and pretending. With you I came closer to you than to any other man I've ever known. Those weeks could have been heaven, if only you'd shown me you loved me.'

'But that's why I couldn't, my little one, because it could have been a mistake, and you might have ended up hating me. Now...' He tipped up her chin, and everything she had ever wanted to read was in his eyes. 'When?' he said softly.

'Soon—very, very soon.'

'As soon as I can fix the licence and the more practical details?'

'As soon as you can fix the licence. Because I'll never let you go.' She looked up at him, knowing that there was no need of coyness or evasions or pretence. At last she knew he wanted her as passionately as she wanted him, and everything they had undergone during the past weeks had forged a bond of understanding between them that would allow nothing less than utter honesty. She remembered something else. 'Max, there's been no complications—it healed all right?'

'Perfectly. Of course you know you've marked me for life,' he said into her hair. 'At the hospital they wanted to know who had been responsible for the fancy embroidery work, and had you used a—— Oh, my darling, I'm only teasing!'

'You'd better be!' She framed his face with caressing hands and abandoned joyously the final constraint of doubt. No more misunderstanding. Max in her arms, hers to love and keep and honour, as she was his in their wonderful new world of lovers' enchantment.

At last he reluctantly put her away from him, kissing the tip of her nose and her brow as he said, 'Come on, my Inca girl, before things get completely out of hand and we miss that plane.'

They walked slowly back to the car, their shadows as one, their laughter and their whispers blending with the sounds of the sea. A glint of moonlight touched a great gleaming teardrop of gold at her throat as she raised her face to his, and high above a great silver plane began to circle low in the heavens. And far above them all the little flower of stars danced in eternal brilliance.

Harlequin Presents...

The books that let you escape into the wonderful world of romance! Trips to exotic places... interesting plots... meeting memorable people... the excitement of love....These are integral parts of Harlequin Presents—the heartwarming novels read by women everywhere.

Many early issues are now available. Choose from this great selection!

Choose from this great selection of exciting Harlequin Presents editions

99 Love Made the Choice
Mary Burchell

100 Dark Moonless Night
Anne Mather

101 Palace of the Hawk
Margaret Rome

102 The Rainbow Bird
Margaret Way

103 The Flower of Eternity
Margery Hilton

106 Yellow Moon
Rebecca Stratton

107 Pagan Heart
Rebecca Caine

108 Pride and Power
Anne Hampson

109 Temporary Wife
Roberta Leigh

110 Witchstone
Anne Mather

111 Such Is Love
Mary Burchell

112 The Waterfalls of the Moon
Anne Mather